THERESA HALVORSEN

# River City Widows

NBBP

*To Stephanie—the idea for this book wouldn't have existed without you*

*And as always, to Brad and my boys for all your support and love*

# Contents

# Chapter 1

"Gabe! Come on—we're going to be late. Get your jacket."

Nothing.

"Gabe!" I barked up the stairs, adding the sharp mom tone. The tone that says, don't-you-make-me-come-get-you.

Nothing.

Seriously?

I'd given him the thirty-minute, fifteen-minute, and five-minute count-downs. He'd responded to each one. Now, when we had to leave, he wasn't answering?

"Polly?" I called from my spot at the bottom of the stairs. I'd almost forgotten about my stepdaughter. She'd gone away to college in Arizona three years ago and would graduate with a history degree in a year. She'd woken me with a knock on the front door, at five a.m. today, asking to crash in the guest room. I'd barely heard from her in the last three years.

"Just a place to stay over spring break," she'd said. Then Polly had wheeled her suitcase into the guest room, unpacked, showered, and made herself breakfast. When I'd asked her why she was here, she'd said she wanted to surprise us and reassured me all was fine. It was just a spur-of-the-moment road trip, she'd said, and had loved the adventure of driving all night.

She was a terrible liar.

"Polly?" I called again. "Did you want to come with us to dinner? If so, we have to leave, or we won't make our reservation."

No response. No whispers of movement over my head, no footsteps on the stairs, no flush of a toilet. Just silence. Had she and Gabe gone out and not told me?

I shivered, a cold puff of air flowing around the family room and kitchen. Someone must have opened a window.

"Guys?" I called again, starting up the stairs. My foot hit the squeaky step I usually avoided, and the board wailed. I cringed, hating the sound. I pulled my to-do list—a tiny spiral notebook with the blue cover—out of my pocket and added a note to get the step fixed.

"We're going to be late for pizza," I called. "It's your favorite, Gabe."

Goosebumps popped out on my arms as I reached the upstairs landing. It felt so much colder up here. I'd have to remind Polly of the rules. No opening windows, even during the summer—it wore down the sashes, and windows were expensive to fix in my 1940s home.

I knocked on the closed door to Gabe's bedroom.

No answer. "Gabe?"

I cracked open the door. It was dark, except for his Hulk nightlight casting green-tinged shadows. There were lumps in his bed.

"Gabe?" I said again. Was he asleep? Maybe he was getting sick. God, I hoped not; it would destroy all my plans for this week.

The lumps in his bed didn't move when I flicked on the light.

"Gabe?"

Stepping into the room, my foot landed on a metal car. I winced and bent over to put it into its container with the other toys.

"Gabe?" The lumps still didn't move. I pulled back the blanket and bedsheets, expecting to find my son curled into a giggling lump, playing some sort of one-sided hide-and-seek. But there was only the laundry I'd folded two days before. The laundry I'd placed on his bed for him to put away. He'd created a nest of clean laundry and then slept on it.

He'd been sleeping. On. The. Clean. Laundry.

I puffed out a sigh. What the heck was wrong with him? Why on earth would he look at a pile of laundry and think, oh, that's a good place for a nap? I gathered up the clothes and tossed them into the basket. I'd deal with it later.

*Later is always better.*

I stuck my head into the bathroom.

No Gabe.

He wouldn't have left. Right?

A dim light shone from the crack beneath Polly's door. I wondered if she'd thrown a scarf over the lamp. I hoped not; the last thing we needed was a fire.

I knocked. "Polly? Is Gabe in there? We need to leave for pizza."

No answer.

I didn't want to just walk into her room. She was twenty-one, and I'd learned when she was about fifteen not to do the quick-knock-and-open-the-door parent thing. She'd been so upset.

Rightfully so, I now acknowledged.

I pressed my ear against the door and recoiled. It felt like a window when snow was falling outside.

She absolutely had her window open.

"Polly?" I cracked open the door. "I'm so sorry to barge in, but do you know—"

She and Gabe sat in the middle of the floor, surrounded by lit candles, the light flickering across the walls. A game sat in front of them, and a white thing spun on the board, like a top. They let out a screech, and I echoed it.

The white piece leapt off the board and shot toward me. I jumped, and it zoomed under my foot hitting and gouging the wall.

"Is that a Ouija board?" I flicked on the light. Gabe leaped to his feet and kicked a candle onto the floor.

Fire!

With a screech of fear, I stomped out the flame, pressing candle wax into the original hardwood floor.

"What—who—floor—why—?" My brain stuttered; words stuck in my throat. "Don't pick up the candle," I yelled as Gabe bent over. He straightened, tears in his eyes. I never yelled at him.

"Candles? On the floor? What were you thinking?" I screamed.

"Sorry, Mom," Gabe whispered. Right then, he looked so much like his father, my breath caught. Even though Gabe had my blonde hair and hazel eyes, I saw Miguel in Gabe's face more and more as time passed. They had the same frown, the same smile, the same snarky quirk of the eyebrows.

I took a deep breath and then another, controlling my temper until I could speak. "What were you guys doing?"

Polly hadn't moved from her spot on the floor, hadn't even looked up. She just stared down at the board with its white rows of letters arcing across the top.

Gabe answered, his shoulders hunched, and his hands stuffed in his pockets. "Nothing. Just Polly brought this game, and I'd seen it in a movie. Wanted to try it," he mumbled.

"What movie?"

He shrugged again.

"Go get your jacket. We're going to be late." Gabe slunk from the room.

"Polly?" My stepdaughter's face was pale in the bright room. She had her father's jade eyes, but her mother's face with high cheekbones and full lips. Her naturally brunette hair was a strawberry blonde now.

"Polly!" She hadn't moved. I toggled the bedroom light. A gust of wind ruffled my hair. I stepped into the room to close the window, but it was shut and locked tight.

Weird.

Polly shook her head, her long earrings catching the light. "Tasia?"

"We have to leave," I said. "We're going to Sergio's, Gabe's favorite, and you have to have a reservation. Blow out the candles, scrape up the wax, and pack up the board if you're going to come." She was going to make us late, and I was never late.

Polly stood, swaying back and forth a little. She blinked, shook her head, and tilted her head to crack her neck.

I hated the popping sound and looked away. The opened suitcase on her bed looked like it had burst, exploding its treasures all over the room. She'd scattered clothes, shoes, wires for chargers, an iPad, and a laptop around my guest room. Hair products and nail polish sat on the windowsill along with the orchid I was trying to get to flower again.

I forced my eyes away from the mess. "Did you want to come with us to dinner?"

"Yeah, it sounds good," she said. She looked around the room like she couldn't remember where she was.

"And could you please pick up your stuff?" It escaped my lips before I could stop myself. Keeping her room clean had been an ongoing battle when Polly had lived with us.

She grimaced. "Yes, Tasia, I remember the rules."

A red haze flooded my vision. How dare she use that tone with me? I'd barely heard from my stepdaughter since Miguel had died, and today she'd showed up, without notice, trashing my guest room?

But before I could order her to stay home, or better yet leave, she said, "Sorry. I'm just hungry and drained. I was joking. It came out wrong."

I was hungry too. Starving. And looking forward to tonight all day, planning my breakfast and lunch calories so I could gorge on Sergio's pizza tonight. That must explain the red still encircling my vision. Just hunger.

I'd never actually seen red before, only read about the experience in novels. Even during the typical fights with my siblings or frustrations with Gabe and Polly, I'd never gotten that angry before.

"Come with us to dinner," I said, trying and failing to keep my frustration out of my voice. "It's for Gabe's birthday week."

I sensed Gabe standing behind me and turned to look at him. He'd stuffed his hands into his pockets, his eyes on the ground. "I'm sorry we're going to be late," he muttered. "I ruined everything."

My anger disappeared, like someone had turned off a switch inside of me. On the night of Miguel's funeral, Gabe had said he'd always do what was right because that's what men did. He'd take care of me because there wasn't anyone else. He'd made promises adults couldn't keep, let alone a child.

I hugged him, noticing how he came up to my waist. Yesterday it felt like he'd been at my hip. "It's okay," I said. "Not a big deal, at the end of the day. Ready to get some eighth birthday pizza?"

He nodded and sniffed, trying not to cry. I pretended I didn't notice and gave him a last squeeze before letting him go.

5

Polly bent over to blow out the candles, holding her hair back. She looked so sad as the smell of candle smoke filled the room. Why was she here? Had something happened? Why hadn't she spoken to me in three years?

"Ready?" I asked. She nodded and shifted through the mess on her floor for a scarf and leather jacket. We turned to head downstairs, and my foot landed on the white plastic triangle from the Ouija board.

Crack.

I winced, bending over to pick up the pieces. What was this thing called? A planchette? I remembered my one time with a Ouija board. I was fifteen and giggling classmates had asked it whether a boy liked them. The planchette had moved across the board, spelling words, likely pushed by one of the girls.

I tried to fit the broken pieces together, but they cracked further, falling into white bits of plastic in my hands.

Dang. It wasn't my property, and yet I'd managed to break it.

Passing the parts to Polly, I said. "Sorry. I didn't see it."

"I know," she murmured. "It was just an accident." She looked even sadder. I went to put my arm around her, to give her a quick hug, but she stepped away, like she used to when she was sixteen and too cool to hang out with her stepmother.

I pushed down the pain.

We went downstairs, into what used to be the formal living room and was now my office. "Okay, guys," I said, clapping my hands and pretending to be cheerful. "Let's jump in the car and get some food. We'll feel better."

A giant thump sounded over our head, and I glanced at the ceiling. The sound, like someone had dropped a hardback book, had come from the room we didn't use anymore.

A chill crawled up my spine. I'd nearly succeeded in forgetting that room even existed.

"You keeping a boyfriend up there?" Polly asked.

"It's my sex slave," I deadpanned.

"Mom? What's a—?"

"Let's go," I said. "I'm sure it's nothing."

*Later.*

6

# CHAPTER 1

I'd figure it out later.

# Chapter 2

The restaurant had given our table away. Of course it had.

"You're over thirty minutes late," the hostess said, her thick eyelashes flapping at us. Then she looked down at her screen, obviously hoping we'd just walk away.

"I understand," I said, my cheeks hot. I knew this would happen. "We had a bit of an emergency," I explained. "And left later than we should've. I'm sorry. When can you seat us?" The restaurant was half-empty. It shouldn't be a long wait.

She swiped at her screen.

"We're completely booked," she said, with a fake pout. "We only accept reservations. And we retain the right to give your table away if you're late."

"Seriously?" Polly said. "You guys are empty."

"Sorry," the hostess said in that I-don't-really-care tone. "I can make you a reservation for another day, but perhaps the Spaghetti Factory would be more at your level."

Gabe's shoulders dropped. Sergio's was his favorite restaurant, and today marked the start of an unforgettable week. He'd be turning eight on Saturday, and I'd promised him the entire week of spring break devoted to whatever he wanted to do. Starting with specialty pizza with every ingredient, including the mozzarella, made from scratch.

At Sergio's. At his favorite Italian restaurant.

Not the Spaghetti Factory.

"Is there anything you can do?" I asked. My cheeks were so hot, I probably could've lit a candle with them. "Can we wait and see if one of your reservations is a no-show?"

She raised an eyebrow. "Our patrons don't no-show. And are generally not tardy."

"Obviously," Polly snapped, looking around at the half-empty restaurant. "You don't want this loser pizza, do you, Gabe?" She put a hand on his shoulder.

"No?"

"Polly," I said. "I've got this."

I ignored the way her lips tightened. "Come on, dude," she said to Gabe. "Let's go outside and let your mom talk to this... person."

The hostess ignored the jab. "Can you get us in tomorrow?" I asked. "Please. It's crucial."

"Look," she said. "I'll be honest with you. We're under new owners. And they just don't want kids here. Bottom line."

"Well, bottom line, I think that's pretty discriminatory," I snapped.

She shrugged. "We're a business. And we don't need..." she looked me up and down, taking in my disheveled blonde hair, my old jeans, and plain sweatshirt. "The family trade."

"But that's—"

"I have to tend to these other customers." And she stepped out from behind the hostess stand in a too-tight black dress and motioned the couple behind me forward. She turned her back on me and guided the couple to their table, laughing and pointing out items on the menu.

My stomach dropped, the room swimming around me. I just wanted to give Gabe a wonderful birthday. And Sergio's was his favorite restaurant.

Was.

Red filled my vision. Spotting the bound menus on the hostess stand, I pushed them to the ground. They left a satisfying thwacking crash, and I slammed out the door.

Polly and Gabe looked up as I stomped to them. "Tasia? You okay?" Polly asked.

"Fine." I spat out the words. The red flooding my vision made it hard to see her or Gabe.

*How dare that woman refuse to seat you? Humiliate you?*

I was going to smash the—

"Mom?"

The red haze disappeared like it had never existed. What on earth had that been? I'd never felt anything like that, never lost control, even in my thoughts. Tears pricked my eyes, along with the insane urge to curl up in a ball and weep.

"I'm okay," I said. I could cry later.

*Later. Always later.*

We climbed into the car, and I put the keys into the ignition. I was so hungry my hands shook. "Where to?"

"There's a pizza place like two miles away," Polly said, looking up from her phone. "That work, dude?"

Gabe shrugged. "Sure. Long as they have sausage pizza, and I can add pineapple."

Polly let out a snort of laughter. "You have weird taste in pizza."

"I know," Gabe said with a sigh.

"Know who else has weird taste?" Polly said, in between directing me to the pizza place.

"Who?"

She launched into a story about a college roommate who put shrimp, onions, and peanut butter on a frozen pizza and then ate it.

"Why?" Gabe asked with a squeal of laughter.

"He'd been smo—he was just really relaxed, and it sounded good," she finished.

Gabe snorted to himself, staring outside at the East Sacramento brick and Tudor houses with their green lawns, flowering crepe myrtles, and giant elms. Lending libraries with brightly colored boxes had popped up in front of several homes. Gabe and I should try to stop by some this week, exchange old books for new.

"Polly?" Gabe asked as we pulled into the parking lot of the pizza place. My heart sank. I hated commercial places like this. But it was nearly eight, and I was too hungry to care. Pizza was pizza.

"Yeah, dude?" Polly said, her face lit by her phone screen.

"Did you come back to surprise me for my birthday week?"

"Of course," she said, a slight beat showing the lie.

Luckily, Gabe didn't notice. He sighed happily. "I knew it."

# Chapter 3

The pizza was terrible with canned sauce and cardboard dough. I poked at a previously frozen mushroom, now mushy with bad reheating. The garlic bread was cold in the middle, and the restaurant hadn't even bothered to throw a bit of dried parsley on the fake butter to make it look pretty.

But Gabe was happy. He ate three pieces of pizza and guzzled down two root beers. Was he turning into a teenager with an appetite to match? Wasn't it too early? I wished I had another mom friend to ask, but they'd all disappeared after Miguel's death.

It was after Gabe's bedtime when we got back, but tonight I'd let him stay up late for a special treat. I'd spent a month on Pinterest pinning pictures, reading recipes, and even watching YouTube videos. And now, I'd give him the first of seven small cakes baked and designed by me, each signifying something he loved. I couldn't wait to see his face each night.

"There's one more thing," I said, unlocking the finicky front door lock and stepping into the room I used for my office.

I froze, one foot still in the air.

What the heck was on the floor? It was green, thick, and smooshed into the throw rug. It almost reminded me of the slime the kids liked to make out of Elmer's glue. I'd outlawed it but—

Gabe tried to push his way in, and I threw out my arm, blocking him.

"Wait," I said. The weird green stuff was on the guest armchair and even smeared on the corner of a wall.

"What is it?" Polly asked. I sensed her standing on her toes behind me, craning her neck. "What's going on? Is someone there?"

"Not sure," I said. The room was gloomy—I'd forgotten to turn on the lights before we'd left—and currently only lit by the porch and streetlamps. The house itself was quiet, oppressive, like something lurked within, just out of sight. I could see my project board, with its multi-colored post-it notes, and beyond that, the shadows of the kitchen table and chairs. I squinted, knowing I was being ridiculous, but fighting the feeling of being watched from the shadows. A faint sound came from inside the house, a whisper, like a muffled footstep, like someone had shuffled their feet on the hardwood floors.

Something was in my home.

"Take Gabe over to Derek's," I whispered to Polly. "And see if he'll come over."

"Who's Derek?"

"He lives in the granny unit," Gabe said. "He's nice."

"You have a strange man living in the granny unit?" Polly hissed.

"He's not stra—"

Was that movement inside? Had a shadow close to the floor shifted, or was it my imagination? I froze, barely breathing, my heart thudding in my chest and ears.

"Just go get him," I whispered.

"Jeez, Tasia, I think it's just some frosting on the floor," Polly said, trying to push past me.

"I know it's frosting." Though I hadn't. "But it wasn't there when we left."

"Are you sure?" Polly's cheeks paled in the porch light.

"Positive. Take Gabe to Derek's place. If Derek's not there, lock him in the car and call 9-1-1." I took my eyes off the shadows to look at her, though my brain screamed something would attack me, rake a claw against my exposed cheek.

"Okay. Be careful." Polly and Gabe's footsteps retreated.

There was another rustle—definitely something in there. The fridge clicked on, and I let out a yelp. I'd unlocked the door before stepping in, right? So it wasn't like a burglar had come in through the front door. Or maybe they'd entered through the back? I rubbed goosebumps on my arms, a freezing wind seeming to billow out of the house.

I should call the cops. Have them go through the house.

A hand dropped on my shoulder, and I screeched.

"It's me, it's me," Derek said. "What's going on?"

Derek, an I.T. manager for an insurance company, had moved into the granny unit after a divorce had left him homeless. In his mid-thirties, he'd shaved his head a few months ago and grown a short beard. His living situation was supposed to be temporary, a few months max, to figure out his finances. But a year later, he was still here and not showing any signs of wanting to find a different place.

I stepped out of the doorway. "Look at the floor."

He peered at the green stuff. "What is that? Silly putty?"

"I think it's frosting. But how did it get there?"

His face tightened. "Call the cops."

"What if it's nothing? The last time the cops came..." I trailed off. "I don't want to remind Gabe of it." In truth, I didn't want to remember the morning when the two kind officers had knocked on the door to tell us about Miguel's death. It had taken months before I was able to see police cars without fighting back an anxiety attack. "Tonight sucked. I don't want to make it worse."

Derek touched my shoulder. "Every almost eight-year-old would love having the cops come on his birthday. The police will come out and show him the cop car, maybe let him sit in the back seat. They try to make it fun for kids, so they're not scared of the police. Let's just call them."

"What if it brings up the nightmares again? I swear, he didn't sleep for six months."

Derek sighed. "You got your pepper spray?"

"Of course," I mentally whopped myself on the forehead for not getting it out sooner.

"Stay behind me." I realized Derek held a baseball bat. "But don't spray it unless you have to."

"I won't," I said. I'd taken a self-defense class and been warned the spray would irritate anyone, including us, in the vicinity.

Derek stepped into the house and bent over to scoop up the green stuff. He sniffed it. "It's definitely frosting."

"Probably from Gabe's cake. Something must have smashed it." My heart pounded painfully in my chest, making it hard to breathe.

Derek flicked on the lights as we went through my office, the family room, and then the kitchen.

"Found the source of the frosting," he called.

"Oh no," I said, following him into the room. I'd worked so hard on the little Hulk-themed cake. Now it was smashed on the floor, bits of it on the counter, and smeared out for multiple feet. How on earth had it gotten out of the cupboard I'd hidden it in?

Something rustled in the family room. Derek and I froze. The house felt tight, like before a clap of thunder hit during a thunderstorm.

"If you're in here," Derek boomed, making me jump. "I've called the cops. And I got a gun."

What? Where had he gotten a gun?

"I'll shoot anyone that doesn't belong in here. You'd better leave, you fucker!"

Another whisper of sound from behind the couch. There was no way a person could fit in the space between the piece of furniture and the wall, but I still tensed, my finger on the trigger of the pepper spray.

"I mean it," Derek boomed. "Just run out the front door. I won't stop you. But if I catch—"

A tiny shadow jumped from behind the couch and ran at us, its claws digging into the throw rug. It yowled and scurried up my leg to my shoulder. I screamed, trying to get it off.

But as soon as my hands closed around the soft fur, I knew what it was.

"It's a cat, it's a cat," I repeated, curling my fingers around the soft puff of fur.

Derek let out a deep breath and dropped the bat. He breathed deeply a few more times, pacing away from me and rubbing his chest. "I think I'm having a heart attack."

"Really?" Did I have to call 9-1-1?

"No. Oh my god. I thought it was—I don't know. A demon, like in a TV show. But it's just a cat?" He peered at the gray and green kitten.

"Just a kitten," I said. "Completely covered in frosting." My hands were sticky, and my shoulder and leg burned with the tiny cuts from its claws. It was going to need a bath, and I needed band-aids.

It started to purr, going limp in my hands. "Where did you come from?" I demanded.

"Derek? Tasia? I called the cops," Polly said, coming in from the front door and holding out her phone. "I heard you screech."

Sighing, I took Polly's phone away from her. "Can we cancel?" I asked the dispatcher. "A stray kitten got into my house. Scared the heck out of us."

Red and blue lights filled the windows.

"I think it's too late," the competent male voice on the other side said. Guess it was a slow night in Sacramento.

"Swell," I said to the dispatcher and anyone in the room. The cat responded by mewing, a soft little sound. "Do you want me to release the officers?" the dispatcher asked.

"Mom?"

Gabe tiptoed in through the front door, backlit by the red and blue lights.

"I told you to stay at Derek's," Polly said.

He shrugged, a small shoulder lift. "I got scared," he whispered. He glanced behind him as the officers approached.

"It's okay," I told him and the voice on the phone. "Just a misunderstanding. I'll talk to the officers."

I stuffed the phone into a pocket.

Gabe slunk further inside and cuddled up against me like he used to. The kitten let out a giant meow, and he startled. "A kitten?"

"I guess so," I said. "It got in, somehow." I tried to juggle the kitten, go outside to greet the officers, and comfort Gabe.

"I'll take care of the cops," Derek said. He moved to the front path, introducing himself, and shaking the officer's hands.

"I get a kitten?" Gabe asked. "That's the surprise?"

Nope, nope, nope, absolutely not. Cats were a lot of work, destructive, and their litter boxes stank. There was no way I was keeping a kitten in this house.

"Gabe—"

"This is my birthday present?" He petted it, regardless of the sticky mess on its fur.

I looked out at the police officers and the mess of cake on the floor.

"I get to keep it, really and truly?" he asked. "I dreamt I was getting a kitten."

"I... I guess."

Gabe made this little soft sound of joy, a sound I'd never heard out of him. My eyes teared, and I had to blink to clear them. But they were good tears, not sad ones. I'd nearly forgotten happy tears could exist.

I passed him the kitten, and he cuddled it to his chest.

"We'll have to make sure it's not anyone's pet, and it needs a bath, and we'll need food, and a litter box, and... baby, you might be allergic. Maybe don't kiss it?"

"I'm going to name him Fluffy," Gabe said, frosting now smeared all over his shirt, hands, and face. The sticky kitten headbutted Gabe's chest, making him laugh. A throaty purr filled the room.

"Polly! Did you see?" Gabe said. "I got a kitten!"

"I did," Polly said. "Let's let your mom deal with the police. I'll help you clean it up. Race you to your bathroom."

Their feet banged on the hardwood as they raced each other up the stairs like they did when they were younger, and Miguel was alive.

"Polly," I called.

"Yeah?" Her voice filtered down the stairs.

"Thank you. For helping Gabe."

"Welcome," she called.

I stepped outside, explaining to the officers who barely resisted laughing that our burglar was a kitten, now named Fluffy.

"Once you name an animal, it's yours," Derek said.

Later. I'd deal with it later.

# Chapter 4

An hour later, Derek, Polly, and I sat around the kitchen table. The remains of the Gabe's birthday cake were in the garbage, the frosting was cleaned up, and I'd spent five minutes trying to figure out how the kitten had opened the cupboard and knocked over the cake, to no avail. Gabe was upstairs in his room, with the now clean and damp Fluffy. He was crashing around, talking to the kitten, and trying to get it to chase random toys.

"No-no-no. Don't jump on that. Lay down here. Play with this." His voice echoed down the stairs.

I poured Polly a half-glass of the chardonnay and a full one for myself and Derek. At Polly's unhappy frown, I topped hers off. I thought I was pretty cool offering her any wine, but I'd forgotten she was an adult, twenty-one at that.

A few months ago, around her birthday, I'd sent her a text asking if she wanted to spend a girl's weekend in Vegas or Lake Tahoe to celebrate.

She'd never responded.

"Okay, Tasia," Polly said with a flick of her thumb. "Who's this guy?"

"He's Derek," I said. "Polly meet Derek, Derek meet Polly, my stepdaughter." I was looking at Polly, or I would've missed the flicker of hurt at being called my stepdaughter, but damn-it-all, she'd disappeared after Miguel's death. She rarely answered my texts asking about how college was going and never returned my phone calls. If she cared about our relationship, she should've tried harder. It couldn't all be on me.

I hadn't realized how much it had hurt. Red flickered on the edge of my vision for a second, a voice whispering in my head.

*She's not yours. Not really family.*

God, I was tired.

"Derek's my tenant," I explained, after taking a big gulp of wine. "He's lived here for about a year and been an enormous help with Gabe. Polly showed up at five this morning, as a surprise," I told Derek. "She's staying here for spring break."

"Came for Gabe's birthday," Polly lied.

I finished my wine, hoping the alcohol would calm the jitters of adrenaline still in my system. It was after eleven, but sleep seemed a ways off. And what was I supposed to do with the kitten? Weren't they nocturnal? Did we have to stay home with it, like we would with a puppy? And what I would do next week when Gabe went back to school?

"Tasia?" Derek said like he'd said my name a few times.

"Sorry?"

Derek gave me a crooked smile, the one he'd used on me a year ago that made me think renting the granny unit to him wouldn't be a bad idea. "You seem tired. I'll let you get some sleep."

"Sorry," I said again. "I was just thinking about how much of a disaster today was."

"Disaster?" Polly asked, looking up from her phone.

"No breakfast in bed, no pizza at Sergio's, no cake. And then we had to call the cops. For a kitten. That somehow got in through the window no one remembers opening." I hadn't even realized the old window still opened.

Polly went back to her phone. "I guarantee Gabe's had the best birthday he will ever have."

"Best birthday?" I asked. "We didn't do any of the things I'd planned."

"Oh come on, Tasia," Derek said. He stood up and took his half-drunk glass of wine to the kitchen, dumping the white wine down the sink, rinsing out his glass, and putting it into the dishwasher. "He got a kitten and a visit from his half-sister. It's been the best day of his life."

"I guess."

*Why does he get an opinion? He's just your tenant.*

"Good to meet you, Polly," Derek said. "Have a good night." He went to the back door to head to his little house.

"Night," she said, not looking up from her phone.

I unlocked the back door and walked into the chilly night with him. Sacramento had dozens of nicknames, from River City to SacTown to Camellia City. My favorite was City of Trees, and nowhere was that more evident than in East Sac. The giant plane trees, maples, and elms lined the streets, taller than the houses and older than the inhabitants. And in the spring, cherry blossoms spread white and pink petals all over the cars, porches, and sidewalks and everyone's allergies go crazy. As a child, I'd always loved East Sac more than other neighborhoods like Land or Oak Park. Getting the keys to this house was one of the best days of my life.

Derek and I walked along the gravel path between our homes. Before Derek, there wasn't much need to go to the granny unit; Miguel and I had used it as a guest cottage and for excess storage. But a few months after Derek had moved in, I'd realized we'd worn a path in the lawn between the houses. So one weekend, he and I had put down a gravel path lined with bulbs. Tonight I noticed the tulips and daffodils had sprouted their tiny stems. In a few weeks, we'd have the brightly colored spring flowers everywhere.

"Thank you for coming over," I said.

"Polly and Gabe showing up, saying someone was in the house, took a year off my life," he said. "They were terrified, though Polly tried to be cool about it."

"I was pretty scared too."

"And then that cat jumped out of the shadows."

"Did it take another year off?"

"At least." He grinned down at me.

"How about you come to dinner tomorrow? My treat. I'd planned to take Gabe to Rosarita's in midtown for night two of his birthday week."

"Yum. They have the best carnitas and their cilantro-lime dressing is incredible."

"Right? Though Gabe won't touch it. He likes their cheese quesadilla."

"As would most near eight-year-olds," Derek said. He looked over my shoulder, and I turned, seeing Polly sitting at the table through the open kitchen window. "I didn't realize you had another child," he murmured.

"She was Miguel's," I said.

Miguel had died nearly three years ago, the day after Polly graduated from high school. I'd forgotten to buy coffee the night before, so Miguel had gotten up while we were still asleep to buy coffee and celebratory donuts. "Wanted to surprise us," said the silly note on the kitchen table. Wanted us to know "he'd be right back, probably before any of us were awake."

But he didn't come home.

The driver of a delivery truck had fallen asleep and run a red light, smashing Miguel's little commuter car into a building. Miguel had died instantly and left us broken. Instead of staying at our home and going to Sac State like she'd agreed, Polly had chosen a different college, closer to her mom and moved out, leaving me to navigate a life without her and Miguel.

I rubbed my forehead. "After Miguel died, Polly never came back, not for summers or spring break or anything. She'd lived with us for about six years since we'd gotten married, and then she was gone." I'd missed her, missed talking about her plans for the future, missed talking about her classes, friends, and teachers. I'd missed pedicures followed by lunches at local East Sac restaurants. I'd missed watching her interact with Gabe as they'd grown up. "I don't know why she's here."

"Sounds like she needs something."

"I know. And it must be big because she won't tell me what it is."

I looked at his tiny house in my backyard. While I liked the house I lived in, I'd genuinely fallen in love with the granny unit. I loved the crooked red shutters and bright blue door, which contrasted with the soft gray exterior paint. As soon as the renovations inside had been done, I'd planted star jasmines around the outside of the house. Tonight, I took a moment to breathe in the sweet jasmine smell, remembering how I'd joked with Miguel that he and I would live in the granny unit when we got old, while Gabe lived in the big house with his family.

Light flashing from the upstairs of my house caught my attention. Gabe's bedroom light turned off and then on, and I heard his voice, though not the words. Must be talking to the cat.

Derek had seen the shift of light too and grinned, the moonlight reflecting off his shaved head. "Gabe's not going to get any sleep tonight. That kitten is going to keep him up."

"I should go check on him."

There it was—that moment of awkwardness when we said goodbye. A moment when we just stood, staring at each other. He took a step toward me, and I took a step back.

"Seven work for dinner tomorrow?" I said, my eyes on his feet and my hands in my pockets.

"Sounds good. I'll pop over then."

"Thanks again. Stop by for coffee tomorrow morning, if you want."

He made a face. "I have an early meeting. Who schedules meetings at seven a.m. on a Monday?

"I gotta get up early to make breakfast in bed for Gabe."

"Then I'll come over. Six?"

"Sounds good."

And I turned away before he could take another step toward me.

When I came in, locking the door behind me, Polly glanced up from her phone and then went back to whatever social media app was her favorite. "What's going on with that?"

"With what?"

"With Derek. Are you like together or something?"

"No. He's just my tenant and a good neighbor. And Gabe likes him. It's nice to have him here in case of emergency." I shrugged. "He's a friendly guy." That was an understatement. I hadn't wanted a male tenant, but knew he'd be perfect after meeting him. His interview had lasted two hours, consisting of both of us drinking coffee and laughing in my kitchen.

"Uh-uh. He likes you." Polly didn't look up from her phone.

"Of course he likes me. We're friends."

Even I knew that was lame.

"He just... he's been really helpful with Gabe," I tried to clarify. "I can't always be there for him, and it's nice Gabe has a guy he can talk about guy stuff with. Or if I'm stuck on a job and have a deadline, he can help with

Gabe. That's it. He likes Gabe and sometimes comes over for coffee." He'd been coming over for coffee four or five times a week lately. But that meant nothing. It was just a habit.

"And he checked out your ass when you were pouring wine," Polly said, finally looking up.

"He did not. You're watching too many romcoms." My cheeks warmed, though. Had he? "We're just friends."

Polly made a face. "Friends don't ogle each other's asses."

I threw up my arms. She wasn't going to believe Derek and I were only friends. "I'm going to bed," I said. "He's joining us for dinner tomorrow at Rosarita's. And will probably come over for coffee in the morning."

"Coffee and dinner? I totally believe you. You guys are just friends."

Whatever. I hadn't forgotten her father and never would. I looked at the framed note in the kitchen—the one Miguel had left the morning he died. "Can you behave yourself with Derek? I owe him for tonight."

"Of course. I'll behave around your boyfriend." She looked up and must have seen something in my face. "I'll stop," she said, her lips turning down, her voice a whisper. "And we owe him. He came running over when he found out you were in trouble."

"When he found out we were in trouble," I corrected. "He loves Gabe." The words were out before I could stop them. And he truly did. Derek treated Gabe like a nephew or a young cousin.

Or the way he would if he was dating Gabe's mom.

"Get some sleep." I poured another glass of wine and headed into the room I slept in on the first floor. I was going to spend an hour with a good book and enjoy my wine.

# Chapter 5

**<u>Monday</u>**

I couldn't move.

I wanted to but couldn't. Couldn't even open my eyes.

Straining against the covers, I tried to push them off. But my arms refused to move. The blankets were heavy against my body but weren't holding me down.

Something else was.

I took a deep breath, then another, the air barely going into my lungs. My toes and fingers refused to twitch.

Move!

Open your eyes!

Come on, MOVE!

Nothing.

Not even an eyelash flutter.

Fear made me nauseous. How would I throw up if I couldn't open my mouth? My heart pounded, my chest hurting.

Something breathed against my cheek, their body pressing against every inch of mine. It held me down, squashed me into the mattress, making the cushion sag beneath me. Beneath us.

Oh, God. Who was here?

What was holding me down?

I needed to open my eyes.

The moist breath against my cheek sped up, panting. Droplets of their

24

saliva formed on my skin.

"Polly? Gabe?" I tried to choke the words out but only produced a raspy gasp.

The thing on my chest giggled, an odd child-like sound.

A female voice whispered, "Get out."

My eyes opened, and I bolted up in bed, throwing the covers aside and jumping out, my arms and legs free of the oppressive weight.

I heard myself saying, "You're okay, you're okay, you're okay," over and over. I flicked on the lamp next to my bed and wiped my dry cheek.

Just a bad dream.

"You're okay," I said. "No one's here."

I shivered, drenched in sweat, thick enough to leave patches on the t-shirt I slept in. What had happened?

My brain filled in a diagnosis. Sleep paralysis.

That's all it was. I took some deep breaths. "Normal," I said aloud. "It was normal. You're okay. No one's here."

I'd read about the phenomenon but had never experienced it.

Holy mother of God, my entire body shook with tremors.

I ripped off my damp pajamas, pulling on fresh ones. I considered wearing one of Miguel's t-shirts, the ones that still smelled of him, the ones I'd saved. But I only had two left and wanted to use them on the terrible nights when I couldn't breathe from missing him.

They were in the closet. I looked at the closed door and couldn't bring myself to open it; maybe something waited in the shadows within for me.

Climbing back into bed, I wrapped my arms around myself, scared to pull the covers up, scared of their weight, and refusing to turn out the light. I reached for my book, but my hands shook too much to hold it. Remembering a tactic my therapist had taught me, I counted my breaths and focused on my feet to ground myself in the here and now.

It kind of worked. Maybe this was where ghost stories had come from—the normal if terrifying phenomena of being caught between REM sleep and waking. Eventually, I was able to hold my book and start reading, start comprehending the words.

It was still so cold though, and eventually, I pulled the blankets up around me, like a cocoon, shivering. Then I pushed them off, the weight against my body bringing back anxiety. But then the shivering started again.

I pulled the covers back up, my heart racing as the blankets pressed against my arms and legs.

Just reaction, I told myself. It would pass.

Maybe the furnace was going out too, and that's why it was so cold. My bedside clock told me it was 2:23 a.m.

I went back to my cozy mystery story about a bookstore owner and her tabby kitty, trying not to think about the breathing on my cheek. And that terrible giggle from my nightmare, so like a baby's, yet not. Like the sound an adult made when they were trying to sound like a baby. And then the whisper telling me to get out.

A knock sounded on my door, and I shrieked.

"Tasia, you okay? I'm sorry."

"Fine, Polly," I called back. "I'm awake. Just had a bad dream."

I sensed Polly waiting at the door. "Me too," she said. "Can I come in?"

"Sure," I called. I didn't want to get out of bed, though. What if something was under there and grabbed my ankle?

*Least it would grab Polly's.*

The thought whispered up, scarcely registered. What was wrong with me?

Polly swung the door open. She'd turned on all the lights on the first floor, and for a second, I thought I saw a shadow standing behind her.

My heart sped up again. "Come in," I said. "Quickly. Close the door behind you, so you don't wake up Gabe." It was silly, but when she closed the door, I felt like she'd closed the shadow out too.

"Grab a seat," I said, pointing at an armchair. "What was your bad dream about?"

She shook her head. "I'd gotten tangled in the covers and couldn't move. Dreamt I was a mummy or something." She shrugged. "It's silly now."

Odd her dream had paralleled mine so much.

"I thought, if you were awake, you might want some hot chocolate." She tugged on her sleep messed hair.

26

A memory I'd forgotten pushed itself up to the surface. After Miguel had died, Polly and I had problems sleeping. We'd meet in the kitchen during those first terrible weeks to drink hot chocolate, look at pictures, swap stories, and cry. We'd cried a lot, free from showing Gabe how broken we were. Those nights had helped me keep it together for Gabe during the day. I'd been able to witness his grief and hug him close when he acted out or said he was sad. It helped me not to break down around him, as I became both his mom and dad when he needed it.

I threw back the covers, shivering a bit, and set a foot onto the floor. Nothing grabbed me, and I smiled at Polly. "Let's go."

I bet we'd wake up to a frosty morning with a white edge on the daffodil and tulip stems. I pulled on socks and an extra sweatshirt against the chill, adding a note to my to-do notebook to look at the furnace.

# Chapter 6

At four a.m., Polly went back to bed, and I spent the time until the sun rose, reading on the couch. I was exhausted, but every time I tried to close my eyes, the awful feeling of being pressed into the bed returned, and nausea swelled. Never had I been so terrified from a dream.

I looked up information on sleep paralysis and confirmed it was a regular, though frightening experience. Many ghost stories started with sleep paralysis, with people insisting a ghost was holding them down. There were even some who swore demon attacks began that way. I rolled my eyes. This wasn't the 1800s when everyone believed everything they heard. Weren't people supposed to learn critical thinking skills in school?

At six, I poured water into the Keurig, preparing for Derek to come over. But by six-thirty, he still hadn't. I tried to focus on my book and not keep glancing out the window at his house. His car was still in the driveway. Maybe I'd misunderstood him.

At six forty-five, a text came through.

*Overslept. Raincheck on coffee. See you tonight?*

I heard his car door slam and saw his sedan pull out of the driveway.

*No problem,* I responded. *Tonight it is.*

I finished my cup of coffee and at seven, started pancakes, eggs, and bacon for Gabe's breakfast. Despite the coffee, my eyes felt grainy, and my body was heavy with exhaustion. My heart—my core—felt cold. Even with the hot chocolate and then the coffee, I'd never really warmed up.

I added a note to my to-do notebook to call a furnace repair person.

At seven-thirty, I delivered breakfast in bed to Gabe. Of course, Gabe was

28

more excited Fluffy had slept on the pile of pillows he'd arranged, than the breakfast I'd cooked.

A voice whispered, *He doesn't care about you, about how much work you put into taking care of him. He'll leave you as soon as he can. And you'll be alone.*

I pushed the emotion down. I'd never thought of things like this before. Was something wrong? I pulled my to-do notebook out of a pocket and made a note to call the doctor. I had to get my hormones checked. Was I premenopausal? There were all these jokes about women's emotions going crazy with menopause. But I was only thirty-seven. Wasn't that too early?

"Can I keep Fluffy?" Gabe asked when I gathered up the plates to take downstairs.

"We have to make sure he doesn't belong to anyone. It's not fair, and it would be stealing."

"He doesn't belong to anyone," Gabe said, cuddling the kitten to his chest. "He told me. He's here to help us."

Fluffy turned around to headbutt Gabe. The kitten started to lick his hair, and Gabe giggled, leaning forward so the kitten could easily get to the locks of blonde hair.

I looked at the cat's backside. "Also, pretty sure Fluffy is a girl. But we'll have to take her to the vet to see."

"How do you..." Gabe stared at the kitten's butt. "Oh, because she doesn't have a penis."

Do cats have penises? I wondered. I mean, they had to, but I thought it was hidden, not like with dogs. Did I need to explain about testicles to my son? And jeez, was I really going to have to google cat penises?

"Mom," Gabe asked before I could deal with that landmine. "Can Fluffy come to Folsom Lake with us today?"

Thank goodness, something I could answer. "No," I said firmly. "She wouldn't like the car ride, and then she'd have to wait for us in the car. It might be too hot for her, and she'd suffer."

"But what if he gets lonely when we're gone?"

"She'll be fine," I said.

"Maybe Polly can stay with him? Or Derek?"

"No. It's a Monday, Derek's at work. And Polly may want to go with us."

"Can we get a camera for Fluffy so we can watch him? And talk to him through it? He gets lonely, he told me. She told me," he corrected before I could say anything.

"Let's make sure Fluffy doesn't belong to someone else first. Okay to leave in two hours?"

Gabe nodded and went back to waving a shoelace in front of the kitten. We'd have to stop at the pet store and get real cat toys today too. I pulled my to-do notebook out of my pocket and added to it. I watched Fluffy bat at the shoelace, her purring getting even louder. Could purring too much hurt a kitten? Was there a point when they'd lose their voice?

I dropped a kiss on Gabe's forehead and grabbed the plates, heading down the hallway toward the stairs. Polly had gotten up, and I heard her footsteps on the stairs. She landed on the squeaky step, and I winced, the sound like nails on a chalkboard.

*Shut up! Why isn't she more careful?*

I swayed, nearly dropping the plates. Where had those thoughts come from?

I took a deep breath. Sleep deprivation was playing with my head.

In the kitchen, I dumped Gabe's dirty plates into the sink. I'd expected to see Polly slumped over a cup of coffee, but there was no one. Maybe she'd gone back up the stairs, and I hadn't heard her. But the room felt... used. Like someone had just left it. "Derek?" I called. But I'd seen him drive away to work.

And I'd locked the back door.

Weird. She must have gone back to bed, and somehow, I'd missed her.

I glanced at the clock. I'd been unable to cancel a phone call at eight-thirty with a demanding client who would want to analyze each of my suggested changes to her sci-fi novel, explaining why I was wrong, and she was right. And after we argued on each point, she'd make the changes I initially suggested.

She rarely bothered me, but today the idea of sitting on the phone with her made my hands shake. Must be too much caffeine mixed with sleep deprivation. My job was to help her, and if helping her meant going over each tiny detail, I would do it. She paid well and never bickered about the price.

Two hours later, I'd apologized three times for snapping and explained five times I was sleep-deprived, but we'd gotten through the notes, and I still had a client.

Hopefully.

I underlined the note to call my doctor.

I went into the kitchen to pack up a picnic lunch and spotted Polly sitting with my coffee mug and a bowl of cereal, staring at her phone.

MY coffee mug. The one I always used. The one Gabe had given ME for Christmas.

Rage bubbled up again, and I had to take a deep breath. I reminded myself Polly didn't know which mugs were whose. And it didn't matter, anyway. A mug was a mug. I pulled out a different one, a random present from a client, and popped a pod in the Keurig.

Maybe more caffeine would help.

"Morning," I said, trying to be cheerful. It had come out deranged. God, something was absolutely wrong with me.

"Morning," Polly muttered. Her phone kept vibrating as messages came in, faster than she could respond.

I sat down across from her with my coffee. "So, what's the plan?" I asked.

"Plan?" She looked up from her phone.

"Polly, why are you here? And don't tell me spring break. You brought too much stuff with you for just for a week."

"God, Tasia. Can't do this right now."

"I mean, I'm happy to have you here, and you will always have a place to visit with me." I gently emphasized the word visit. If she wanted to move in, we would have a long conversation, starting with why she wasn't in school.

Polly rolled her eyes. "I just came for Gabe's birthday. Why is that a big deal?"

I wondered where the Polly had gone from the early morning with the hot chocolate. We'd laughed instead of crying as we swapped "remember when" stories about our lives with Miguel. Now she was sarcastic and prickly.

*A real child of yours, one that really loves you, would never speak to you that way.*

I tried another tactic, though I felt the red haze beginning to take over. "Don't you have a job missing you? Don't you need the rent to pay for your apartment?"

Footsteps flew down the stairs, and I jumped.

"Gabe?"

The lights flickered, and something thumped over our heads. It was the same sound from last night, like something had fallen to the ground. I'd forgotten about it in the chaos of finding Fluffy the previous night. I'd have to go into the locked room to see what was going on.

The lights flickered again. Swell. The last thing I needed was the electricity to go out.

I looked at Polly. She kept texting.

Hadn't she heard any of that? Weird.

"Polly? What's the plan?"

"I'm still figuring things out," she snapped, grabbing her phone and stomping upstairs. A minute later, her bedroom door slammed. She reopened it. "I didn't mean to slam it," she called down the stairs.

I didn't answer but glared at her half-eaten bowl of cereal and coffee mug still on the table. Guess it was my job to clean that up. Fluffy jumped onto the table, startling me, and began to lap up the cereal milk.

"No," I said, picking her up and dropping her onto the floor. "Cats shouldn't drink milk." I cleaned up the mess and looked at the time. I didn't want cranky Polly to come to Folsom Lake with us. Friendly, hot chocolate drinking Polly from the early morning was who I wanted.

I hesitated and then texted her, *We're going to Folsom Lake for a picnic lunch and swimming in a few minutes. Did you want to come?*

My phone buzzed. *Thanks, but I got things to do.*

I sent her the thumbs up emoji, got Gabe, packed up, and climbed into the car.

# Chapter 7

Folsom Lake, in the old gold mining town of Folsom, was a good thirty minutes from our house in East Sac. The lake formed from damming the American River was one of Gabe's favorite places to visit during the hot summer weekends. When Miguel was alive, we'd rent a boat and race around the clear water, towing Polly and Miguel in giant inflatables until one of them went flying out. And we'd laugh, throwing up the flag, circling the boat back to pick them back up. Then we'd get tacos from a food truck and eat them on an overlook of the lake, watching the sunset.

Now Gabe and I only went to the beach, and we never rented a boat.

It took us two trips to carry our ice chest, towels, chairs, and sunshade from the car. Gabe had brought his sand toys and, most importantly, his gold-panning tray. He set them close to the water edge. The lake was a still sapphire today, with few people on the rocky sand, and I didn't have to worry about his toys floating away. He ran into the water, up to his knees, and then back out to where I sat, watching him.

"It's freezing," he said.

"Spring isn't the best time for Folsom Lake," I said. "It's all melted snow right now. Make sure you come out if you get too cold. Like if your fingers turn blue. Or white. Make sure you check and let me know. And let's put more sunblock on. The sun is hot, and you'll get a sunburn."

"You just put on sunblock." He squirmed away from me.

And I had. He still had white smears across his back. But what if I missed a spot and twenty years from now, he had cancer?

*It would be your fault.*

I shook the thought away. One missed spot, just the one time, wouldn't cause cancer.

"You're right," I told him. "No more sunblock. Have fun. But don't go too deep into the water."

"I won't."

But instead of running back into the water, he got to work digging a big hole. What was it about boys and digging holes on beaches?

A few minutes later, he ran into the water to wash the sand off, and before I realized it, I was on my feet, fighting the urge to pull him out, scared he would fall, hit his head on a rock, and drown in front of my eyes.

I counted to ten, breathed in and out, and focused on my feet. I hadn't been this anxious in a while. Maybe I needed some anti-anxiety meds. I'd tried them after Miguel had died but hadn't liked the fuzzy feeling. Anti-depressants had worked better.

Gabe ran for his gold-panning tray, a shallow, circular tray gold miners had used in the rivers to find gold dust and nuggets. "My teacher said there's still gold in the hills," he told me, like he'd told me fifty times before. "I'm going to find it," he said, running back toward the water.

"Don't go in too deep," came bubbling out of me before I could stop it. I sighed, sat back down, and opened my book. He was fine. He'd never gone into the water more than his waist, and there weren't any speed boats out today creating artificial waves as they whipped close to the beach. The lake was mirror smooth.

And might hide a monster.

I shook the thought away. Paranoia was not like me.

My phone buzzed, and I ignored it. I should be able to enjoy this time with Gabe without the world interfering. I focused on the feel of the warm sun on my skin and the surrounding quiet. Folsom Lake was beautiful, not as beautiful as Lake Tahoe, but still picturesque and with fewer people.

Gabe came running back, his tray full of sand. "I got it, I got it," he said, pointing at the sparkling bits of sand, as my phone buzzed again.

"Maybe," I said, inspecting the wet sand. "But how are you going to get the gold out of the sand?"

"The way the miners did it," he said. "I'll wiggle it back and forth." He demonstrated, wet sand flying everywhere.

"Damn it," I yelled, flicking the sticky sand off my book.

My phone buzzed yet again and again.

"Sorry," he said.

"I know you are, but you have to be—" I ripped my phone out of my beach bag, ready to throw it into the lake.

But a picture of a giant white balloon caught my eye. Polly had sent the image along with a bunch of missed phone calls and texts with exclamation points.

My heart dropped.

*What is this?* she'd texted. *What is wrong with your house? Do I need to evacuate?*

I couldn't figure out what the picture was. Why was there a giant white balloon stuck to something white? And was the inside of the balloon sparkling?

*I don't know what this is a picture of,* I texted back.

She sent another picture, and I caught a corner of my kitchen cabinet.

*This is the scariest thing I've ever seen,* she texted back. *And it keeps growing. I think something's in it. I swear if it's bugs, I'm out of here.*

"Mom," Gabe called. "I got a piece of gold." He stuck a finger, sparkling with an infinitesimal bit of glitter, in my face.

"One minute," I said, blowing up the pictures on my phone and trying to figure out what the balloon was.

"But Mom! You gotta—"

"One minute!"

*It's leaking water,* Polly texted. *What do I do?*

*Put a bucket under the... growth.* I responded. *Is Derek—*

*I tried Derek, but he wasn't home,* buzzed through before I could finish the other text.

Duh. He was at work. Feeling silly, I used Google to look up giant-balloon-in-the-ceiling. "Oh," I said out loud. "Oh no."

"Mom?" Gabe asked. "What's wrong?"

We had a leak. Water from upstairs was pooling under the latex paint in the ceiling and creating a giant bubble of water.

*Turn off the water to the house,* I texted.

*How?* she responded. *I know how to do it at the sink or toilet, but don't know about the house.*

Crap. Derek would know.

*Google it,* I typed. *We're coming home.*

"Sorry, baby," I said to Gabe. "We gotta go home." My heart broke. It was day two of his birthday week, and so far, nothing had gone according to plan. But if we had a leak, I had to get a plumber out ASAP, or there was no way we'd have the big party on Saturday.

"Oh." His shoulders dropped, and he sighed.

I held him to me, but he didn't wrap his arms around my waist. "I'm so sorry," I said. "There's an emergency back at the house, and I have to take care of it. But I will get you McDonald's on the way home." It would only take five minutes and might make up for ruining his day at the lake.

"I don't want McDonald's." He pulled away and plopped down in the sand.

I started gathering up our stuff. Normally I brushed the sand off the items, and put everything back in the correct beach bag, but now I threw towels, sunblock, and snacks together. I'd figure it out later.

"Go get your toys, please," I said.

"No. You promised Folsom Lake. With a picnic. I haven't even gone swimming!"

"Gabe, I'm truly sorry. But things like this happen. We have to be flexible." I broke down the sunshade and folded the chairs into their little bags. "Go get your toys," I repeated.

"I want to stay here." He wiggled his butt into the sand like I wasn't going to blast him off the beach.

"Well, you can't." I gathered up the stuff, managing to collect all of it for one trip by draping the bags across my back like a pack mule. I started to walk away, pretending I was going to leave him and his sand toys behind.

He didn't move, just started digging small holes with his hands on either side of his body.

"Gabe," I snapped. "We have to go." My phone buzzed again, but I couldn't reach it with all the stuff strapped across my back. "Get. Your. Toys. And. Let's. Go."

He kicked at the sand with a heel and stood up. I ignored the stomping while he picked up his toys in the slowest way possible.

I let all the things strapped against my body fall and joined him, picking up the brightly colored shovels, buckets, and other crap. The red haze filled my vision, making it hard to see the sand and toys, and my hands shook violently as I fought not to fling the toys to the ground, stomp on them, destroy them.

It took forever, but we finally got all of his playthings. We walked to the car, the chairs, sunshade, and bags strapped to my body, making my gait uneven, while Gabe carried his stuff.

Within a few feet, I was ten steps ahead of him. I turned around to glare, noticing he was taking the slowest steps possible.

"Let's go!" I screamed, spittle flying from my mouth.

Gabe jumped and started running, knowing I'd hit my breaking point.

I loaded up the car while Gabe buckled himself in. Turning the key in the ignition, I sent a text to Polly telling her we were leaving and turned the air conditioner on high. It was boiling in the car. I pulled out the parking spot too fast, whipping the wheel hard, venting my frustration.

Luckily, no one was around.

I glanced into the backseat. Gabe had his arms folded against his bare chest, sniffing.

The red haze disappeared. "I'm sorry," I said. "We'll come back, maybe later this month," I said. "Maybe invite some of your friends?"

"Like a party?"

"We already have a party planned for Saturday." I hated myself. I couldn't believe I was ruining his birthday week again; couldn't believe I'd screamed at him. I wasn't a perfect mom, but I'd thought I was pretty good at the no-yelling part. "But maybe like a mini-party at the lake the weekend after. You guys can go gold-panning again."

"And can I invite Tyler and Nathaniel?"

"Sure," I said, hiding my wince. Tyler and Nathaniel were identical twins I couldn't tell the difference between and their mom, Alice, was an alpha mom. She'd divorced her husband about a year ago but still lived in their house in the Fab Forties neighborhood. She always wore pretty sundresses and heels, with flawless make-up, her hair styled with the beach-wave look I couldn't figure out. Alice was on every board at the school and sent these annoying emails telling us about themed days the kids needed to dress up for or provide snacks for. And I'd show up at the school with cupcakes I'd barely managed to complete with chocolate frosting and sprinkles I'd found in the back of the pantry. Then she'd walk in with themed cupcakes with multiple layers of cake, tricolored frosting, each one garnished with candy she'd made herself.

"So McDonald's?" I asked.

"I want a Big Mac."

"No Happy Meal?"

"A Happy Meal and a Big Mac. And don't worry, Mom," Gabe said, proving once again he was turning into a wonderful human, with or without my help. "When we get home, I can see Fluffy. I know he's missing me."

"She," I murmured more to myself.

Thank God for that kitten. I hoped she didn't belong to anyone, or if she did, I could convince them to let her stay with us.

# Chapter 8

By the time Gabe and I made it home, Polly had figured out how to turn off the water to the house. But there was water all over the kitchen, despite the towels Polly had put under the dripping bubble in the ceiling. And the bubble was huge. Easily three feet across. Where was the water coming from? I was going to have to go into the room we never used, have to bring in plumbers and contractors. They'd have to see the room I pretended didn't exist.

Sunlight streaming through the window made the bubble almost translucent, and reflections rippled across the kitchen. I wanted to touch the stretched paint but was scared it'd pop and spray the kitchen with water. And then the water would get in the drawers and cabinets and take hours to clean up.

"Swell," I muttered. I went to adjust the towels and realized they were soaked through.

"I did the best I could," Polly said, her voice very young.

"Totally get it," I said, though I didn't. What good were wet towels? Red flickered on the edge of my vision, and I took a deep breath. "Thank you for turning off the water and putting down the towels. I just think we need some more."

"That's all the towels I could find," she said. "There were a lot in the dirty clothes, though."

I sighed. I hadn't done laundry yesterday like I usually did on Sundays. Polly arriving, then the Ouija board, then Fluffy had distracted me.

I found a bucket in the garage and put it under the dripping bubble, tried to start a load of laundry, cursed, and called a plumber. They promised to have someone out within a few hours. I set up Gabe with his Happy Meal and Big Mac and pretended I didn't see him dump out a half bottle of ketchup for the fries. Polly eyed the food hungrily, and I cursed myself for not texting her to find out if she wanted any. I was doing a terrible job on this mom thing.

*But it wasn't like she was really my daughter.*

I pushed the thought down. I'd promised Miguel that Polly was my family too when we'd gotten engaged.

I was a horrible person. Couldn't do anything right.

"Polly?" I asked, fighting back tears of dejection. "I'm so sorry. Do you want me to make you something? A grilled cheese, a hot dog?"

"I'm okay," she said. "I'll grab something later."

An hour later, Gabe confessed he couldn't stand still because he had to pee, and with no water to the house, we couldn't flush the toilet.

*Have a huge favor,* I texted Derek.

*Whatever it is, sure.*

*You should know better.* I added a smiley emoji, so he'd know I was kidding.
*What's going on?*

*We had a leak and had to turn off the water. Can Gabe use your bathroom?*

*Sure. You don't have to ask. It's your place. I'm just living there.*

*Thank you. I hate using the owner key without your permission.*

*No big deal. Did you get a plumber? Are we still on for dinner?*

Even over text, his way of asking was intimate, like we were going on a date. Or maybe it was only my imagination.

*Yep to both!* I responded. *You, me, Gabe, and Polly.*

*Sounds like fun.*

I sent him the thumbs up emoji and grabbed the key to let Gabe into Derek's.

Once there, I looked around his house. I'd rarely been in here since he'd moved in; he'd always come to my place for coffee or a dinner as a thank you for watching Gabe. When Miguel and I had bought the main house, the converted unit had been falling down, a storage dump for old junk from the woman who had lived in the main house before us. We'd put in a new kitchen and bathroom, with dark cabinets and Corian countertops. I'd insisted on replacing the old carpet with wood-looking tile. I loved how this house came together, probably because it was so tiny; it had been easier to do what I wanted regardless of cost.

Derek had decorated the tiny space well. There was a cozy loveseat in front of a big-screen TV, a video game console below it. The kitchen was tidy, if not immaculate. It looked like he enjoyed cooking but didn't scrub the counters down each day. A desk sat in a corner with a laptop, a stack of books, and a charging station. Hardy succulents grew on two of the windowsills. His bedroom door was open, but I didn't go in. I could see an unmade bed, but there weren't dirty clothes all over the floor or anything.

I shook my head. It didn't matter whether there was trash everywhere as long as he paid the rent each month. And he did. Our friendship was a bonus I hadn't expected.

* * *

Three hours later, I was still cleaning up water from the leak, and there were holes in the walls of the kitchen, loft, and the room we didn't use. Not to mention the holes in the kitchen ceiling.

After taking a picture of the most gigantic bubble he'd ever seen, the plumber popped it. But rather than the water dropping straight down as he'd promised, it had sprayed across the room, hitting the kitchen table and doing what I'd feared, dribbling inside the cabinets and drawers with kitchen appliances, plates, and silverware.

I had to ask Alice, the hated alpha mom, to take Gabe to and from his robotics class, which—for some reason—was still running during spring break.

An hour after Gabe left, the plumber called me into the kitchen to announce he'd figured out where the leak was. He explained how he couldn't find the leak at first, which is why he had put so many holes in the walls, then talked about how he would mend the leaky pipe. I fought not to tell him that I didn't care how he repaired it, just to get it fixed.

"And you're sure it won't leak again?" I snapped.

"It shouldn't," the small man assured me. "And I'll give you the name of a contractor I use to patch the holes. You're lucky." He leaned on my kitchen counter, getting bits of plaster everywhere. "It doesn't look like much of your drywall is wet, and you caught it early, so you shouldn't have any mold problems."

"Guess it's a good thing."

He passed me an invoice, and I handed him my credit card. I added a note to my to-do notebook to transfer money out of savings. I was going to have to pick up some extra freelance gigs.

"Do you think I should contact my insurance company?" I asked.

"Is your husband handy? I bet he is. A lot of you with these older houses are. It's a lot cheaper to do it yourself than pay for a contractor."

"No."

He shrugged. "Then my contractor is the guy to call." He pulled out a business card and handed it over.

"I have thirty people coming over on Saturday," I said. "Do you think the holes can be patched by then?"

The plumber shrugged. "Depends on how busy he is. If your husband calls, maybe he can talk him into it."

This happened periodically because I still wore my wedding ring; people thought I was still married or newly divorced. And I'd given up correcting them. They were always too curious and asked too many questions.

It wasn't their business. It was mine and Gabe's.

And Polly's.

I showed the plumber out and called the number on the card. Luckily, the owner's son was also a contractor, and they'd had a cancellation. They could come out first thing tomorrow.

Finally, something went right!

Then I described the number of holes in the kitchen, loft, and upstairs room and was told to contact my insurance company. I hung up, called my agent, and left a message.

I was staring at my bank account on my laptop screen when Gabe came running into the house, leaving the front door wide open. He charged up the stairs, his feet hitting the squeaky step, calling for Fluffy. My chair scraped on the hardwood when I got up to close the door. He hadn't even said hi to me.

I went to slam the door but caught it at the last minute before it could close in Alice's face. Why had she bothered to get out of her Tesla, in her Jimmy Choo sandals? Surely walking up my un-swept walkway would've deterred her. She could've gotten a bit of dust on her perfectly manicured pink toes.

I rubbed my head. Stupid hormones.

*Nothing's wrong with you. It's her that's the problem.*

"Sorry," I said. "I almost didn't see you. Thanks for picking up and taking Gabe. I had this terrible leak, and the plumber just left. I totally owe you." Her flowery perfume turned my stomach, and I started to close the door.

"Things happen," she said, with a toss of her coppery hair. "But there is something I need to tell you."

Swell, she was going to sell me on some sort of multi-level marketing plan. Probably lipstick or essential oils. This was why I avoided the school moms whenever I could.

"Oh?"

"I just wanted you to know," she said in a whispery voice. "He was agitated when I picked him up."

"Gabe? Why? What happened?"

"He said you guys were at Folsom Lake but had to leave earlier than expected. And he wasn't able to pan for gold or eat his picnic lunch like you'd promised."

My heart stopped. Yes, he'd thrown a bit of a tantrum when we left, but by the time I got him McDonald's, he'd seemed fine. Heck, I still had the peanut butter and jelly sandwich from the picnic if he wanted it. And when we'd gotten home from Folsom Lake, he'd stared wide-eyed at the bubble, took some pictures of it with an old digital camera, and then ran up the stairs to make sure Fluffy was okay. And when Fluffy had gotten into one of the holes in the walls, he'd popped open the can of tuna to get her to come out, giggling the whole time.

He'd had the best afternoon, I'd thought. Yes, he'd been bummed about Folsom Lake, but I'd made it up to him.

Right?

I hadn't realized he was upset. I knew my son better than anyone. How had I missed it?

"I know you have a lot going on," she continued. "But birthdays, especially birthdays at this age, are rites of passage and something they're always going to remember. And divorced parents need to make whatever time they can spend with their children a priority. There's a great book about navigating birthdays for divorced parents. It totally helped me with Gerald. I'll loan it to you. But maybe his dad—"

"Is dead," Polly said, coming up behind me. "I don't think you know what you're talking about," she continued. "Tasia is doing an amazing job giving Gabe a birthday lasting an entire week. She doesn't have to do that. Most parents are happy with a one-day birthday."

"Besides," I said, the red haze making it hard to see. "Weren't you in charge of the handmade cards Gabe's class made for him when Miguel died three years ago?" I marched outside, and Alice fell back a step or two. "Didn't you organize some sort of casserole thing? Insist I join some support group?"

Alice's cheeks reddened, her chest flushing. "Oh my God. I... I got Gabe conf... I'm so..."

I leaned into her face. "Don't speak to my son or me again."

Slamming the door in her face, I balled my fists, my breath coming fast. God, I felt fantastic. Maybe there was something to this being a bitch thing. *Fun!*

Fluffy came running down the stairs and twined between my legs. "Gabe," I yelled. "Come and get your cat." I stepped over the purring animal, the red haze fading.

"I got her." Polly scooped up the kitten. "Maybe go get a cup of coffee or something. Take a break. Aren't we doing Mexican with Derek in a few hours? You should get ready."

I shook my head. "I have to make Gabe's cake."

"Then go. I got Gabe. And Fluffy." She kissed the top of the kitten's head, and the kitten sneezed, making the cutest little sound.

We giggled in harmony, and the knot in my chest loosened.

"Polly," I said as she went up the stairs. "Thank you for being around today and helping with the leak and Gabe. Thank you for coming back here."

She smiled, but it was strained and didn't reach her eyes. "Glad it worked out."

# Chapter 9

Three hours later, we were eating pizza. The pizza with the canned sauce, cardboard crust, and the frozen mushrooms. At the same pizza place as the previous night.

And it was my fault.

Derek had arrived at precisely six-forty-five with a small gift for Gabe and a promise a more significant gift was coming on Saturday. And the present was perfect—an action figure from the latest Marvel movie Gabe had asked for fifteen times every time we went to Target. Either he'd told Derek about it, or Derek had good instincts when it came to toys for almost eight-year-olds.

Then we'd hopped into my SUV, Derek beating Polly to the passenger seat by yelling "shotgun!" before she could. Polly had agreed with a smile and climbed into the back with Gabe. Gabe had walked his action figure back and forth across the seats and onto Polly's leg, making crashing noises until a song came on the radio Polly remembered from high school. She started singing, belting it out, with a pretend microphone. She and Gabe had danced in the back seat, and Derek and I had laughed, Derek playing the drums on the dashboard. Then a red beetle Volkswagen had driven past, and we'd all smacked each other, yelling "red one!" at the same time. Then dissolved into laughter and "that-one-hurt."

It felt like a family, a real and whole family.

We were still laughing when we got out of the car and went into Rosarita's.

"Four, please," Gabe had told the hostess. She'd used a pen as a bookmark in a molecular biology book while Gabe marched his action figure up and down the hostess stand.

"Did you like molecular biology?" Polly had asked her as we walked to the table.

"It's okay," the hostess had said. "I'm having a lot of problems wrapping my brain around it, but the teacher at Sac State is outstanding. And I have to take it to get into vet school."

"I hated it," Polly had said. "I changed my major because of it."

When had she changed her major? I'd wondered. She should be graduating soon with a degree in history. As far as I knew, that didn't involve molecular biology. Had she changed her major and not told me?

The hostess had shrugged, set the menus down, and we scooted into the teal upholstered booth. "I have to warn you though," she'd said. "We're out of chips."

Chips were Gabe's favorite part of Rosarita's. He'd gobble down two bowls, dripping salsa all over the place before his food ever arrived. And then he'd be too full to eat his tacos, I'd take them home, and he'd eat them for lunch the next day. It was a tradition.

I wasn't going to let anything ruin tonight.

"Sorry, what?" I'd said, trying for a laugh, though I wanted to scream. The haze wasn't red now; it was black. Black and tarry, blocking my vision. "There's no chips? At a Mexican restaurant?"

The girl had shrugged. "I'm sorry. They told me to tell you, we've run out. I think they're taking ten percent off everyone's meals, but check with your server to be sure."

"And you can't make more? Out of tortillas? You know, the stuff tortilla chips are made out of? Tortillas?" I'd said, enunciating the word. "The stuff all Mexican restaurants need to have for their burritos. Enchiladas. And. Tacos."

*I bet they have the chips. They just want to humiliate you, like the other place. There's no respect for widows anymore.*

"I'm sorry," the girl had said, her neck and chest turning a blotchy red. "There was an accident with the..." she trailed off, staring over my shoulder, afraid to make eye contact.

"You have to be kidding me," I'd said. "No chips. The most important part.

47

At a Mexican restaurant. Let's go," I'd said to Gabe, Polly, and Derek. They'd looked at each other and then stood up, their eyes on anyone else other than the hostess.

I almost shouted that I was going to blast them on Yelp but stopped myself at the last minute. My family headed toward the door, Derek's hand on Gabe's shoulder and Polly bending over to whisper in his ear.

*Never let anyone take advantage of you. That's all everyone wants, just to use you until there's nothing left.*

Once we were in the car, I'd turned to the back seat where Gabe and Polly were buckling into their seats. "Okay," I'd said to Gabe. "Where to? How about a Mexican restaurant that actually has chips?"

Gabe had sniffed, his face turned toward the window. He'd run his fist under his nose, sniffing again. Polly had looked like she'd seen a car crash.

"What, guys?" I'd asked. "This isn't a big deal. There's lots of Mexican restaurants. We'll find a new one. It'll be a new birthday tradition."

"But this one is my favorite," Gabe had whispered, his chin wobbling. "I just like their coloring book. I don't care about chips."

My heart stopped.

Derek had glanced at me and then away, out the window.

I'd closed my eyes. I was the worst mom. Ever. In the history of moms. We'd had to cut our day at Folsom Lake short, and now I'd destroyed his night at his favorite restaurant. With his favorite coloring book.

Belatedly, I'd remembered how he'd take it home each time to finish the puzzles and pictures. How he'd always left other restaurant's coloring books behind, but these, these stupid ones from this stupid restaurant he'd loved so much, he'd wanted to make it a part of his birthday weekend.

And then I'd screamed at the hostess. About chips. And they didn't matter to Gabe.

"Stay here," I'd said, unbuckling my seat belt and going back inside.

The hostess had looked up from her book, her lips pulled down in an unhappy line.

"I'm sorry," I'd said before she could say anything else. "I was out of line, and I apologize. Today was a bad day, but that's not an excuse."

"It's okay." She'd shrugged, a quick shoulder movement, staring some-where at my feet.

I had to do something. Something to make up to this poor hostess and Gabe.

"Can I buy a coloring book off of you?"

She'd blinked.

"One of the coloring books you give out to kids," I'd clarified.

*What an idiot.*

"I'll give you a twenty," I'd told the girl. "You can keep the change." I'd rifled in my giant purse to pull out my wallet. "Consider it a tip," I'd said, inspired. This was fixable, I told myself and the black haze. I didn't need its help.

"Sure, I guess," she'd said slowly, raising her eyebrows. She'd pulled one of the paper booklets out of the hostess stand and put it where I could grab it. "Do you want crayons too?"

"Yes, please," I'd said. This was totally going to work. Assuming I could find my wallet. My fingers closed on the fabric, and I opened the zipper.

No cash. Of course not. I'd given Derek most of my cash to buy the litter box for Fluffy yesterday after the police had left. And parking at Folsom Lake had wiped out the rest. I'd closed my eyes, tears coming to them. I couldn't fix this. Just like everything else since Miguel had died. Despair filled me, burbling up from my chest. For an instant, I'd wanted to curl up on the ground and quit. Quit trying to make things perfect.

I was a horrible human being. I couldn't do this. Not anymore.

"Just take it and go," the hostess had whispered.

"Thank you," I'd muttered and shuffled back out of the door.

I'd buckled myself back into my seat, passing the coloring book back without a word. Everyone in the car stared out different windows, refusing to make eye contact. My cheeks flamed, and I took a deep breath.

I wasn't going to cry, not in front of everyone.

I wasn't.

"Okay, baby," I'd said. "We'll go to Mexican later. I apologized to the hostess. And I'm sorry to all of you for my behavior. This mom gig is tough, and I'm—where do you want to go now?"

"Pizza?"

"I don't have a reservation for Sergio's."

"How about the place on the corner by our houses?" Derek had said, naming the same place we'd been at yesterday with the cardboard pizza crust.

"Yes!" Gabe had said.

So that's how we ended up eating crappy pizza again.

Gabe picked at his crusts, not really eating. "What's wrong, baby?" I asked.

"Think Fluffy is okay?"

"I'm sure she is," I said. We'd locked her up in his and Polly's bathroom before leaving, scared the kitten would find a way into the open walls again.

"But she's missing me," Gabe said, an uncharacteristic whine coming into his voice.

"Then hurry and finish," I said. "And we can go home to play with her."

"Have you ever played with a laser pointer with a kitten?" Derek asked, getting out his phone. He showed Gabe some YouTube videos, and Gabe cackled. Gabe looked at me and covered his hand to whisper to Derek. Pain centered in my chest. Gabe had done the same thing with Miguel when he'd wanted to share a secret with his father.

I took a deep breath, and Polly glanced up at me from her phone. I didn't know how she knew, but somehow, she did. She gave me a sad smile, then her phone vibrated, and she went back to it.

When the check came, Derek reached for his wallet. "I got it," I said. "It's a poor thank you if you had to pay for dinner, too."

"I don't mind," he said. "It's this dude's birthday."

"And we'll celebrate it on Saturday, assuming the contractor patches the holes in the house."

"If not, we'll figure out something," Derek said, watching me put my credit card down.

We? When had this become about we?

*Cut him out of your life now. Better that than a broken heart.*

# Chapter 10

I fumed about Derek's comment, fighting back the red haze as we drove home.

"Did you have any homework on spring break?" Derek asked Gabe.

"A little," Gabe said, wiggling around in the seat. He'd had too much root beer at the pizza place and would race for the bathroom when we got home.

"When are you going to work on it? Don't want to forget—"

"You're not his father," came out of my mouth before I could stop it.

Derek stiffened next to me. "No, I'm not," he said, his voice soft. We rode back to the house in silence except for Gabe making crashing sounds with his action figure and the buzzing of Polly's phone.

Derek climbed out of the car the second we pulled into the driveway.

"Thank you for Captain America," Gabe said to him, with no prompting from me. He high-fived Derek, and they did a complicated fist bump. How long had that been going on? Gabe demanded my keys and raced toward the front door, unlocking it and leaving it swinging open.

Derek said goodnight to us and headed back down the gravel path toward his house.

"Derek..." I said, but he didn't turn around. I started to go after him.

I needed to apologize. And I should invite him in for birthday cake. It was a gold miner themed cake to go with the day we'd spent at Folsom Lake, as short as it had been.

"Mom," Gabe yelled from the house. "There's something on the floor."

I let Derek go.

The cake, the second one I'd specially made, was smashed like the first, the gold frosting smeared across the kitchen, reaching the family room couch.

And Fluffy danced in the mess, covered with the sugary goo again. She'd somehow gotten into the cupboard. Maybe this whole cat thing was a terrible idea.

"I'm sorry, baby," I said as Gabe scooped up the kitten, giggling at the mess. "That's two cakes you didn't get a chance to have. Tomorrow will be better," I promised. And I meant it. I would figure this out, even if I had to leave the kitten out in the garden.

Gabe used a damp paper towel to wipe the frosting off the kitten. I'd expected Fluffy to claw Gabe to pieces, but she didn't. If anything, she relaxed even more into Gabe's hands, arching her back against the damp paper towel and purring like mad.

"It's okay, mom," he said. "I only need cake on my actual birthday."

"I will make this up to you," I said. "Tomorrow, we have the train museum and Old Town. And the candy store. And lunch this time, I promise."

"And I'll stay with the contractors," Polly said.

I closed my eyes. There was a hole directly over my head. How had I forgotten about the contractors? Maybe I was going insane. That would explain things.

"Thank you," I mouthed to her. She winked at me.

"Tomorrow will be better," I promised yet again. "Now, get to bed." I lightly smacked Gabe on the butt.

Gabe went running up the stairs, Fluffy following, one of their feet hitting the squeaky step on the way up.

I poured myself a glass of wine. I'd clean up the cake in a few minutes. "Want some?" I asked Polly.

She looked up from her phone. "No," she said. I waited to see if she'd say more, but she kept texting.

I took a sip of the wine, willing it to work. "Thanks for your help today," I told her. "And now we know how to turn off the water to the house."

"Yep." Polly's attention was totally on her phone.

"Can you make sure your window is closed tonight?" I asked her. "It was so cold last night."

"I haven't opened a window," Polly said.

"It's the only explanation—" The doorbell rang, and I jumped.

"Dude," Polly said with a dramatic sigh. "I told him just to text me when he got here. Not to ring the doorbell."

"Him?"

"Just a date. Be back later."

"Oh. A date? Where are you going? Where'd you meet him?"

She rolled her eyes. "On an app."

"Do you..." I trailed off. She had her phone, and I was sure she'd been out on dates when she lived in her apartment. She was an adult who didn't need me for this part. "Okay. Be safe." The words were out before I could stop them. I winced.

She smiled a little. "I will. Thanks, mo—thanks, Tasia."

And she was gone, the front door slamming on her way out.

"Mom?" Gabe called.

"It was just Polly," I yelled up the stairs. "She's heading out with a friend."

"Oh," Gabe appeared at the top of the stairs, Fluffy wrapped around his shoulders like a rich woman's fox stole. "I thought she and I could play a game."

"Not tonight," I told him. "You're supposed to be in bed. And I bet Fluffy wants to hang out with you."

"She said she was fine playing a game with Polly." He tilted his head to the side like he was listening, and a shiver rolled down my spine. "Now she says she and I can play together. Night, mom."

"But you're supposed to be..." Never mind. It was his birthday week, and there wasn't school tomorrow or anything.

I cleaned up the cake and settled down on the couch with my glass of wine and half-finished book. The house was super cold again, and I had to pull on socks and grab a blanket out of the linen cupboard before I was comfortable. I sipped my wine, trying to concentrate on the book. But the cozy mystery was dull. I'd already identified the murderer, and it wasn't even a clever plot.

Footsteps sounded on the stairs, and Gabe whispered my name.

I looked up. "Hey, bab—" But Gabe wasn't there. I had a direct line of sight to the stairs, and Gabe wasn't coming down them.

Weird. I could've sworn I heard something.

And Gabe wouldn't have said my name, he would've said, "Mom." I looked at my half-finished glass of wine. That didn't explain anything.

It was just sleep deprivation. After Miguel had died, I'd heard all sorts of things, seen movement and shadows all around me. My doctor had put me on anti-depressants, and the whispers and shadows had gone away. It had been a year since I'd been off of them, but maybe all the stresses from the recent days were stirring up the old emotions.

I tried to go back to my book, but the house felt oppressive, like I'd forgotten to do something. Shivering from the cold, I got up to check the locks on the doors and windows. I looked into the kitchen—everything was away, and there weren't dirty dishes sitting in the sink. I checked the washing machine; no wet laundry inside, waiting for the dryer. No one was expecting a phone call or email from me that I could remember. I turned up the heat in the house, though it didn't seem to be doing any good, and went back to the couch, tugging the blanket up to my neck and leaning my book next to me, so I could read and keep both hands covered.

Trying to concentrate on the words, I kept startling at every noise, feeling like something stared at the back of my head. Half expecting to see someone standing behind me, I turned around twice.

Of course, there was nothing there.

I finished my wine, feeling sleepy. It was time for bed; time to go into the room I slept in, complete the chapter, and pass out.

I jumped when a giant thump shook the house, right over my head. The lights flickered when I looked upward. Was that thunder? We rarely got thunder and lightning in Sacramento, but it had felt just like it.

"Gabe?"

Maybe he was in the room we didn't use, playing some game with Fluffy. After Miguel had died, I'd locked the door of the master bedroom and told Gabe it was off-limits. I couldn't stand sleeping in the same room Miguel and I had shared. Maybe the plumber had left it unlocked and Gabe had gone inside.

I'd have to go upstairs to check. But I couldn't find the courage to move; my brain was screaming at me to freeze, that staying still made the difference between life and death.

Pushing aside the blanket, I stood up. This was ridiculous. There was a child in the house, and I was a grown woman. It was my responsibility to check on him, check the house and make sure no one was here.

I took a few steps and almost fell, my feet tangled in the blanket. I could've sworn I'd left it on the couch. How had it...?

The combination of sleep deprivation and my full glass of wine were playing tricks on me. Obviously, I hadn't left it on the couch, or I'd caught my foot in it and dragged it with me.

Stepping over the squeaky step so Gabe wouldn't hear me, I went upstairs and jiggled the handle to the master bedroom. The door was locked like I'd instructed the plumber to leave it.

I did not want to go in there. What was a big deal about a bump? The plumber would've told me if there was any damage.

I could go in later.

A soft sound, like a whisper or a moan, came from inside the room.

It was probably Gabe, playing hide-and-seek with that damn kitten. I reached up and pulled the key off the top of the doorjamb, unlocking and swinging the door open. The door creaked in the quiet house, startling me. I pulled my to-do notebook out of my pocket and added a note to WD40 the hinges, trying to get my hands to stop shaking.

Everything was how I'd left it three years ago; the bed made, the bureau drawers closed, and everything put away. There were footprints in the dust on the floor from the plumber. I should come up here and clean before the dust and cobwebs took over. A book lay next to the bed, where it had fallen off the bedside table. A heavy fantasy hardback; Miguel's favorite genre. That had explained the noise. I blew the dust off and tucked it under an arm, going into the adjoining bathroom.

Miguel's pants and shirts still hung in the closet, the hangers covered in dust and the colors looking dingy. When he'd died, I hadn't been able to pack up his things. His toothbrush and razor were still on the bathroom counter, for crying out loud.

It'd been so stupid keeping all this stuff here. It wasn't doing anyone any good. Tomorrow, I'd bring up some trash bags. Maybe Polly—

Movement in the bathroom mirror made me freeze. Out of the corner of my eye, I saw a shadow flit behind me and into the closet. I froze, my heart pounding. My palms grew sweaty.

"Miguel," I whispered? "Are you here?"

A rustle sounded from the bedroom. "Miguel?" I whispered again.

"Mom?"

I let out the breath I'd been holding.

"Mom? Your old bedroom door is open."

"I'm in here," I said.

I met Gabe in the bedroom, Fluffy draped across his arms like a stuffed animal.

"What are you doing out of bed?" I put my hand on his shoulder, leading him out of the room. I closed and locked the door behind me.

Gabe shrugged. "Fluffy said to check on you."

I patted the kitten, and she batted at my finger, her tiny claws catching my skin. "She did, huh?"

"What were you doing in there?" Gabe asked.

"I thought I heard a sound. But it was nothing. Let's get you back to bed. I don't want to miss the train museum tomorrow."

# Chapter 11

<u>**Tuesday**</u>

I woke up, staring at the curtains in the room I slept in. Someone was standing over my head with a knife in their hand. My brain screamed at me to get up, to move, to do something. But I was frozen again. My breath caught in my chest. I couldn't breathe, couldn't move, couldn't—

The buzzing from my phone startled me, and I turned my head. The light from the screen lit up the room, chasing back the shadows.

I grunted a blurred "hello?" into the device, my heart pounding. Just a dream. The shadow from the lighted power strip under my curtain was casting a weird monster-like shadow.

Exactly what I needed.

I threw a pillow to block the light from the power strip and said, "hello," again.

"Tasia?" The voice was slurred and so young.

"Yes?"

"Can you come get me?" slurred the voice again.

"Polly?"

"My name's not in your phone?" Now the voice sounded hurt. "You should put my name in your phone."

I pulled my phone away from my ear. Sure enough, Polly's name was on the screen, along with the time of 1:57 a.m.

"What?" I was not one of those who could jump out of bed and instantly know what was going on. "Where are you? What's going on?" I clicked on the bedside lamp and sat up in bed. The phone must have woken Gabe. I heard him thump down the stairs, his feet heavy.

"My..." Polly belched. "This guy ditched me. Stupid Tinder."

"Are you drunk?"

"Yes." For some reason, this came out clearly.

"Can you take an Uber?"

"No." She slurred, rolling the O sound.

The red haze rolled up my vision. It felt normal now. "I can't leave Gabe alone," I said like I was speaking to a child. "You need to take an Uber."

"... take me to a random place... rape me. Happened to this... chick. Or... whatever... promised... never take Uber. Scary. Don't wanna get raped."

"So call a cab," I snapped out.

*She's not even yours. And she wants you to risk the child that's your blood?*

"... expensive. Please. So pissed. Don't know... anyone. Don't know...." She sniffed.

The redness receded.

"Do you know where you are?"

"Hang on."

A male voice came through the phone and said, "She's at The Bronze. She can stay until I'm done cleaning up, but after that, I gotta kick her out."

"Who are you?"

"Steve. I'm the bartender."

Swell, peachy keen. My stepdaughter, who had appeared out of the blue yesterday morning and trashed my guest room, was now asking for me to get her drunk butt. I hadn't heard from her in a year, but had to offer her a place to stay, pay for her to eat out, and then get her when she'd made poor decisions.

At 1:57 in the morning.

I pushed down the red haze. Time to call my doctor.

*You're fine. Doctors don't know what they're doing.*

I threw the covers back and got out of bed. I could do this. It was just one terrible night in a bad week.

"Can you text me the address, please?" I said to Polly who had the phone again. "I'll come get you. Stay around other people."

"Owe you."

Yes, she did.

I hurried into leggings and a hoodie. God, what was I going to do with Gabe? Could I leave him here? He'd never know I left. Unless he had a nightmare. Or wanted a drink of water. Or Fluffy woke him. Or if there was another leak. Or the house caught fire.

But I didn't want to wake him to shuffle him into the car with me. He didn't need to see Polly stumbling around drunk. It was his birthday week, and so far, I'd done a terrible job with it.

I scrolled through the contacts on my phone, wishing my parents were still alive. I tried to think if anyone owed me a big enough favor to be woken in the middle of the night to stay with my nearly eight-year-old while I picked up his drunk sister.

Oddly enough, I couldn't think of anyone. When Miguel was alive, I had friends. What had happened to them?

My fingers stopped on a contact. Derek was the logical choice. God, I depended on him too much. And I was a bitch to him just a few hours ago. Why would he help me?

My phone buzzed with the address, and I pulled up my map app. Polly was over thirty minutes away at a bar in Roseville. I'd be lucky if I made it there by 2:45, and I was pretty sure the bartender would've gone home by then.

I pressed on Derek's name.

He grunted into the phone, the same way I'd grunted a few minutes ago.

"It's me," I said.

"Hey you." His voice was husky with sleep.

"I'm sorry about earlier," I whispered.

"I'm sorry too," he said, his voice even huskier. "I shouldn't have overstepped. It's just—"

I stopped him before he could tell me... whatever we both kept not saying. I didn't think I could handle that too. Not tonight.

*Always later.*

"I have a favor to ask," I said. "And I know I owe you huge. I promise I'll pay you back once this leak and birthday mess are done."

I explained about Polly, and he snickered. "Been there. You're a good mom for going to get her."

Great, now I felt terrible for telling her to get an Uber. I was not a good mom to either of my kids.

"Can you come over to be with Gabe, just in case something happens?"

"Be there in five."

Derek showed up at my back door with a box of tiny trash bags. "Just in case she throws up," he said. "That way, you don't have to have your car detailed."

"Thank you." There was stubble on his head, and he'd pulled a ripped t-shirt on over a pair of jogging shorts. I wondered if he slept bare-chested or in anything at all. A part of myself I'd thought dead and buried woke up and purred. I had the strong desire to step close and run my fingers down his chest, to find out if he worked his chest muscles when he went to the gym.

Swallowing, I stepped back. I needed to say something, but I'd already apologized and thanked him. What was left?

"I put some blankets on the couch in case you wanted to go back to sleep. Gabe's a heavy sleeper, but I thought I heard him come down when the phone buzzed. Maybe he heard it?" I said with a shrug. "Or needed a glass of water. But I just checked on him, and he was asleep."

"Brought a book, though I'll try to go back to sleep." He yawned, his jaw cracking. "Go get Polly. This isn't a big deal."

"What are friends for?" I quipped.

"Is that what we are?" Derek asked.

When I didn't answer, he grabbed the blankets and moved to the armchair, settling in and curling a blanket over his legs. "Drive safe."

# Chapter 12

It took me nearly forty minutes to get out of Sacramento and to Roseville. Why had she chosen a bar in Roseville? Why not downtown Sacramento?

My phone kept buzzing with random texts from Polly, asking how much longer, telling me the bartender was giving her hurry-up looks, how she'd already thrown up twice and how terrible she felt.

I drove faster down the 80 until flashing blue and red lights filled my rear mirror. I glanced down—I was doing 90 mph. Pulling over, I turned on my cabin light and rolled down the window.

"Morning," I told the officer.

"Morning." He shone a light into my eyes, then into the backseat, taking in the random toys Gabe had left. I wiped my sweaty, shaking hands on my leggings and reminded myself I hadn't done anything too wrong.

"Where are you off to?" he asked, the bulletproof vest strapped across his chest making him look bigger and more menacing than he would be without it.

"My ste— I'm picking up my daughter. She had too much to drink, and her date left her."

"What bar?"

I pulled my phone off its little stand and read off the address. As I did, the phone buzzed. Polly again, asking how long before I got there. I showed the police officer the text. "I understand I was speeding, though," I said. "Wasn't paying close attention."

"Were you texting while driving?"

My stomach dropped, and I felt nauseous. I hated getting in trouble.

"No, sir. You can check. There's no responses."

His lips twitched. "You shouldn't offer anyone your phone."

"Of course." God, I was an idiot.

"I will issue you a ticket for speeding, but not for the cell phone usage."

"Yes, sir. Thank you, sir. I will drive slower." Tears welled up, and I didn't know if I was grateful or upset.

He nodded, his movement deliberate. "I know you're doing the right thing, but it's too easy to become a stain on this freeway driving that fast."

"Yes, sir," I said, letting out a hitching breath. I was in my late thirties, for crying out loud. Tearing up would not get me out of this.

He typed a few things on his keypad and passed me the document, along with my license and registration. I took them back, my hands shaking so hard I almost dropped them.

"By the way," the officer said. "Good on you for not having her take an Uber. You hear horror stories, especially this late at night with drunk pretty girls."

Swell.

For the remainder of the drive, I kept an eye on the speedometer, frustrated I couldn't drive faster and terrified I'd get pulled over again. Ten minutes away, I realized the text messages from Polly had stopped. God, I hoped she was okay.

I pulled into the parking lot and struggled to find the address in the poorly lit strip mall. It took two tries, but I finally found the bar the second time I circled the lot. Polly sat cross-legged in front of the closed business, no one else around.

Had the bartender just left her? Who did that?

I was going to smash in the windows, pour out all the liquor, light a—

Polly's eyes opened, and she tried to stand up. I put the car in park and got out to help her. She was so drunk, she could only stumble to the car. Once in the passenger seat, she closed her eyes, and I had to buckle her in. I passed her a water bottle. Gagging slightly, she tried to pass it back.

"It's a long drive," I said.

"I know," she muttered. "Sorry." She uncapped the water and took a

62

careful sip. I passed her a trash bag.

"You're so prepared. For everything."

"No, I'm not," I muttered. If I'd been prepared, I would've had coffee, and Miguel wouldn't have gone out that morning. My eyes filled with tears, the old bruise aching again. I pushed the thought away.

"Course you are," she slurred. "But I keep forgetting to tell you."

I negotiated a tricky turn. It was nearly three a.m. The bars were closed, and work hadn't started for most people yet. It was quiet and oddly peaceful on the roads.

Hypnotic even.

I rolled my neck. Falling asleep would be bad. I didn't want to take a father away from another family.

"What'd you forget?" I asked. Maybe talking to Polly would help me stay awake.

Polly started. She'd drifted off.

"What did you forget to tell me?" I asked again.

"Member the Ouija board?"

Remember it? It had made us late for Sergio's.

"Of course. What were you guys trying to do?"

"Things total fake," she slurred. "... the planchette moving fast. I thought Gabe... moved... but nope. Started spinning without us... then you interrupted."

A shiver ran down my arms and goosebumps popped up. Suddenly, the quiet streets didn't seem so friendly. Over the freeway, fog rose, cloudy shapes outlined by my headlamps twisting in the darkness. Typical for Sacramento, but the mist formed shapes I couldn't seem to grasp. Now it would've been nice to see another car or two.

I turned on the radio to chase away the shadows, spinning down the sound, so it was just background noise.

"Weird," I said. "I don't know much about Ouija boards."

"Just silly," Polly slurred before slumping back in the seat and closing her eyes. I took a deep breath and turned up the radio a little to keep me company.

The planchette had shot out the door at me. If Polly and Gabe hadn't pushed it, who had?

"Oh," Polly said, sitting up. I suppressed a shriek. "Told Gabe I moved planchette. So no nightmares."

"That was nice of you," I murmured. We were about ten minutes from the house. "Go back to sleep," I said.

"No," she said. She sat up, blinking. I could tell she was trying to get the world to stop spinning. She covered one eye with her hand like she was taking a vision test. "Wanted tell you... before forget. And while drunk. Dated anyone since Dad?"

"You're not telling me something. You're asking a question."

She nodded, her head flopping like it had come unattached from her spine. "Thought so. Girl, what about sex?"

Ummm... "I'm not having this conversation with you," I said. "Even if you're not going to remember it."

"Point," she slurred. "Can't mortalize, dad."

Mortalize?

"He's gone." Her voice hitched out, and she took a deep breath. She held up a hand like I'd said something. "He's gone... therapist said accept."

We pulled into the driveway, and I turned to look at her. My therapist had told me the same thing. Told me that turning Gabe's birthday into a big event would help us both embrace the future and let go of the past. Maybe it would help all three of us. Polly took her hand away from her eye and covered my mouth like I was going to argue.

"Dad's gone," she said. "Not coming back. Wanna die alone? Derek likes you. Really. A lot. And cute."

"Don't I have to like him back?"

She grinned. "Pends what you want," she slurred. "Should bang him." Then she grabbed a trash bag and threw up.

I helped a wobbly Polly into the house, where she collapsed onto the couch and started snoring. I moved a trash can next to her head while Derek swung the blanket he'd been using over her.

"Any problems?" I whispered as we moved toward the back door.

"Your house is freezing," he said, slipping his shoes back on.

64

"I know. I think the holes in the walls are making it colder. Or maybe there's a problem with the furnace. But I'll deal with it after I deal with the leak."

"It's so cold the stairs are creaking," he whispered. "It kept sounding like someone was going up and down the stairs."

Oh! That made sense. The cold was warping the old boards making them pop and pinch. No wonder it sounded like footsteps. Maybe the cold was causing the thumps too.

I walked Derek back to his house. "I can't thank you enough. Hope you can go back to sleep."

"I'll manage even if I can't. I haven't done a day of coffee survival in a while. Probably due."

His lips parted as I turned to face him, and I stepped away, staring at my feet. "I will figure out how to repay you. Promise. Soon." Turning, I went back to my house before he could respond. I sensed him watching me walk away and tried to walk normally, hoping my hips weren't swinging too much.

God, what was wrong with me?

My family room and kitchen felt icy, and I pulled an extra blanket for Polly out of the linen cupboard. There had to be a problem with the furnace. I blew out my breath, expecting to see it mist before me. God, I felt shaky and overstimulated. I wasn't used to being up in the middle of the night, let alone two nights in a row.

I adjusted the trash can next to Polly's head.

She flicked one eye open. "Thank you," she said. "Sorry, I'm a pain."

I sat down next to her and ran a hand down her arm. "I never got to do this with you," I said. She'd been a good teenager and never come home drunk from a high school party. "Glad I was able to do one mom thing."

She closed her eyes, and I put a bottle of water and some ibuprofen on the side table. I brushed a strand of her hair off a cheek.

I heard footsteps on the stairs and glanced at them. But there was nothing—of course not. Just the stairs contracting in the cold. Derek was a genius. What else could it be? I tucked the blanket around Polly and stood to go back to my room. The squeaky step sounded, and I peeked at the stairs again.

In the moonlight, a shadow stood on a step.

A scream strangled in my throat, and I made a terrible gaspy sound.

Polly touched my leg. "What's wrong?" she asked. I looked down at her, then back at the stairs.

Nothing. There was nothing there. A giant thud sounded upstairs, shaking the house.

# Chapter 13

I stared at the spot on the stairs, my heart thumping. There was no shadow there. I hadn't seen anything, just a trick of my tired brain.

Polly started snoring. Guess she hadn't noticed the...

Nothing. Zip, zero, nada.

I pulled out my to-do notebook and noted it was time to call my doctor and therapist. Something was very wrong. This week with the leak, Gabe's birthday, and Polly coming home had been too much, and I was going insane.

I moved to the armchair, staring at the spot on the stairs where I'd seen the shadow. Collecting another blanket, I pulled it over my shaking knees, feeling like I was standing guard over Polly. But what about Gabe? What if something was upstairs with him?

There was nothing on the stairs, I told myself. I had slept little in the last two nights, which made me suggestible. Lots of people saw weird shadows, and there was always an explanation.

And tonight's explanation was sleep deprivation and brain chemistry out of balance.

I needed to go up the stairs to check on Gabe.

It took everything I had to stand up, go to the staircase, and take the first step, my heart pounding and knees trembling. And then I had to dig deeper to climb to the place where the shadow had stood. Stepping on the wood, I didn't feel anything. No sensation of cold, no feelings of wooziness or nausea like in the paranormal romances I'd read.

I was being silly. But the shadow had seemed so real, wearing a bell-shaped skirt, with curls piled on its head.

Flicking on every light I could find, even the decorative ones I never touched, I went to Gabe's room and creaked open his door.

He lay curled up on his bed, a foot sticking out from under the covers. The comfortable green from his night light lit the room. Fluffy made a "prrrrtt" sound and started purring. She'd shoved Gabe mostly off the pillow and was still lying on half his face. He'd probably wake up with a stiff neck. I weaved through the toys, and Fluffy let out a little meow when I repositioned her so Gabe could have more of the pillow. But she didn't seem upset by it.

I patted the soft fur, and she yawned at me, a cute little tongue sticking out. *Nothing but trouble.*

I ran a hand across Gabe's cheek, ignoring the voice. Gabe opened his eyes.

"Mom?" he whispered. "Is it time to get up? Are we leaving early for the train museum?"

"Not yet," I told him. "Just checking on you."

"Are you sad?"

I sat down on the bed and brushed his hair back. "Not really. Why?"

He grabbed Fluffy and cuddled her to him. Fluffy responded by letting out a little meow and purring even louder. I'd never owned a cat before, but surely this one was unique. I couldn't believe she let Gabe hold her like a stuffed animal.

"Because when you check on me, it's because you're sad."

"I'm trying to be less sad now. Have you noticed?"

He shrugged and cuddled Fluffy closer.

"Go back to sleep."

I crept back downstairs and curled up in the armchair, where I could see Polly on the couch and watch the stairs. Alert for any noise, any movement out of the ordinary, I catnapped a bit.

But there was still nothing.

Around six, Polly grunted and rolled off the couch, white as a sheet. She guzzled the bottle of water, draped the blanket around her like a cape, and lurched up the stairs, all without noticing me in the armchair.

*She gets what she deserves.*

I threw back the blanket and staggered into the kitchen, staring at the

68

Keurig, wondering why no one had invented IVs of caffeine. I took my coffee into my office and checked my project board with all the things I'd planned for Gabe. Breakfast in bed, Folsom Lake, the train museum, the zoo. Some of it I'd done, but most of it not very well. Would I give him a good day today?

A knock sounded on my back door. I shrieked before I could stop myself.

I opened it to Derek wearing jeans and a t-shirt from a local band. He wasn't super muscular, but he kept in shape, and watched what he ate. The jeans and t-shirt looked good.

And now I was the one wanting to check out his ass.

"Morning," I said. "Do you want coffee? Don't you have work?"

"I can take a day off today—work from home."

"That's nice?" I leaned on the doorframe, wondering why he was telling me this.

"So you can go to the museum with Gabe and Polly. Though Polly probably doesn't feel up to it."

"I doubt it." I pointed at the empty spot on the couch. "She stumbled upstairs a few minutes ago. She looked terrible. I wonder how much she drank."

Derek shook his head. "Probably some of those super strong craft cocktails that don't taste like alcohol. She's just twenty-one, right?"

I nodded. "You're saying she doesn't have the experience to know when to stop."

"Been there," Derek said. "She'll feel better by tonight. But I thought I'd stay here to deal with the contractors so you can take Gabe to the museum and Polly can sleep."

My heart leapt and then dropped.

"I shouldn't ask you to do that," I said. "In fact, don't. We'll be fine." I sensed the red haze creeping up the corners of my eyes.

*Nobody's this friendly for free. Just wait.*

He frowned. "I do things like this all the time for you. What changed?"

Polly's words about just banging him ran through my mind, and my cheeks grew hot. The red haze retreated. I hoped I wasn't blushing.

"Tasia," Derek said. "Let me help. You can't do everything yourself. If you go to the museum in the morning, you'll be back by mid-afternoon and can deal with the contractors yourself."

I couldn't let Gabe down again. I had to give him at least one good day.

"Look," Derek began. "I know how much this week means to you."

"Okay," I said, giving in, though I didn't want to. "I will figure out a way to thank you."

Derek smiled. "You can always bribe me with your excellent coffee."

With a laugh, I let him into the kitchen, got him a cup and we drank together, comparing local news stories pulled up on our phones and talking about the things affecting our town. A few minutes later, the contractors, a father/son team, arrived. The son was in his early twenties and the father in his late forties. You could see the family resemblance in their amber eyes and light hair.

"When do you guys think you'll be done?" I asked after they looked at the number of holes.

"Doesn't look too bad," the father, Ted said, his eyes crinkling at the corners. "Maybe today, probably tomorrow. Hopefully, just a straight patch job. But sometimes, especially in a house this old, we find other problems." Ted looked around. "Though the cold might affect things. It's freezing in here."

"It always is now," I said. "I'm hoping once you guys get the holes patched, the temperature will stabilize. Do you do furnaces by any chance?"

"Negative."

Gabe came down the stairs and looked at the contractors, dropping his eyes and turning shy. He hadn't done that in a while—the stress must be getting to him. He was wearing an Avengers shirt and cradling Fluffy, her legs hanging to his belly. "Are we still going to the train museum?" he asked.

"Of course," I said. I adjusted Fluffy, so she was more comfortable looking but still in Gabe's arms. "Derek will stay with the contractors."

Derek looked up from his phone and grinned at Gabe. "Hey, dude," he said. "Which train is your favorite at the museum?"

I made pancake batter and spooned it into the melted butter on the skillet, half-listening, while Derek and Gabe talked. Miguel would've loved Gabe's obsession with trains.

Interrupting a monologue about how people used to sleep on trains for days at a time and how families would dress up to go to the dining car for dinner, I asked Gabe to set the table. I took out my to-do notebook and made a note to look into historic train rides. Maybe Sonoma County did some.

I touched Derek's arm. "Do you want some pancakes?"

"I'd love some."

The kitchen filled with the smell of warmed pancake batter. I threw blueberries in a few and added fresh slices of strawberries to the plates.

I set the golden pancakes down, and Derek took a bite, groaning dramatically. "Dude," he told Gabe. "You've been holding out on me. Why didn't you tell me your mom cooked breakfast so well?"

Gabe laughed.

"I never knew you liked pancakes so much," I said, wondering why Derek had never come over on a Saturday or Sunday morning.

"Any breakfast food. Waffles, pancakes, French toast. Crepes. They're the key to my heart."

The contractors dragged in their supplies and started laying plastic over the floors. The young one, Jameson, barely more than a teenager, stared at the pancakes.

Why not? It couldn't hurt.

"Would you like some pancakes?" I asked the duo. "I have plenty of batter. It's no trouble."

"No, thank you, ma'am," Ted said. Jameson shot me a longing look and then went back to work, carrying in supplies while Ted measured one of the holes.

"It's not a big deal," I said. "Everyone in the house is having some."

"He gave you the puppy dog eyes, didn't he?" Ted pointed a finger at his son.

"He did," I laughed.

"Fine. We'll take a quick break."

Five minutes later, Jameson, Ted, Derek, Gabe, and I sat around the table, passing syrup, jam, butter, strawberries, and whipped cream. Gabe gave everyone a lecture about trains and the vast part trains had played in Sacramento's history. Then Gabe explained the itinerary. Train museum, walking around Old Town, including a visit to The Candy Barrel, with their vast barrels full of candy, then lunch at a burger place in the K Street Mall.

"He's like you," Derek said. "A plan for everything."

I suspected it was Gabe's way of trying to make sure I didn't mess up the day like I had yesterday.

"Miguel hated all the planning," I said. "He said it took the fun out of life."

A giant thump shook the house, and footsteps raced down the stairs. We all froze.

"Must be the cat," I said.

Fluffy jumped onto the table to inspect the butter. "Grab her," I said to Gabe. "See?" I said to the room at large. "She knew I had butter out and came running down the stairs. Or the thump was probably Polly. That's more likely," I babbled. I got up and went to the stairs, half expecting to see the shadow again. But the house was quiet, and no shadows stood on the stairs.

"Do you have a ghost, ma'am?" Ted asked.

"What? No. Absolutely not. There's no such thing."

Ted shrugged. "Sometimes home repairs stir up things. Bumps, whispers, cold spots. They disappear after a few weeks. Nothing to worry about. Especially in these houses."

"Ghosts don't scare us," Jameson said. "We see them all over this neighborhood. I think it's the most haunted area of Sacramento. There's this one house in the Fab Forties with this blonde lady who likes to peek in when we're using the bathroom, giggle, and leave."

"Really?" Gabe asked, his eyes wide.

"No," I said. I looked back and forth between the two men, holding their eyes with mine. "He's kidding. And there's no such thing as ghosts. There are no ghosts here." I said it louder and more firmly than I meant to, and it seemed to echo through the house.

"Come on, Gabe." I pushed my blonde bangs out of my eyes. "Grab your jacket. Let's go. I'll clean up later."

*Later is always better.*

# Chapter 14

I never understood why boys loved trains as much as they did, but the California State Railroad Museum was a colossal hit for any child in Sacramento, and Gabe in particular. We paid our entrance fee, Gabe jumping behind me, and entered the massive room with its transcontinental train. You don't realize how big a train is until you're standing next to one or inside of one. Taking our time, I let Gabe read all the little placards and take notes in his train notebook. We walked through the dining car, Gabe asking excited questions to the elder docent who lived for children like Gabe to come to the museum. The docent walked us through the entire train, explaining the daily lives of people traveling and living on trains. We passed through the sleeping car with its staged models and through an engine room, Gabe's favorite part.

"Have you been to Disneyland yet?" the docent asked.

"No," Gabe said. "But I heard Walt Disney built a train track in his backyard, and it inspired Disneyland. That's why there's a train around every Disney park."

I raised an eyebrow. I hadn't known the trivia behind the trains at Disneyland.

"And if you're really good, they'll let you sit up in the engine and blow the horn," the docent said.

"No way," Gabe said.

"Scout's honor," the older gentleman said, his hand on his chest.

"Scout's honor," Gabe repeated, writing it into his notebook. I knew he had a new catchphrase. We went upstairs to the model train display and watched the trains go around their tracks, past a little village, and through a mountain pass. Gabe started planning an absurd idea to put in a model train track in the backyard, just like Walt Disney.

My phone buzzed. *Call me*, Derek texted.

Now what? I punched the little phone icon on the text.

"One of the contractors was hurt," Derek said without saying hi.

"Hang on. Why don't you go into the gift shop?" I told Gabe. "Go pick out a poster or something for your room. Under twenty dollars."

"Can I choose multiple things?"

"If the total is under twenty dollars." I squatted in front of him and kissed his nose, something I hadn't done in years. I knew the math would keep him busy for a while. We went into the store, and I stood in the doorway.

"What happened?" I asked Derek, trying to keep my voice down. "Which one of the contractors was hurt? Is he okay?"

"The young guy, Jameson."

"How bad? And what happened?"

"Not too bad, but Ted is going to take him to Sutter's ER for stitches."

"Oh my God. What happened?" I demanded.

"It was just a head wound, but it bled a lot, and they couldn't stop it."

I winced. There was probably blood all over my house now.

*Blood never comes up.*

"How'd he hurt his head? Did he lose consciousness?"

"Well..." Derek trailed off like he didn't want to tell me.

The red haze rose. "I swear to fucking god, Derek, you'd better tell me." The words came out through clenched teeth.

"He tripped and slammed his head into the wall."

Did Jameson getting hurt mean they could sue me? I hadn't even been home. But if it was just Jameson's carelessness, I wasn't responsible, right? Or would I have to pay for the medical bills because it happened on my property? Didn't Ted and Jameson have insurance?

"But he'll be okay," Derek said.

God, I hadn't even asked. I pulled my to-do notebook out of my purse and made a note to send flowers to the hospital.

"Did he trip over anything? How did he fall?"

Gabe came running over with a pen, a poster, and a wooden train whistle. "Mom, Mom, these three things are twenty-two dollars. That's only two dollars over. Can I please get them?"

"One minute," I snapped. "I have to get this figured out."

His shoulders dropped.

The red haze faded away. "I'm sorry, baby. Let me finish this phone call, and we'll figure it out. Go look at the pins. Do they have anything you don't have?"

"Yes!"

"Pick out one thing from there."

"In addition to the twenty dollars?"

"Yep." Anything so I could go back to this call. "So is Jam—"

"Can we buy a model train track?" Gabe asked.

"Maybe. I need to get back to this phone call, though. Go get your pin."

Gabe danced in place and went running over to the display.

"So it's just a few stitches," Derek said. "And Jameson doesn't know what happened. He says he tripped over his feet. He just wasn't watching."

Derek wasn't telling me something. "Did something else happen?"

"Nope," he said, a bit too loud. "But they're stopping work for the day. Ted said he'll come back out to finish up. But they did patch all the walls. The drywall needs to dry, and then they'll paint."

"Okay. Thank you for taking care of that. We'll head home."

Gabe was somehow standing next to me, three pins in his hands in addition to his other souvenirs. "But mooommmm. You promised lunch," he yelled. "You PROMISED!"

People in the store stared, and my cheeks warmed.

"You don't need to come back," Derek said. "Everyone's left, and I cleaned up the blood."

He shouldn't have done that.

"Polly is still asleep, and I'm going to head back to my place," he continued. "I'll work from home for a bit until you get home. Stay out, enjoy your time. There's nothing you can do."

"I definitely owe you dinner," I said. "Like a fancy dinner." The words were out of my mouth before I could stop them. "And..." Polly's comments from last night about banging him jumped into my mind. I pushed the thought down. "And a great Christmas present," I said, feeling stupid. "And birthday. And—" Nope. Nothing else to say or give.

He laughed. "Polly just came downstairs and wants to talk to you," he said.

"Hey you," I said when her voice came onto the line. "How are you feeling?"

"Like I did twelve shots," she mumbled into the phone, sounding so tired and young. "Can you pick me up some Gatorade?"

"There's Pedialyte in the fridge. That's probably better for you. And I think goldfish in the pantry. One time..." I glanced down at Gabe. I shouldn't be telling my adult daughter about my overindulgences in front of my son. "I found goldfish helped," I finished. "Back in the day."

I felt her smile into the phone. "There's a story I want to hear."

"It's not that interesting."

"Thanks, Tasia," she murmured.

"Thought you'd be sleeping all day," I said.

"It's too cold. The ghost woke me clumping up and down the stairs. We're going to have to figure it out." She passed the phone back to Derek.

"Ghost?" Derek asked.

"There's no ghost," I said. "Polly's playing around. And you said it last night. The footsteps sound is the house contracting. And the furnace isn't working. And the damn cat is thumping all over everything."

"No, there's a ghost," Polly called from the background. "I saw her this morning. I hadn't seen her in a while. Wonder if the Ouija board stirred her up."

"You guys did a Ouija board?" Derek asked.

"I didn't," I said. "Polly did. And those things are just pieces of plastic." I pushed away the memory of how the planchette had zoomed out the door and at my feet.

"I'll be at my house," he told me. "Here's Polly."

Polly giggled. "Derek took off through the back door. He forgot I was talking on his phone. Guess he doesn't like ghosts. I'll bring him his phone. See you soon?"

"In a few hours," I said. "Feel better." I hung up and stuffed my phone back into my purse, going to tell Gabe he could only have one pin purchase in addition to everything else. Blowing his train whistle, he agreed.

I did not have a ghost. There was no way. Miguel would've seen it when he was alive.

# Chapter 15

We got back around four, with plastic bags full of old-fashioned candy from The Barrel Candy store on 2nd street, a random hat with a pinwheel on top Gabe insisted on, and leftovers from lunch. As I pulled into the driveway, my phone buzzed with a text from one of my clients. They had questions about some of my edits and were under a publishing deadline. They would pay double my hourly rate to meet with me immediately.

I left Gabe to hang up a train souvenir poster in his room and explained to the client why I thought their protagonist's character arc needed work. The call took two hours, and I iced Gabe's third cake while talking. I hoped Gabe would be able to blow out the candles on this one. We'd have to make sure Fluffy was truly locked up in the bathroom and the cake hidden from her while we went out to dinner. I still had no idea how she'd gotten out of the bathroom yesterday and into the cupboard I'd hidden the cake in.

By seven, I'd wrapped up the call. I stepped over the matchbox car racetracks set up all over the downstairs and went up to look at the damage from Jameson. Though Derek had tried, the reddish-brown stain on the throw rug looked permanent. I sighed. I'd try again with another cleaner, but I was pretty sure I wouldn't be able to get the blood out. Poor Jameson had got himself good. I could see where he'd fallen too; there was a new hole with uneven edges in the loft's wall.

I stepped closer to the hole.

It was unbelievable Jameson had fallen hard enough to punch a hole through the wall. I touched the rough edges, peering inside. It was deep and shadowy. Shouldn't there be insulation behind the hole? I shaded my eyes and stuck my face into the darkness, trying to see what was in the space.

My heart pounded. What if something moved within?

"What's on your project board for dinner for tonight?" Polly asked from behind me.

I screeched and spun away from the wall.

"Sorry, sorry, sorry," Polly said. "I thought you heard me."

I patted my chest, the same way Derek had two nights ago. "Obviously not. And it's Greek tonight," I said. "Pitas and kabobs."

"Really? Gabe likes Greek?"

I shrugged. It wasn't my favorite either, but Gabe liked the novelty of dipping pita bread in tzatziki, hummus, and baba ghanoush.

"You feel up to coming?" I asked her. Polly's color was better, but she was still pale with dark circles under her eyes.

"I'm starving," she said.

"Me too." I'd have to deal with this hole later. I was too hungry and brain-fried to worry about it now. And it wasn't like it was going anywhere. Hopefully, I could convince Ted to patch it for free. Assuming Jameson was okay.

"Gabe," I yelled as Polly and I went downstairs. "Get your shoes on and let's go get some dinner." Luckily, the Greek place wasn't so popular you needed a reservation, and on a Tuesday night, would be mostly empty.

A few minutes later, Gabe clumped down.

"What took you so long?" Polly teased. "Did you go to New York to get your shoes?"

Gabe twisted his face. "How would I get there?"

"Dig a tunnel? Do you have a secret tunnel in your room? And you didn't tell us?"

Polly pretended to go upstairs to check, and Gabe tugged her back down, laughing.

"No, silly," he said. "Let's go, I'm hungry."

Polly poked him in the belly, making him laugh harder and wiggle away from her.

For a moment, my heart hurt. Why did Miguel have to miss this?

# Chapter 16

Derek had declined dinner tonight, and I was kind of glad. I enjoyed his company, but maybe too much. And I was looking forward to spending some time with Gabe and Polly, just the three of us.

*She's not yours.*

I rubbed my head. When Miguel had died, I'd felt like I was going crazy. The anti-depressants had helped, but they made me feel so numb to everything. I didn't want to go back on them. It was just an adjustment period with Polly being home. Everything would be fine. I just had to wait it out.

Gabe was unhappy with my decision not to invite Derek to dinner though and pouted on the way to the restaurant. He'd been looking forward to telling Derek all about the train museum and had brought his notebook full of his drawings and information about trains. He kept asking if he'd done anything wrong or made Derek mad. I finally had to text Derek and get his promise to join us for dinner tomorrow night.

When we got home from dinner, our breath stinking of garlic, I proudly presented Gabe with the small cake I'd decorated while on the call with my client. Because we'd been to the train museum, I'd gone for a train theme—an old-fashioned steam train with a caboose and a track that went between mountains snaked across the cake. I was so glad I'd had the first two cakes to experiment on, and he hadn't seen the clumsy renditions of Hulk.

I lit the candles, and we sang Happy Birthday, Gabe grinning and conducting us like he was at the Met. He leaned over to make a wish, and the candles blazed blue for a second. I wrenched him away and thought I heard his name whispered.

Fluffy jumped onto the table, and Polly let out a yelp. I scooped the kitten off before she could get burned, and the moment was gone. Gabe blew out the candles, proudly telling us he'd wished to blow the whistle on the train at Disneyland one day.

"One day," I echoed and put "look into Disneyland tickets" into my to-do notebook. We cut the cake and sat around with ice cream, rehashing the day.

I was so happy something had finally gone right.

But we were going to have to do something about Fluffy. She hadn't touched the cake but had gotten out of the bathroom we'd locked her in and knocked everything on the kitchen counters to the floor. I'd had to clean up the pieces of a plate, splayed napkins, and throw mushed fruit from the fruit bowl away.

After the cake, we played a few rounds of Uno, Polly and Gabe flipping the cards back and forth and laughing.

"All right, baby," I said when Gabe had gotten rid of his last card, jumped to his feet, and danced around the table while Polly clapped. "Time for bed."

"But Mom, I promised Nathaniel and Tyler I'd play Fortnight tonight. It's not a school night."

"Okay, okay. Just this one time," I said, kissing his nose. He made a face. Not a playful one, but an annoyed one. Guess he was getting too old for mom kisses. "But keep the shouting down."

He jumped up, put his plate in the dishwasher, and ran up the stairs. Fluffy got in his way, stopping Gabe on the landing and staring up at him. Gabe ran back to me.

"Thank you," he said, giving me the quickest of hugs, so quick I could barely get my arms around him before he went running off.

"Want to watch a movie?" I asked Polly. Maybe she had another date.

"I'm good," she said, looking up from her phone. "I'm going to head up myself. Still not feeling great."

A bit lonely, I made a cup of tea and settled onto the couch to read. Gabe shouted upstairs about battles, getting onto a boat, and something about chickens. He had to get chickens onto a ship? Their games were so silly, but the parental controls I'd put in made sure he stayed safe on his online games. I smiled, realizing how old I sounded, even to myself.

I'd quit on the cozy mystery from last night and grabbed a different one; one from Reese Witherspoon's book club. This one was at least interesting, even though it was a genre I rarely read. But it didn't seem to be helping with the cold patch in my heart. I missed Miguel on nights like this. Nights when things had gone well, and I wanted someone to share a conversation about my day, someone I could talk about my plans for the future with.

Tears sprang to my eyes and fell onto my Kindle. After a while, I went for the tissue box, bringing it into the room with me. I hadn't cried like this in a long time, and I sobbed over what could've been.

*It'll never be the same.*

The stairs creaked, and I looked up. Nothing. I rubbed the goosebumps on my arms and blew my nose. I took another sip of tea. We were going to turn into icicles before I could get the damn furnace fixed. Thank goodness it was spring, and we'd be in hundred-degree weather in a few weeks.

Wind struck the house and rattled the windows. The giant maple trees lining the street waved their branches, making shadows from the streetlamps move over the houses. I closed the blinds between Derek's house and mine, shutting out the warm glow from his windows, and went to the thermostat. It said it was sixty-four in the house, which couldn't be right. It was cold, but there was no way the temperature could drop that fast. Maybe the thermostat was broken. Adding a note to my to-do notebook, I went back to sit on the couch, cuddled under a blanket.

I made it two pages into my book before I heard, "Tasia?"

I startled, dropping my tea mug onto the coffee table. The cup shattered, spattering hot liquid all over the family room.

Polly and Gabe stood on the bottom stair.

"Gosh-dang-darn-it-all," I said. "Stay there." I threw a bathroom towel on the mess, and we got busy wiping up the tea and cleaning up the shattered mug. I had to take a deep breath when I threw away the pieces—it had been Miguel's. But it was just a mug. Having the cup or not didn't change anything. He was still gone.

Gabe curled up on the couch, pulling the blanket I'd been under over his legs. I joined him under the blanket, and he passed me a purring Fluffy. She kneaded my lap, poking me with her claws until she found a comfortable place to curl up. This kitten was painful.

"Were you sad about dad?" Gabe whispered, wiggling into my side. The tissue box with the used tissues was still on the table. Nothing was getting past this kid.

I tucked an arm around him and kissed the top of his head. "Sometimes I miss him," I said.

"Me too," he said.

"Me three," Polly said.

I held out my hand, and Polly took it, sitting next to me on the couch. We made a little sandwich, with me in the middle, and Fluffy vibrating. She walked back and forth across us, putting her two front paws on our chests, headbutting each of us, licking our noses and cheeks until we giggled.

"Do you guys want to watch a movie or something?" I asked. "I know it's late, but I'm giving up on the whole idea of sleep this week."

She and Gabe exchanged a look. What was going on?

"Sure," Polly said. I picked up the remote, and we flicked through a few movie offerings before settling on the latest Marvel movie. A bang sounded upstairs, and I glanced up. Gabe shivered, and I tucked the blanket more around him while Polly pulled up the hood on her sweatshirt. It sounded again. Jeez, maybe something was wrong with the house if it was contracting this much.

Thumps sounded on the stairs like something was going up them. The squeaky stair went off, and as one, we turned toward the sound.

"I think there's something upstairs," Gabe whispered, hiding his face in my side.

"I think so too," Polly whispered. "It woke us up. It's the... ghost," she mouthed the last word to me, hoping Gabe wouldn't see it.

"Don't be ridiculous," I said. "There's no such thing. It's just the house. It's old, and I probably need to get a contractor out to look at...." I didn't know what. Maybe we had termites, and the wood was rotting. Or perhaps they hadn't found all the leaked water, and it was... making things move. But all of these sounds had to be the normal, if unusual, sounds old houses made.

There was no other explanation.

Air shifted around us like someone had just run by.

"It's the wind against the house," I said. "Someone left a window open again." My voice cracked on the last word. My hands shook, and I tucked them against my body so Gabe wouldn't notice.

Fluffy stood and jumped onto the back of the couch, behind our heads. She puffed up and let out a low, low growl.

I clenched my jaw to keep my teeth from chattering. My knees trembled.

Something was coming.

The movie kept playing, Chris Hemsworth saying, "Then finish it, because I'm with you until the end of time," but everything else went silent. There was nothing. No hum of the fridge, no sleepy birds outside, no ticking clock from the mantel. Utter silence, other than the movie and our ragged breathing.

"Tasia, something's wrong," Polly whispered.

"Miguel?" I said.

Multiple thumps sounded upstairs like something was rolling. The sound moved to the top of the stairs and rolled on down, connecting with every step.

Fluffy hissed, and Polly let out a half screech.

The stairs were empty, no shadows, no movement. But something had just rolled down the stairs. Something was here with us.

Gabe let out a sob, curling so hard into me he was going to leave a bruise.

Then there were three sudden slams.

"The upstairs doors," Polly whispered.

The doorknobs rattled, and the doors opened and then slammed again.

And again.

And again.

Gabe put his hands over his ears and shrieked. Fluffy paced back and forth behind our heads, growling, and hissing, her fur stuck up like a porcupine's.

"It'll be okay, Fluffy," Gabe sobbed, grabbing the kitten and clutching her to his chest, one hand on the cat, the other still around his ears. Fluffy hissed and spit, but it wasn't at Gabe. It was at whatever was in my house.

A scream sounded, and my blood chilled. A child's laugh followed.

"Go to Derek's," I said to Polly. "Take Gabe with you. Right now."

She scooped him up, trying to balance him and Fluffy. Fluffy fell to the floor and ran to the back door.

"No," Gabe yelled, reaching for me, one arm outstretched.

"Go with Polly to Derek's," I told him. "I'm right behind you."

Polly ran for the door.

"No, Mom. Don't leave us," he shrieked. Polly wrestled the door open somehow, fighting to keep Gabe in her arms. They ran out, Fluffy at their ankles. I hoped she wouldn't get lost.

I turned toward the stairs. The entire house shook with bangs, cracks, and thumps. All the doors, every one of them, opened and slammed, the doorknobs rattling.

Open and close. Open and close.

Between that and the movie, the din was terrible.

Then it all stopped, except for the fight on screen.

The back door hung open, streetlights and the moon letting in a little light.

I took a deep breath. I had to know. Was Miguel trying to get our attention? Had he been here the whole time?

I took one step, then another. Behind me, the back door slammed, and I jumped, letting out a screech.

A shadow slowly descended the stairs. I could see its dark legs moving beneath a skirt. One step, then two, coming toward me. I backed up until my spine hit a kitchen wall. I couldn't look at the face; my eyes seemed stuck on the torso where the breasts were. In my peripheral vision, I saw a long neck and narrow shoulders below a shadowed face.

I slid along the wall until I found the open back door, swearing the entity was becoming more solid as the seconds passed. There was a cinched belt and curled hair within the shadow. Practical one-inch heels under the skirt, the blouse tied off with a bow at the collar, gave the impression of a woman from the fifties.

I moved out the door, the warm air of the spring evening surrounding me. The scent of jasmine and honeysuckle filled my nose.

I slammed the door on the shadow and backed toward Derek's. I needed to keep an eye on the house. Even with the back door closed, I heard the inside doors slamming again. The lights went out and then on. Then off.

I ran into something and let out a screech as arms encircled my waist.

"It's me, it's me," the voice whispered into my ear.

I leaned into the warmth, into the strength. Thank God for Derek.

# Chapter 17

We sat in Derek's tiny living room, Gabe curled up in a ball on my lap, Fluffy in his lap, purring like mad. Derek, Polly, and I needed to talk about what happened, but Gabe came first. I'd tried laying him down with Fluffy in Derek's bed, but when I started to go out into Derek's living area, he'd shivered and begged me not to leave him alone. So, I'd scooped him up and moved out onto the loveseat. I cuddled him and Fluffy close while Derek made hot chocolate with shaking hands.

Polly sat with a pad of paper, a pen, and her phone, pecking away at the screen like she'd gone mad. She was using Google to get information about ghosts, about the house, about God knew what. I didn't know what she hoped to accomplish, her cheeks pale, and her eyes dark with fear. But her hands didn't shake when she wrote notes.

Derek gave Gabe hot chocolate and offered me a cup with a dribble of brandy in it. I sipped it, feeling my heart slow and my hands stop shaking. No wonder they gave brandy to scared people in old movies. If this kept up, I'd become a convert to the intense flavor.

And probably an alcoholic.

I bit back an insane giggle. Something had chased us out of my house, and I was worried about adding brandy to my shopping list?

"This is my fault," Polly said, throwing her pen down and making all of us jump. "It was the Ouija board. I think we summoned something."

"Shhh..." I said. Gabe's eyes were closing as Fluffy kept up her massive purring. It took a few more minutes of running my fingers up and down Gabe's spine before his eyes fully closed and his breathing evened out. Fluffy's purring quieted, and she closed her eyes, her paws folded in front of her chest.

When Gabe was a limp weight, I nodded at Polly to continue.

"Your house has always been weird," she said, whispering. "And when dad died, it got worse. But I never felt like it was... mean. I'd see shadows sometimes, hear whispers. But nothing like what just happened."

I shook my head, disagreeing but not wanting my voice to wake Gabe.

"It's an old house," Derek said. "It's normal for there to be lots of cracks and clicking sounds as the old wood contracts and expands. Electrical and plumbing problems are completely normal."

"Is it normal for all the doors to slam closed while the lights flicker?" Polly asked.

"No. But it's a windy night."

I hadn't heard the wind since coming to Derek's. Maybe it had died down. Or maybe, my house was genuinely haunted.

"With the holes in the wall and the construction..." Derek trailed off when Polly and I shook our heads at him.

"They patched all the holes, other than the one caused by the contractor," I reminded him. "You weren't there. You didn't hear..."

"It's a ghost," Polly said. "There's no other explanation."

"But where did it come from?" I asked. "The woman living here before we did... um... Ruby? Ruth?" I shushed Gabe when he shuddered against my chest. Fluffy started purring again. I waited until my son quieted before whispering, "Ruth had been eccentric. We noticed she'd lived primarily downstairs, sleeping in the bedroom I sleep in and using the kitchen, bathroom, and downstairs rooms. The upstairs was a mess of rotten furniture, boxes, trunks, clothes, and that type of thing. And the downstairs was gross in a different kind of way. She hadn't been able to keep up with the cleaning before she'd died, and the kitchen was thick with grease and dead bugs. And the bathroom..." I shuddered. "We had to rip everything out of the downstairs bath. But there was never anything ghostly."

"I still think the sounds might be a weird combination of a power surge and the wind," Derek said. "I bet if we look again, we'll all agree that's all it was."

Polly shook her head. "The scream—"

"Was probably the wind," Derek said.

"It laughed at us," Polly insisted.

"And I saw her," I said. "This shadow came down the stairs at us."

"You did?" Polly said. "I've only seen her out of the corners of my eyes. But I agree. It's definitely a woman."

Derek threw up his hands but listened as I whispered what I'd seen, as I fought not to shiver and wake up Gabe. Derek took a seat next to me, swinging his arm around my shoulders. I couldn't resist curling into him, Gabe still on my lap. I was so cold and too tired to worry about where our relationship was going.

"Not trying to be rude," Derek said when I was done. "But it could've been your imagination. Maybe you guys ate something at the Greek restaurant. Maybe it's making you all hallucinate."

"My stomach feels fine," Polly said.

Mine did too, but I said, "I'm not going back into the house to test it out," I said. "Not tonight. And I'm not taking Gabe there until we're sure." God, I'd given him the worst birthday present ever. A ghost.

A hysterical giggle escaped my lips, and Derek handed me my hot chocolate. I took another sip, beginning to feel a little buzzed.

Polly's lips turned downward at the sight of us. Despite her words last night, despite how scared we all were, she wasn't okay seeing me with another man. And I shouldn't be cuddling with Derek. Not until I figured out my own feelings.

I sighed and pulled away, repositioning Gabe as an excuse. Gabe muttered in his sleep, and Fluffy opened her eyes, purring until Gabe settled back down.

"I think we need to figure out what kind of ghost we have," Polly said. "And where it came from."

There were different kinds?

"Fine," I said. "But not tonight. I need to figure out how to get to my purse and car keys so we can find a hotel."

"No way," Derek said. "No one is going back into the house. Even if it's just electrical problems combined with a windstorm—which I'm sure it was—it's safer to go back in the morning. After we get some sleep."

*Later is always better.*

I looked around Derek's tiny house, with its loveseat couch and breakfast bar stools. Through the bedroom door was the giant king-sized bed. I knew we were all tired, but I wasn't comfortable with the four of us sleeping all together.

"I'll take the couch," he said. "The bed is big enough for the three of you."

"No," I said. "It's barely midnight. We should go to a hotel."

"With what clothes?" he asked. "With what money? You don't even have shoes on."

I glanced at my socked feet. One of my socks had a hole in it, and my chipped nail polish peeked through. Well, that was embarrassing.

Polly pulled back the blinds and peeked at the house. "All the lights are on, but they're not turning off and on anymore," she reported dropping the slats, so they rattled against the window. Gabe didn't even move. "Maybe we could go back."

Derek shifted. "I vote we head in once it's daylight. I mean, once we get some sleep. Day or night doesn't matter if it's electrical problems."

"Besides, the hotel clerk will think we're fleeing some domestic dispute," Polly quipped. "Tasia may end up with CPS called by some mandated reporter."

Oh God, that was all I needed.

"Let's stop debating," Derek said. "You'll all stay here. Moving Gabe to the car will wake him up. And this isn't a big deal. I'll sleep on the couch, and the kids are here, for crying out loud."

Why was this man giving so much of himself to my family and me? We wouldn't have survived the last few days without him. I owed him so much more than I could ever repay him.

I cuddled Gabe closer and dropped a kiss on his head.

"Okay," I said into Gabe's hair. I did not want to deal with stuffing Gabe into the car or trying to go back into the house for my purse.

Fluffy jumped off the loveseat and started sniffing around the living room, finding a stray button under a chair and batting it around. I tried again to stand up without waking Gabe, but he was too heavy and Derek's couch too low. Without being asked, Derek collected Gabe into his arms. He carried him into the bedroom, his hands gentle, and placed him onto the middle of the bed. Fluffy stalked into the room and curled up at Gabe's feet. Gabe muttered and curled up on his side. My poor son was going to need to see his therapist again. I brushed the hair off his forehead.

"Don't sneak past me to go back into the house," Derek said in a low tone.

"It's my house," I said. I met him in the bedroom's doorway.

"But let's do it together in the morning."

I had to admit it. The idea of going back into my house terrified me. And I certainly wasn't going to allow Polly or Gabe back into it until I was sure there wasn't a ghost.

"It's not your responsibility," I said. "You took today off of work—"

"And it's my choice if I want to take tomorrow off too. I have plenty of PTO and—"

"Fight later," Polly whispered. She scooted between us, crawled onto the bed, and rolled over with her back against Gabe's. She pulled out her phone and swiped across the screen, the light from her screen adding shadows to her face.

Derek rubbed my arm, one quick rub. "She's right," he whispered. "Things will look different in the morning. Let's get some sleep."

There was more I wanted to say but instead said, "Good night. I'll wait for you before I go back. Promise."

"Sweet dreams," he said.

I sensed Polly hanging onto every word, though she was staring at her phone, so I nodded at Derek and closed the door.

"Bowchickawow," Polly quipped.

"Stop that," I said. I curled up in the bed next to Gabe, cuddling him to me. I hadn't slept with him in years and was determined to remember holding him while he slept, even if it was under horrible circumstances.

"He likes you," she whispered. "The way Dad did." Her back was still to me. "I remember he'd look at you the way Derek does."

"I still miss Miguel," I whispered back. The pillows smelled like Derek, and I had an odd feeling I was cheating. I hadn't dated anyone since Miguel's death, hadn't wanted to, hadn't felt an attraction toward anyone. "I miss him so much, every day. I see so much of him in Gabe."

"Me too," she whispered. "All his good parts are in Gabe. 'Night."

"Polly? Why are you here?"

"I flunked out of college," she murmured.

"What?" If I could've sat up and shouted, I would've. But instead, I whispered. Loudly. Fluffy began purring again, walking across Gabe and headbutting my forehead. I got the message; I wasn't supposed to wake Gabe.

"What happened?" I asked. "Are you okay?"

"Jeez, Tasia. I think a ghost chasing us out of the house is more important right now."

"But Polly, what are you going to do? Does your mom know?"

But she'd popped in headphones and was ignoring me.

I stared at the ceiling, Gabe's warm body cuddled close to mine and Fluffy chewing on a strand of my hair. What were we going to do?

# Chapter 18

**Wednesday**

This time Derek let me have the baseball bat. I held the reassuring weight against my shoulder while he took the pepper spray. The three of us, Polly, Derek, and I stood together, on the gravel path between our houses, looking up at mine. We'd trampled the tulip and daffodil stems in the night, and I hated how broken they looked. I'd have to clip them back and hope the bulbs came up next spring.

I waved at Gabe, watching us out of Derek's living room window. Gabe lifted Fluffy's paw to wave back.

"Tell me everything you're doing," Polly reminded us for the umpteenth time. I managed not to roll my eyes but only because her voice shook.

We'd decided Polly would stay outside, and I'd keep my phone on speaker so she'd hear everything we were doing. Then she could call 9-1-1 if she needed to.

"We're stepping away from you," I said into the phone like I was speaking to someone going deaf. "And now we're walking toward the house." I backed away from her. "One step, two steps...."

We were just a bunch of idiots whistling in the dark.

I took a deep breath. My house looked the same as it always had. My home. The home Gabe had grown up in. The home Miguel and I had bought together and fixed up. I loved the damn thing.

And I hated it. It just wasn't the same without Miguel.

I pushed my pounding heart down and took a shaking step, my mind commenting I now knew what a shaking step was. Derek wasn't doing much better, the pepper spray jiggling as he tried to hold it steady.

I touched the back door's handle and jerked my hand away, terrified something inside would turn the knob and come out at us.

"What happened?" Derek demanded.

"Tasia!" Polly screamed.

"I'm okay," I said. "Just nervous." After wiping my sweaty palms on my leggings, I opened the door. I half expected a fog to rush out at me, to hear a crazy laugh, or for a spectral arm to reach through the crack and pull me in. Shaking away the images, I vowed to never watch a horror movie again.

I used the bat to push the door all the way open. The kitchen was a mess. The paper towels were unfurled and strewn around the kitchen; my tea bags opened and dumped onto the floor, along with the remainder of the fruit from the fruit bowl. Guess it hadn't been Fluffy destroying the cakes and knocking things off the counters.

"What are you seeing?" Polly demanded, making Derek jump and nearly drop the pepper spray.

"It trashed the kitchen. Hope it didn't destroy anything else."

We walked in, one step at a time, heading into the family room. This room looked okay, though the TV was still on, and Netflix demanded to know if we were still watching. I flicked off the screen.

There wasn't any noticeable damage downstairs I could see. The areas of fresh plaster looked about the same, waiting for a coat of paint, and there were no new holes in the walls or ceiling. We glanced into the tiny bathroom, the water in the sink trickling and the toilet paper unrolled to a puddle on the floor. I flicked off the water. The room I slept in had the bedsheets pulled off the bed, and one of my drawers had underwear and t-shirts hanging out of it. I quickly straightened the drawers, knowing it could've been so much worse.

We went into my office, and I gulped. All my post-it notes on my project boards had been peeled off and stuck onto my laptop, the lamp, the chairs, and even the ceiling. Was this intentional? Was the ghost trying to tell us something? I looked at the rainbow of colors. I'd never get them back into a semblance of order.

"You're supposed to be talking! What's happening?" Polly screamed through the phone.

I let out a yelp and dropped my phone with a thump onto my desk.

"Tasia! Derek! I'm calling 9-1-1."

"No," I yelled. "I just dropped the phone. My post-notes are all rearranged. And the kitchen is a mess. But otherwise, everything else seems fine."

"Not your post-it notes," Polly gasped, trying for humor, but not hiding the shaking in her voice. None of us were going to want to live in this house again.

"Ha, ha," I said, trying to play along. "We're about to go up the stairs. Need us to tell you each time we take a step?"

"Yes, please," Polly said. I could hear the eyeroll in her voice, but the shaking stopped. Good—I wished mine would.

Derek and I stood on the landing staring up the stairs. "Did you honestly think the noises you heard when you were watching Gabe were just the house contracting?" I asked him. "Or did it sound like footsteps?"

"I'm sure it was the house shifting. It's the only explanation. Ask a contractor."

"But what about my office and the kitchen?"

"I don't know," he muttered. "Maybe someone broke in. That's more reasonable than ghosts. I mean the way your dresser drawers looked; it was like someone had broken in and was searching for something."

I doubted anyone had broken in to trash my tea bags and move my post-it notes. But I didn't say anything, taking a deep breath, and staring up the stairs. We needed to go up, needed to inspect the upstairs.

"Right behind you," Derek said.

But my legs wouldn't take the first step. The house I loved so much felt threatening and troubling. Like a shadow was going to come running at me, closing their fingers around my throat and stopping my breath.

I heard my breath pick up. I panted, the air wheezing in and out of my open mouth.

"Okay," Derek said. "Time to go."

"What's going on?" Polly demanded. "Do I need to call 9-1-1?"

"Tasia is having a panic attack," Derek said. "Nothing more than that."

My vision swam, and I struggled to get my breathing under control. I sat on a step and put my head between my knees. I hadn't had a panic attack in about a year, an achievement I'd celebrated.

Taking deep breaths, I fought to get my breathing under control, one breath at a time. Derek rubbed my back.

"I'm okay," I finally said, the feeling receding, though I felt like I'd run a marathon. Sweat soaked my shirt and dripped from my hairline.

"I'll check the rest of the house," Derek said. "Go outside with Polly."

"No. It's my house."

Derek helped me to my feet. "I love how stubborn you are," he said.

"I'm still here," Polly said. "Just FYI."

"Let's go upstairs." My cheeks warmed as I realized how that sounded, especially when Polly let out a giggle.

It was odd, but the panic attack had helped a bit. I felt more clear-headed.

Derek kept his hand around mine as we started up. His hand was warm, and larger than Miguel's had been, with long fingers curling around mine. We walked up, one step at a time, stopping to pause and listen to the quiet house.

We reached the squeaky stair, and I stepped over, climbing to the next tread. I didn't want to hear that sound ever again.

"I was doing a ton of research last night," Polly said, her voice a little muffled through the phone. "Apparently, ghosts only have a limited amount of energy they can use. Maybe this one used up all its energy last night."

I knew nothing about ghosts; wasn't even sure I believed in them.

We made it up the stairs, and I took a deep breath. Nothing had happened. I let Derek's hand go.

"Now what?" he asked.

Polly and Gabe's bedroom doors were open, and plaster bits from the walls sat beneath the doors, paint flecked off the door jams from the slamming. And the springy doorstops were bent, with holes in the walls where the doorknobs had hit. But I didn't spot any other damage inside the rooms—Gabe's room was controlled chaos, and Polly's had clothes all over the floor, but that was normal. The master bedroom was still closed, probably because I'd locked it.

But the tiny loft was different. The hole made by the contractor falling into the wall was bigger. Much bigger. And inside was just darkness.

The house seemed to take a deep breath.

"Think that's what the booming was?" I asked, picking my way through the plaster and bits of drywall. "It was busting down the wall?"

Derek moved closer to the hole pepper spray ready. I pointed the bat at the space and waited. Nothing moved within.

"What wall?" Polly asked.

"The one the contractor fell into," I told her. "The hole he left is bigger."

"It was trying to tell us something," Polly breathed. "There's something in the wall. Or maybe behind the wall. Take a picture. I want to see it."

I texted her the picture.

"Can't see anything," she said. "What's in there?"

My heart hammered. If there was a dead body, there was no way I was coming back into this house. I'd hire movers somehow and put us into an apartment until I could buy another home. I'd sell this house for a dollar if it was the best offer.

Derek took a deep breath and shone his phone flashlight into the space. There were dark objects inside, furniture maybe. We froze, staring into the area, waiting for something to move. The house was eerily quiet.

Derek stuck his head into the hole.

"There's a room in here," he said. "I can see a bed. A crib, maybe. And a rocking chair. I think it's a nursery?"

I thought back to the baby's giggle I'd heard twice and shuddered. Going up the stairs was the hardest thing I'd ever done, but somehow stepping close enough to see into the hole was worse. I peered over Derek's shoulder. Sure enough, there was a crib, rocking chair, chest, and a rotted rug on the ground.

"It's an entire room," I said. "It's tiny, but there's a room hidden in here."

Derek pulled away a bit of the drywall, and I stepped in.

"I always wondered why the master bath was so small when it seemed like there was plenty of room," I said. "I thought maybe it had something to do with the chimney or a weird attic space. Miguel and I never bothered to inspect it, though."

The large chest sat in the middle of the floor with dried flowers on it.

"This is sad," I said, touching the flowers. They melted away, turning to dust. "You can feel it in here."

"Why would someone wall up a nursery?" Derek asked. "And not just use the room as something else?"

I thought about my unused master bedroom. "Because it was easier to forget," I said.

"Did the lady that lived here before have kids?" Polly asked.

"No," I answered. "I remember when we bought it. Miguel had been worried a grand or great-grandchild might come after us, wanting an inheritance or something, but our lawyer assured us Ruth didn't have any kids."

We finished inspecting the room. Other than dust, there was nothing else in here; not even a discarded baby sock. I inspected the chest. It was wood, with wrought iron details, like so many chests from the forties and fifties. This one was in gorgeous condition, though, full of intricate carvings. I ran my finger over the inlays, dirt building up in front of the skin. Derek sneezed.

"I guess, open it?" I asked.

"Open what?" Polly demanded.

"A chest."

I put my hand on the lid, but Polly spoke. "Wait, take a picture. You never know."

Derek sighed and took some pictures. This room felt gloomy and confining, and it wasn't just that it didn't have a window. I couldn't imagine anyone ever using this space, let alone for a baby.

I shivered and glanced over my shoulder. Something was watching us. "I want to get out of here," I said. "Let's take the chest outside into the sunlight."

Derek shrugged and lifted the chest, staggering under the weight. "Can you get it down the stairs?" I asked.

"Yep."

A sigh whispered through the house, loud enough for Polly to hear. "Was this what you wanted?" Polly's voice came from the phone. "Did you want us to find this?"

Was she talking to it? The ghost? Was that a good idea?

Luckily, there was no response.

We went down the stairs, the house quiet and waiting. As soon as we made it down, the thumps started up again. The heavy-sounding footsteps, like something was stomping around the upstairs in anger.

Or pain.

I put my hands over my ears. The sound kept going over and over in a circle right over our heads. Right over the kitchen, where the nursery was.

"Stop!" Polly's voice commanded. "We have your chest. Now let us figure out what to do with it. This is our house, and you must stop immediately."

The sound stopped, and the house felt... different. Lighter. Like a presence had left. I heard a ticking clock on the mantel and the refrigerator grumbling to itself.

"See," Derek said. His voice shook. "Just the house contracting."

# Chapter 19

We carried the carved chest into the backyard and placed it onto the concrete patch where a patio set could've gone if I still owned one. We had when Miguel was alive. We'd spent the spring and summer weekends barbecuing, eating smoked chicken, sausages, and homemade mac'n cheese on our outdoor table, surrounded by the blooming garden.

I'd given away the patio set last year and never came out here anymore. Miguel had loved gardening, loved seeing things grow and change through the seasons. He'd spent hours in nurseries deciding which plants went well together and whether they needed lots of light or shade. Now his favorite roses were dormant and looked like they'd developed a fungus. I felt a pang of regret. I'd let that happen.

*It doesn't matter anymore.*

I added a note to my to-do notebook to talk to the gardener.

Polly appeared with a blue canister from Derek's house and poured a circle of salt around the chest.

"What the heck are you doing?" I asked.

She shrugged. "They put a circle of salt around evil things in that show with those hot guys. Salt is pure or something and keeps bad things away. I already put some around the windowsills, and before we go to sleep, we should put some in the doorways."

"I'm not tripping over salt," Derek said.

Polly shrugged. "It's supposed to help keep bad things out. Or... inside, I guess," she said, pointing at the chest.

None of us moved. "Probably time to try to open it," I said. I stepped into the salt circle and pulled on the lip of the box. But nothing happened, not even a little. I tried cramming my nails into where I thought the crack between the lid and box itself should be, but broke two nails instead. Upon closer inspection, I realized there wasn't even an opening there.

"I can't find the top," I said.

"Maybe it opens in the bottom?" Polly said. "Like with a drawer or something?"

We tried the top, bottom, and sides, but nothing worked. Thirty minutes later, after poking, shaking, and finally rolling the box, we quit.

"We could pound a hole in it," Derek said, picking up the bat.

"It's so pretty," I said, tracing the outline of a hummingbird. "I'd hate to do that. And we don't even know if opening this will make the ghost go away."

"But I think the house wanted us to find this," Polly said. "I think the ghost-chick did. And so she'd want us to open it, even if we have to break it."

"If it's so important, the damn ghost can open it, itself," Derek grunted, sitting on the ground, dark shadows beneath his eyes. We were all sleep-deprived and coming off adrenaline overloads. And where were Gabe, Polly, and me going to sleep tonight? It wasn't going to be in my house.

"Hello?" a female voice called from the front yard.

We froze, staring at the chest in its circle of salt.

"I hear you outside in the backyard. I'm coming around." Footsteps came down the gravel path toward us and the gate clanged open.

Alice came around the corner, holding a bag of bagels and a carafe of coffee. "Hello, chickadees," she called out again. "I'm so embarrassed about what happened yesterday, so I thought I'd bring by..." she trailed off, seeing the ornate chest on the concrete patio area. "What are you guys doing?" she asked.

How would I explain this? We're conducting a science experiment to see if a ring of salt would contain any evil ghosts that may or may not be in this box. Nothing to see here.

Yeah, right. I could totally see the alpha moms, with their Starbucks, whispering about how I'd lost it, during school drop-off. Maybe one of them calling CPS on me, and then I'd have to deal with—

I shook my head. I needed sleep.

Alice approached, circling the box. "Ring of salt?" she asked. "Did the chest do something? And you guys are watching too much Supernatural. Salt rings don't do any good. And even if rings of salt did work, you've been crossing it too much, and it's smudged. If you're going to do a ring of protection, you can't break it. But salt is poor; too many things can interfere with it." She shrugged. "I've seen Wiccans use chalk circles with incantations that work better than salt."

My mind reeled. Was this alpha mom with her coppery red hair and manicured nails talking about rings of protection, like a college professor?

Polly, Derek, and I eyed each other.

Alice squatted next to the chest. "So what's going on with you?" she purred, running a hand over the top.

She jerked away, her cheeks paling under make-up. Inside the house, all the doors slammed.

She breathed out, blinking, and cradling her hand against her body. "You have a ghost. Do you know what kind?"

# Chapter 20

We ate Alice's bagels and drank her coffee, sitting in Derek's tiny living room. Gabe spilled sesame seeds everywhere and fed Fluffy cream cheese when he thought I wasn't looking. I winced. I'd have to pay for a cleaner to come out to Derek's house. And I hoped the cream cheese wasn't going to make the kitten sick.

"No more cream cheese," I snapped at Gabe.

He looked up, his eyes wide and shocked.

*He should listen to you. You're his mother. The most important person in his life.*

"Sorry, baby," I said, fighting down the red haze. "Cream cheese isn't good for cats."

I leaned back on the couch, and Derek put his arm around the back like it was how he usually sat on the sofa. His arm wasn't entirely around me, but it was halfway there. One slight movement, and he'd have it over my shoulders. I saw Alice's bright eyes file the action away. The alpha moms were going to get an earful at school drop-off on Monday.

I leaned forward, and Derek brought his arm to his lap.

Alice set down her coffee mug. "So a ghost," she said, waggling her eyebrows. "Tell me everything. Yours is the fourth house in East Sac with a ghost I know of."

"I don't even know where to begin," I started.

Alice shrugged. "So begin in the middle. Why are you guys here and not in your house?"

"We got scared last night and ended up spending the night here," I said, realizing how stupid I sounded.

"You're lucky it appears contained to the house and didn't follow you here," Alice said.

My stomach dropped. Was that possible?

Gabe stopped playing with Fluffy and curled into me, his head against my chest. Fluffy started purring and climbed onto Gabe's lap, head-butting him until Gabe petted her.

"Gabe," I said. "Why don't you go outside? It's a beautiful day."

"Not with the chest out there," Gabe said.

Damn, I'd forgotten.

"How about you go over to my house?" Alice said. "My boys are home and playing video games. Michelle, my nanny, is there and making cookies."

"Can I bring Fluffy?"

"No, sweetie," Alice and I said together.

"We need him here," Polly said. "To protect us, like he's been protecting you."

"Go put your shoes on," I said.

Five minutes later, we were still trying to get Gabe to leave. He didn't want to leave Fluffy, couldn't remember how to tie his shoes, wanted his Nintendo Switch, which was trapped in the house, but didn't want anyone to get it for him, and finally wanted a glass of water.

I knelt in front of him. "What's going on, baby?" I asked, rubbing his shoulders. He was looking at the ground, his hands stuffed in his pockets.

"What if the ghost follows me?" he whispered.

Alice joined me on the floor. "It won't," she said. "I'm an expert. I have a master's in parapsychology, and I know all about ghosts. There's no way a ghost can get into my house. You don't get a degree in parapsychology without learning how to protect a family."

"Can you teach us?"

"I will talk to your mom about it. But why don't you go play with your friends? It's the best place for you."

"I'll walk you there," Derek said. He corralled Gabe out of the house.

"He's going to need more therapy," I said.

"We all need therapy periodically," Alice said. "It's not a bad thing. We need to end the stigma around seeing a therapist. It's like going to a doctor when you're not feeling good. And he'll be fine. Kids his age love the idea of ghosts."

"The idea," I said. "You didn't see him last night. That... thing..."

"Ghosts can be frightening. But most don't mean to be. They're just lost and confused. Like the living."

Polly leaned forward. "So ghosts aren't contained to houses? They can move to other houses?"

Alice shrugged. "It depends on what's tying them to where they're at and if they're sentient or not."

"Sentient?" I asked.

"There's different kinds of ghosts, including ones that interact with us in a knowing way. They're called sentient ghosts. But most ghosts aren't. They're repetitive ghosts and are just doing the same thing they were doing when they were alive. I've written a lot of articles about this." She pulled a notebook out of her Louis Vuitton purse. "Tell me about what's been going on and how long it's been going on?"

Polly started telling Alice about the Ouija board, but the words were hardly out of Polly's mouth before Alice stopped her.

"Those are exceptionally dangerous. You're shouting, doorway open, into the spirit world, asking for something to come through. If the problems started right after you used one, you probably have a demon or a nasty spirit. And they're very hard to get rid of. I'm not sure you're going to be able to live in the house again."

"How would we know?" I asked.

"Heard any growls?" Alice asked. "Foul smells? Odd feelings? Anyone gotten scratched or hurt?"

"Just the contractor," Polly said.

"The contractor?"

"He fell into a wall," Polly said.

"Did he feel like he was pushed, or did he trip?"

I shrugged. "He said he tripped, but it was over his own feet."

Alice chewed her lip. "Could go either way. Demons can be subtle and can ramp up over time. So it might start with small things, foul odors, bruises you can't explain. Items moving or being misplaced—that type of thing. Then things get worse over months or years. And then there's the emotional piece too."

"Emotional?"

"Unexplained anger, odd thoughts. Increased depression or anxiety. Though those things can be ghost related too. One of the women I've had classes with believes ghosts can manipulate our emotions or make us more susceptible to certain emotions. But demons can do that too. Have you noticed anything like that?"

"I'm a widow for the last three years," I said. "Of course, I've been depressed. Gabe and Polly too." But things had gotten worse since Polly had come back.

*Polly's messing everything up.*

Alice was watching me, her eyes half-closed. She put a hand on my arm and, when I tried to pull away, tightened her grip just for a second.

The red haze rose. Why would she touch me without my permission? Why would she violate me with her perfection?

Alice pulled a necklace off from around her neck—something golden and expensive-looking—with a tiny charm dangling. "Try this on."

Bile filled my throat. I did not want to wear the necklace.

"No thanks," I said, crossing my legs and shifting my body away from Alice. "Not my style." I didn't want anything this rich bitch would want to give me. It probably cost a thousand dollars, which would be nothing to her and everything to me. I could do so much more with an extra thousand dollars and wouldn't waste it on a stupid necklace.

I wanted out of this room. Away from her.

I scratched my shoulder, feeling itchy and hot.

"Tasia?" Polly asked. "You okay?"

I got up and went outside, slamming the door behind me. It was cooler out here, petals from the cherry trees floating in a light breeze to coat the street.

My car was going to be filthy.

Derek was just coming back from walking Gabe to Alice's. "You okay?" he asked.

"Why wouldn't I be?" I snapped. "There's a ghost in my house, a parapsychologist in your house, my stepdaughter flunked out of college and appeared without notice, looking for a place to live. My son is going to need massive therapy, and I ruined his birthday. The birthday I've spent months planning is totally ruined!"

Derek tried to touch me, but I stomped away. "Oh, and did I mention recently I was a widow?" Alice and Polly stood in the doorway of Derek's house, watching me. "Everything is just perfect," I screamed, not caring who saw or heard me.

"Let's come back in," Alice said. "Grab another cup of coffee."

"It's too hot in there," I said. "Too many people. Too much noise. I'll come back in later."

*Later. Later. Later.*

*They can't control you.*

*Can't tell you what to do.*

*You know what's best for you.*

Fluffy ran outside, rubbing against my legs. She stood on her hind legs, digging her claws into my knee, meowing. I wanted to kick her away, but instead scooped her up, pressing my face against the fur. She smelled like fresh grass and clean water. Purring, she licked my cheek, her nose cold.

I giggled like Gabe would have; I couldn't help it.

"I'm sorry," I told them. "I know you're trying to help. It's just been so much." Tears leaked down my cheeks, and Fluffy batted at one.

"Keep holding the kitten," Alice said. She stepped closer and slipped the necklace over my head.

For an instant, everything went black, like I'd gotten up too fast. Fluffy headbutted my nose, and I put her down. She shot into the bushes and then back into Derek's house.

"Feel better?" Alice asked.

"A little." And I did. Things seemed a little brighter, a little clearer.

"Let's go back in," she said.

We traipsed back in, and I sat next to Polly on the couch. Derek handed me a glass of water, and I sipped.

"I'm okay. Again, I'm sorry," I said. "I don't know what happened there."

Alice looked at her watch. "Okay, so you have a bigger problem than I thought. I need to talk to some people, but I need you to keep the necklace on. And don't go back into the house for a little while."

"Has that thing been controlling Tasia?" Polly asked. Derek let out a small wordless sound.

"No," Alice said. "I promise you, no. But things our subconscious pick up on influence us all the time—it's what drives our advertising industry and social media. We feel things without understanding why. And we often act on them, like Tasia has been doing."

"So the ghost has been making me think things?" I asked.

"No," Polly said with a thinking frown. "I think she means the ghost is emoting around you. If someone is angry or sad around you, you can pick up on those feelings. Someone tells you a sad story, and you cry in sympathy and then are depressed for a little while. So if the ghost is sad or angry, you'd be feeling that, and it would influence your feelings. Is that right?"

"Exactly," Alice said. "You explained it well. And I think in Tasia's case, she's been around those extra emotions for a while, and it's affecting things. The longer you're around something, the more used to it you get. So you don't question odd emotions or even thoughts."

I didn't like the idea of something manipulating me without my knowledge.

"Parents and kids do it all the time," Alice said. She touched my arm again and smiled. "It's like when you and your spouse fight, not in front of your kids, but your kids start acting out. It's because they picked up on the emotions."

"So what does this necklace do?"

"Helps to block it," Alice said.

I looked down at the golden charm. There were tiny words written on it; too small to read. "I can't keep this," I said, starting to take it off.

"It's yours," Alice said. "It wasn't expensive, I have plenty, and there's no sentimental value." She looked at her watch again. "I have to get going, but do you know anything about the house or who lived in it before you?"

I shook my head. "Only a little," I explained what I knew about Ruth. "But we got the house for a steal and then did a lot of remodeling."

"And the empty room, the nursery was never found?" Alice asked.

I shook my head. "Not that I know of. And I can't imagine Miguel keeping an entire room from me."

"Interesting," she said. "Did you guys find any trunks, journals, or anything when you moved in?"

I shrugged. "There was a ton of stuff. There was even stuff in here." I pointed around Derek's house. "But we had the house emptied by professionals. Most of it went to an antique store."

"I remember when you bought the house," Polly said. "There were some cool trunks and dressers with stuff in them. Looking back, the clothes were totally retro from the forties and fifties. Gorgeous skirts and fabric. And I remember there was this one trunk full of nothing but journals,"

"Journals?" Alice paled. "And you just donated them?"

I shrugged. "I didn't know. Miguel did it all."

"Okay," Alice said. She closed her notebook. "Here's your homework. You'll have to hit the internet and try to find everything you can about the house. The Sacramento Historical Society has done a great job of putting a lot of stuff up, but you may need to head to the library anyways."

"On it," Polly said. "I'll go find a coffee shop and dig in."

"You go find the antique store," Alice said to me. "They may still have some of the stuff or know who it got donated to."

"But Gabe and I..." I stopped. I needed to get this resolved.

"What's wrong?" Polly asked.

"Today, Gabe and I were supposed to go to the zoo and Fairytale Town." There were discounts on Wednesdays, and the sunny warm weather was perfect.

"You don't have to go to the antique store today," Alice said. "The ghost will still be here tomorrow."

"No, I do." I sighed. I still wanted to have Gabe's birthday party on Saturday. Make this week up to Gabe somehow.

"Take him with you to the antique store," Polly said. "They may have some model trains he can talk you into buying."

"Whatever you think is best," Alice said. "Today or tomorrow probably doesn't make too much of a difference. I'll be back at seven with friends tonight, and we'll do a ghost hunt. Everyone clear?"

Wait, what?

"A ghost hunt?" I asked.

Alice looked at her watch again. "Yep. It's the best way to sort this out and maybe get rid of the ghost." She saw my face. "It's only a couple of friends from the parapsychology department at Sac State. They... we do these all the time."

I waited for the red haze to rise, for me to order Alice out of Derek's house, but the necklace just warmed.

"What happens in a ghost hunt?" Polly asked.

"We set up some cameras and recorders and try to get some footage," Alice said. "It's not a big deal. I've got to get out of here. I'm super late picking up Nathaniel from his soccer practice. See you at seven, chickadees." She blew us a kiss and left.

Thirty seconds later, my phone buzzed.

*Keep the necklace on,* Alice texted. *I'll bring similar ones for the rest of you tonight. And Gabe should plan to spend the night at my place.*

There was the alpha mom I knew so well from school emails.

# Chapter 21

I'd never been inside the antique store we'd sold Ruth's things to. Miguel and I had always planned to pop in, but we were always too busy, too tired, or too late for something. We'd always said we'd do it later.

But later was usually too late.

Besides, with Gabe, we were still in the IKEA stage of furniture. I didn't want to spend a lot of money on antiques he'd accidentally gouge, stain, or scratch while building a racetrack attacked by legions of dinosaurs across the downstairs.

"Do not touch anything," I said, grabbing Gabe's hand as we crossed from the bright sunlight into the shadowy interior of the shop. In the doorway, I stopped, blinking. The building was full—ceiling to floor, with... stuff. Furniture, glass cabinets, lacy white clothes on racks, and fancy light fixtures warred with rusty signs, broken and tarnished bits of metal, and quilts. Glass curio cabinets held jewelry, dolls, china dishes, and random small items. Paths between the furniture gave shoppers the chance to see things from all angles. Lamps, vases, books, and postcards rested on dressers, tables, and desks. Neatly labeled baseball cards sat in boxes, along with old faded photos and bits of dingy embroidery.

How could anyone find anything in here? It was dusty, smelled odd, and wasn't air-conditioned. The air was sticky and warm, though it was only April. The building must be terrible in the Sacramento hundred-degree summers.

We began to walk up and down the aisles. There had to be someone working here. Gabe pressed his nose against a case full of model trains.

"Can we get one?" he asked.

"Maybe," I said. "But probably not today."

"Aw, Mom."

We kept wandering until we located a vast antique desk where a woman with blue, purple, and turquoise hair sat, squinting at a computer.

"Can I help you?" she asked. She'd pushed her sleeves up, and I stared at the tattoos on her arm—waves, octopus, and seahorses mixed with seashells. I'd never realized tattoos could be pretty.

"I'm not sure," I said, tearing my eyes away from her arms and feeling a little silly. And tired. So very exhausted. At some point, I needed a full night's sleep again. "We sold the owners of this store a bunch of stuff we found in our house a few years ago. Just wanted it gone, and you paid us, like a hundred bucks, or something. I was wondering if maybe you still had some of it. Or a list of where the things went."

She nodded. "You're welcome to look around and see what we still have, and we could offer you a discount, depending on what it is. If you give me your name, I can try to find the transaction, but the previous owners were terrible about inventory."

"You're very sweet," I said. "But I'm looking for something specific. We think there were journals in a trunk, and I need those."

"That is going to be harder," the woman said. "The previous owners were supposed to give all the journals they found to the historical society."

"Yes," I said, snapping my fingers as the memory came back to me. "They told us that."

"They lied," the woman said. "Or they'd planned to give it to them and then never did. The owners were ready for retirement when they sold us the business. In truth, they should've retired ten years before they did." She ran her fingers through her multi-colored hair. "And I shouldn't be so hard on them. They did the best they could. But I'll show you where all the journals ended up. Come on."

She led us behind the counter and into a back room. This part of the shop was lighter and better organized. The owners had stacked bits of junk, faded furniture, and broken things on shelves, reaching the length of the back of the store. "We're trying to organize this," the woman said, pointing to the shelves. "Before we try to clean and organize the store itself. That way, we have a place to put stuff. But it's hard. The entire store was such a mess."

"How long have you owned it?"

"My wife and I bought it about six months ago," she said. "Luckily, we ran a similar antique store up in Seattle." She looked around the room, her hand stuffed in a back pocket. "It'll get done. And we've found a lot of treasures in here that have helped us stay afloat." She led me over to a massive stack of plastic bins. "These are full of journals."

I winced. There had to be over fifty boxes, filled to the brim with neatly stacked books.

"These," she said, pointing at another stack of bins. "Are full of photo albums. Our first step was to separate them."

"The historical society doesn't want them?" I asked. "Can't you tell them to pick them up? Let them figure this out?"

She shook her head. "The representative they sent took one look at the boxes and turned white, I kid you not. It was the funniest thing I've ever seen. But they're all volunteers, mostly retired, and this is too much work for them. So we're paying high school kids to help us organize them. But anyways, your journals might be here. Or they might be in a random box we haven't opened yet."

"Holy cow," I said. Gabe's party was on Saturday, and this could take months to go through. If Ruth's journals were even here.

"The journals are kind of organized by year. Do you know how old the ones you're looking for would be?"

"Not really," I said. "Maybe from the forties or fifties?"

"Ah. Doing a genealogical search? I heard once about a family who found out they had African American ancestors because they were looking for stem cell donors. They were totally shocked but ended up going through a bunch of old journals, trying to figure out who their relatives were."

"Nothing like that," I said. "Just trying to learn about the person who owned the house before us."

"Do you have her name?"

"Ruth Evans."

"Well, hopefully, she put her name in the journal. Otherwise, you may be out of luck."

# Chapter 22

Two hours later, I wiped my running nose with a disintegrating tissue. The dust and mold endemic in antiques was stirring up my allergies. If we had to come back, I'd take an allergy pill first.

Gabe had been helpful in the beginning, moving journals into different piles. Two hours in, he'd reached his breaking point and wouldn't last much more.

"I like your drawing," I said to him, grateful the owner with the colored hair had offered crayons and paper.

"It's not done," he growled, scribbling in a giant black circle.

Okay. Jeez.

I went back to opening each journal, trying to decipher the spidery and faded writing of people from the 1900s forward. It was taking forever. We hadn't found any journals with the name Ruth on the front few pages. And even though I'd spent two hours flipping through the fragile paper and disintegrating covers, there were hundreds of journals left. People had been really into documenting their daily lives. But I guess things hadn't changed. Today, they just recorded their feelings on Twitter, Facebook, and Instagram. And blogs. And vlogs. And live-streams.

I stretched out my back, reaching my hands over my head.

"So have you seen the ghost?" the owner said to Gabe. Her name was Piper, and Gabe had told her everything that had happened in the last few days. And God help me, I hadn't stopped him.

"Not yet," Gabe said. "But I heard it last night. It laughed at us."

"That sounds terrifying," Piper said.

"It happened. Scout's honor."

"I believe you," Piper said. "You're really brave."

"Thank you," Gabe said with a smile, going back to his drawing.

"I've gone to estate sales and thought I've seen things," Piper said. "Some pieces, you pick them up, and you can feel things about them or about the people who owned them. But I've never met anyone who has actually lived in a haunted house."

It was like she'd thrown water on me. I lived in a haunted house. And not a fun one like at Disneyland either.

"Let me help you," Piper said, joining me on the floor.

"What if someone comes in?" I asked.

She pointed at her phone. "I have an app that tells me when the front door opens. And it's usually slow on Wednesdays anyways. It's a good day to clean and organize."

We worked in silence until Piper asked, "So this woman, Ruth, was in your house until she died? She lived there her whole adult life? That's kind of sad. I wouldn't be who I am if I didn't move around a lot."

I shrugged. "And Ruth wouldn't have been who she was if she had."

"Fair," Piper said with a wink. "So now Ruth's angry? And scaring you guys?"

I shrugged. "I guess. When we moved in, our neighbors told us all about her. They said the kids would dare each other to hang out in the front yard because she would yell to scare them off. Typical old person stuff."

We went back to the journals until Piper said, "Ruth! I found Ruth Evans." She waved the brown book around and passed it over.

Sure enough, the faded writing on the inside cover said "Ruth Evans," with something unreadable underneath. "When is it from?" I asked, flipping through the pages. The writing was so faded, I could barely make anything out.

"Use your phone flashlight," Piper suggested, showing me how to angle the light so it threw a faint shadow on the writing.

"I think my boss is out to get me," I read out loud. "I told her yesterday how much I hated daisies and what was waiting on my desk today? Daisies!!!!!

Then I had to spend the day looking at them and thinking about how much I hated them. But I can't throw them out. And I can't take them home. He'll smash them, rip them apart until the bits are everywhere, and I have to clean them up. So, they'll stay on my desk until they die, and I can throw them out. Later. Everything always has to wait until later."

I looked at Piper and shrugged. "I guess this could be her. How many Ruth Evans could there have been? Let's see if there's more."

Over the next hour, we kept sorting, eventually finding over twenty-five journals, stretching from 1942 forward. It looked like Ruth kept journals starting with her marriage and then going forward until she died. But she didn't write in them every day, only when she felt like it, and there were gaps for months. And she didn't always use dates, and when she did, there were never any years. This was going to take a while.

I opened another journal at random.

*Why won't he leave me alone, why won't he leave me alone, why won't he stop crying?*

I snorted. I remembered that feeling when Gabe was a baby and not sleeping through the night.

*So very tired. Don't know what's real anymore. Dreading the nighttime, he's so much worse at night.*

The poor woman. I'd lucked out with Gabe—he'd been a good sleeper with no hint of colic. I flipped a few pages at random and kept reading.

*Talked to a priest. But he said there was nothing to be done. I just had to pray more.*

I felt so bad for Ruth. They hadn't known about postpartum depression until recently, and it sounded like Ruth had a terrible case of it. Imagine telling a depressed person they just had to try harder.

Closing the book, we gathered up all the journals we'd found. I hoped there were answers somewhere in them. I couldn't in good conscience sell my house, knowing it came with a ghost.

"Tasia?" Piper said, drawing me over to the pile of photograph albums. "These have Ruth's name in them, too. Is this your house?"

I squinted at the black-and-white picture. "It's hard to tell," I said. "So many of the houses in our neighborhood look the same. They were all built around the same time by a lot of the same builders. Can I flip over the picture?" I asked.

"Sure," she said with a shrug. "It's not like there's a gigantic market for photo albums. Just be careful. A lot of the pictures get stuck to the backing and won't come off."

I peeled the layer of cellophane off and used my nail to flake the picture off. There was writing on the back, but time had faded the ink. I shined my flashlight on it but still struggled to make it out.

"321 35th street," I read. "That's my house." A chill ran up my spine. I reattached the picture and flipped the pages. "I guess this is Ruth."

The woman was pretty, with dark hair curled and puffed out around her face. She looked like she was dancing in the black-and-white picture, her arm around another laughing woman. Their lips were so dark, you could almost see the heavy red lipstick they'd worn in the late forties. I flipped the page. Ruth, and presumably her husband, stared straight ahead, small smiles on their lips. He wore a military uniform, and she wore a dress with a light dress with a full skirt and lace at the collar. I realized by the flowers in her arms it was a wedding picture. I wondered why she hadn't gotten a wedding dress. Maybe she was already pregnant, and the wedding had to be fast. I peered closer, seeing the excitement and happiness shining through their eyes. You could almost feel the love coming off the page. I touched their faces and blinked back tears. I'd been so happy on my wedding day, too.

"Add it to the stack," I said to Piper, wiping my face on my shoulder.

I offered to pay Piper for the journals and album, but she waved my offer away. "You guys were super helpful sorting the journals and not trashing the storeroom. Journals never go for much anyways unless they're some famous person. We're even. Could you come back, though, some time, and tell me about the ghost? I'm so curious."

"I will," I said.

"We have a book club too," Piper said. "If you're interested. We're always looking for new people if you like to read."

"I love to read." And a book club sounded nice. I'd been in one before

Miguel's death, and I missed the conversations over snacks and wine.

We exchanged phone numbers, and I took Gabe's hand as we went outside.

The sun was bright and warm, and I felt like I hadn't seen it in a while.

"Want to stop for ice cream?" I asked Gabe.

"Sure!"

# Chapter 23

Derek's doorbell rang at six-thirty. We were eating Chinese food, Polly and I on the loveseat, Derek and Gabe on the breakfast bar stools. They'd wanted pizza, and I'd refused, in near tears. It had been a challenging few days.

I wiped my fingers on my napkin while Derek stood up to answer the door. What was the protocol of having ghost hunters over? Did I have to feed them? Should we have waited for dinner? What were they going to do in my house other than set up cameras? How many people were even coming?

Polly and I had spent an hour watching a ghost hunters show on Netflix, so we'd know what to expect. But the show was ridiculous and blatantly fake, filmed entirely with night cameras and an obnoxious host who kept looking at the cameraman, demanding to know if they "felt" anything. And then comments about vortexes and hundreds of people dying in that location during a historical event he and the producers had uncovered after "extensive research."

No wonder no one believed in ghosts.

Derek opened the door, showing in a person in their mid-twenties with dark black hair, cut into a shaggy bob, large glasses, and bags of equipment. I couldn't tell if it was a he or she.

"Hi!" He/she shook Derek's hand and then came charging up to me, carrying the bags like they weighed nothing. "I hear you've got a pretty active ghost right now. Pretty exciting. Can't wait to see it."

"Hi," I said back. "Who are you?"

"Oh! I'm Oak. I'm sorry. This is where we're doing a ghost hunt, right? You do know Alice?" She/he fished out a phone and checked an address. "This is 321 35th street, right? She said you'd be in the granny unit, not the big house."

"Yes," I said. "I'm sorry. We're so sleep-deprived. I didn't mean to be rude."

"No worries," he/she said. I couldn't tell from the voice either if this person was a he or she; it was throwing me off. "I'm always early. I think being late is a sign of disrespect. Our most valuable commodity is time and being late robs people of that commodity." He/she glanced at their phone again. "Though I am earlier than I thought. I can hang in the car if it's easier." He/she looked at the little white cartons of food and blinked. "I'm sorry. I'm interrupting your dinner."

"Of course not," Polly said. "It's just Chinese food, and there's always so much. Do you want some?"

"Thanks." He/she held out their hand. "I'm Oak. My pronouns are she/her."

I guess that cleared it up.

"Polly," Polly said. She passed Oak a plate and a set of chopsticks. "Help yourself. And I'm she/her, as well."

"Gabe," Gabe chimed in. "I'm a boy, so he/ him?"

"Derek," Derek said around a mouthful of Kung Pao. "He/him."

Was I missing out on a new social mores? We had to identify our gender now?

"I'll explain later," Polly whispered to me.

"Nice to meet all of you," Oak said. She filled up her place with rice, chow mein, and various meats in various sauces.

"So, how long have you been hunting ghosts?" I asked, feeling surreal.

"I'm about to get my master's in parapsychology," Oak said. "But I've been hunting ghosts since I was about ten. My dad hated my "obsession-with-the-occult," so I'd sneak out and go to the cemetery across the street. I made my own electrostatic meter and waved it all around, pretending I was finding ghosts. Then I started actually getting EVPs and stuff on cameras. Shadows, faces in windows, orbs, that type of thing."

"What are orbs?" Polly asked. "I keep seeing references to them."

"Dust, mostly," Oak said. "People catch the particles with their flash, and it looks like opaque circles. A lot of people think they're ghosts, but trust me, it's dust. It does look pretty spooky, though, so I get it."

"That explains a lot," Polly said.

"There's so much conflicting stuff out there about ghosts. I was obsessed when I was younger. I almost failed fifth grade because I wasn't doing homework or trying for the tests. They thought I had a learning disability until they found out I was reading college-level essays on parapsychology."

"What's your dad think of it now?" Polly asked.

"He's okay with it, though he thinks I should have a "real" career. But you can make pretty good money doing ghost hunts and participating in research. Oh! Alice did say we're doing this for free," she clarified as my heart stopped at the idea of being charged for a ghost hunt I wasn't sure I wanted. Between the holes in the walls, the speeding ticket, and the thousand-dollar dinner I owed Derek, I had no extra money for this odd ghost hunter.

Derek's doorbell rang. "Come in," he called.

Alice stepped in, wearing black jeans and an old Sac State sweatshirt, her hair in a ponytail. She had a gigantic bag over her shoulder.

"Okay, dude," she said to Gabe. "I brought Danny, Nathaniel, and Tyler with me so they could walk you to my house for the sleepover." Danny was Alice's oldest son, a hulking sixteen-year-old who played soccer and football. I bet he tutored the cheerleaders in math while they pretended not to know the answers.

But the thought was unfair and felt faded. Like it wasn't my thought, but someone else's.

Gabe hugged Fluffy, told her to be good, then hugged me. Breathing in his smell, I centered myself. I could do this. I could get rid of this ghost for him and Polly.

Gabe hugged Polly and, without missing a beat, wrapped his arms around Derek's waist too. Derek startled but returned the hug, ending it with some sort of complicated fist bump. My chest hurt, and I didn't want to analyze why.

"Glad you could come," Alice said to Oak. "Did you grab the van from the university?"

"Ben's bringing it," Oak said around a mouthful of chow mein.

"Ben?" Alice said.

I looked up at the other woman. I'd only heard that tone during PTA meetings when someone introduced the idea of not needing a peanut-free classroom.

Oak shrugged. "He was the only one available. And he knows a ton. And you said you were worried about—"

Alice made a slight gesture.

"Anyways," Oak continued. "Ben's an expert. And he can totally set up the equipment and get the feeds going. I haven't done it by myself yet and don't want to screw it up."

"But he's—"

Derek's doorbell rang. An older gentleman with a trimmed, graying beard stood outside, along with more bags of equipment.

"Ben?" I asked.

He nodded, and we did introductions, offering dinner and having it refused.

"Oh shoot," Ben said, looking around Derek's tiny family room. "This isn't going to be big enough for the equipment."

"I think it's plenty big," Alice said. "We can bring in a table to set up the monitors. It'll be fine."

I raised my hand. "What is going on? What monitors? Why are you setting up in Derek's house? My house has the ghost."

They ignored me. "There isn't enough room," Ben said to Alice. "And this house is old. I bet just setting up the equipment and plugging it in will trip the circuits. And there's not enough room. It'll be a safety hazard, and we know you don't like that."

What was going on? Why were Alice and Ben arguing like siblings?

"Hold it," Derek said. "What do you want to do to my house?"

"You didn't even ask them?" Ben said to Alice.

"I was getting there," she snapped.

Oak jumped in. "When we do a ghost hunt, we need a place to monitor the camera feeds—the more monitors, the better, because it's hard to catch stuff, and we need plenty of cameras. We have a van, but it's stuffy and hard to sit in for hours. So we like to set up external monitors at another location when we can."

"Why not inside my house?" I asked.

"Because sometimes the ghosts throw things, or we have to evacuate. It's okay to lose the cameras," Oak said. "I mean, it's not..." she ran her fingers through her black bob. "But it's justified. Also, it's good to have someone away from the action monitoring us. Sometimes they can spot things about to happen or see some activity just kicking in and can warn us about it."

"Wait," I said. "Ghosts throw things?"

"Most of the time, nothing happens on ghost hunts," Ben rumbled. "We're lucky if we get a single EVP or odd picture we can't explain. But sometimes things happen, and we like to be safe. Especially if you have as active a ghost as Alice says."

"I haven't seen it yet," Alice said. "But I trust Tasia. She doesn't imagine things."

"And I saw it too," Polly said. "A quick flash out of the corner of my eye, but I saw her. I'd gotten the feeling she was... nice."

"That's good information," Oak said. "Considering it then chased you out of the house. Maybe you guys made it mad?"

"Less speculation," Ben said. "More action. Let's get set up in the van."

"I agree," Oak said. "Now that I've seen this granny unit. There's definitely not enough room."

"Okay," I said. "I have no idea what all this is about. What are you guys going to do to my house?"

Ben gave Alice a dirty look. "I'm sorry no one explained it to you. We're going to set up several cameras in your house to run for about twelve hours. While we're setting up, Alice and Oak will go into the house with GoPros and recording devices—"

"For EVPs?" Polly asked.

"You got it," Oak said, with a huge nod.

I raised my hand. "What are EVPs?"

Polly looked up from her phone. "Electronic Voice Prints. Ghost hunters record themselves asking the ghost various questions. Normally the ghost hunters can't hear the answers, but the recording picks up on it. It's like this." She held up her phone.

A male voice with a Boston accent asked, "Is anyone here? Can you hear me? Is there anything you'd like to tell us?" A long pause. Then another question, "Did you used to live in this house? Do you remember what year it—" Another voice cut in, distorted, thin and difficult to understand. But the voice with the Boston accent continued asking the questions like it hadn't heard the other voice.

"That's an EVP," Polly said. "The far-away sounding voice. No one in the room heard it, but when they listened to the recording, they could."

"Oh, come on," Derek said. "That was just background noise. That was obvious."

Alice shrugged. "I've experienced it. We've heard nothing in the room but noticed voices on the recording afterward. But in Derek's defense, many people think they hear something when they're not. Human beings are good at finding patterns that aren't there."

"Or it's trickery." Derek said.

"Trickery?" I asked.

"Of course" Alice said. "Just like in all industries, there are scam artists. People will do "ghost hunts."" Alice did the quote marks with her fingers. "Then they'll claim they can get rid of your ghost. For a fee, of course."

"But not all people who ask for a fee are scammers," Oak said. "A lot are trying to make a living, using their expertise, which they totally should get paid for."

I rubbed goosebumps on my arms. The thin voice from Polly's phone had creeped me out. "Was that voice asking for help?" I asked.

Polly read off her screen. "This voice was recorded during a ghost hunt in an abandoned hospital. Most of the hunters agree, the voice is saying, help us."

A chill went up my spine, and I had to stand up. Was that what the hunters would find in my house?

"After we're done for the night," Ben continued. We'll review the data and get you some of our findings by... Friday night. Alice mentioned this was a rush job."

"But I'm hosting a party on Saturday," I said. "It's my son's birthday, and I really want this to be over with by then."

"Over with?" Oak said with a frown.

"Getting rid of the ghost. That's what you guys are doing, right?"

Ben harrumphed.

Alice touched my arm. "I'm sorry if I gave you that impression," she said. "I... we might find something to help you identify what the ghost wants if it's a sentient ghost. But if it's a shadow, they're more difficult to get rid of. And a repetitive ghost you just have to live with."

"Hold it," I said. "You never mentioned shadow ghosts before. And why can't you get rid of the ghost? Don't ghost hunters do that all the time? And what about me having to wear this necklace and all the emotional issues the ghost is causing?"

"That's right," Alice said, snapping her fingers. "I forgot." She pulled a woven bracelet out of her bag and twisted it around Derek's wrist. Polly got another charmed necklace, this one silver with a green stone.

"Which necklace did you get?" Oak asked, stepping close to Polly. Polly held it out, and Oak brushed her fingers across it.

"Make sure you don't take it off. Alice mentioned there might be some emotional interference from this ghost."

"Do you have one?" Polly asked.

Oak pointed to her gold stud earrings, the small silver band she wore on a finger, and a woven necklace with crystals threaded throughout. "I'm good."

"Time's a-wastin'," Ben said. "I'd like to be done by midnight."

I rubbed my head. I wanted a nap.

"Ma'am," Ben said. "Are you okay with this? We're mostly just collecting information for the university. Some of it may help you decide what to do, but it may not help you get rid of the ghost."

"I guess," I said. "Some info is better than none. And call me Tasia."

Ben nodded. "Let's have Alice and Oak set up the equipment. Tasia can give a tour, and Alice can explain about ghosts. Polly and Derek, you can stay here or come and hang out with me in the van. But it's tight."

"I need to go into the house too," Polly said. "I have to pack up stuff for the hotel."

"Okay, the more, the merrier," Alice jumped in. "Derek, you all right staying with Ben?"

Derek shrugged. "I guess. Though I still think if you truly look, there's a logical explanation."

Oak nodded. "Absolutely. And we look for that too. Sometimes an outside light reflects weirdly inside a house and makes people think they're seeing a shadow ghost when they're totally not. And a carbon monoxide leak or even just eating rotten food can make people hallucinate too. Did you know the Witch Trials in Boston may have been caused by the townspeople eating rye bread that had gone bad?"

"We have a carbon monoxide detector as part of our standard equipment," Ben said. "If it's okay with Ms. Tasia."

"It's all fine," I said. Least we were trying something.

# Chapter 24

I took a deep breath and unlocked the back door, my heart pounding. I reminded myself Derek and I had been there earlier in the day, and it had been fine. There hadn't been any problems—no shadows, no thumps, no baby laughs. But my hands still shook.

Alice and Oak had GoPro cameras strapped to their heads. They'd asked if I wanted one, but I refused. I didn't want someone to see my clothes and toiletries, analyzing the shape of my socks and underwear as I packed them.

Alice looked at the unfurled paper towels and tea strewn across the kitchen floor. "Did it do this?"

I nodded. "The mess was here this morning when we came in to check the house. On Sunday and Monday, we had two smooshed cakes too. I thought the kitten did it, but I couldn't figure out how she got to the cakes. They were in a cupboard, and the second night, we even locked her into a bathroom. She still got out, but now I'm thinking she didn't destroy the cakes."

"Wow," Oak said. "Super powerful entity. Lots of energy at their disposal." She used her phone to take pictures of the kitchen, snapping dozens. "Never know what you might see when you analyze the pictures," Oak continued. "I've seen twenty pictures of the exact same thing or area and then the twenty-first has some change in it. The changes can be subtle, but I've caught shadows and objects, like rocking chairs, moving on camera."

"You love this, don't you," Polly asked.

"It's truly fascinating," Oak said. "Especially what we don't know. My goal is to explore the psychology behind ghosts. I'm interested in the emotional overlap. When this is done, can I interview you guys for my thesis?"

"Of course," Polly said. "I haven't lived here for a while—"

"Perfect," Oak said. "You're more likely to notice some emotional things then. Some odd whispered thoughts that seem out of character. Asking yourself what was wrong with you seems to be huge. You know, why were you thinking a certain thought? That type of thing."

I touched the necklace around my neck, my mind exploding. How long had the ghost been interfering with my emotions?

"I'm going through a lot," Polly continued. "I think I noticed some weird thoughts, but with all that's happened this last year, it's probably normal."

"Either way," Oak said. "In fact, having you say that adds validity to my findings. Tasia," Oak asked. "You okay? You look pale."

"I'm okay," I said. "When this is done, I'll have some stuff for your thesis."

"Brilliant," Oak said, her grin huge.

She and Alice took shots of the unpainted areas in the walls and ceilings where the holes had been.

"So this all started with the construction?" Oak asked. We were standing in the odd spot between the family room and kitchen, where I could see the stairs and my office doorway.

"No," Polly said. "I did a Ouija board. I know it was stupid."

"Lots of people do them," Oak said. "It's not your fault. I'm not convinced they're portals, but I think stores shouldn't sell them. There's just too many stories."

"I forgot to ask earlier today; did you close the portal when you used the Ouija board?" Alice asked. "Tell the ghost goodbye or anything? Not that I think it does anything, but some swear by it."

Polly shook her head. "We only had thirty seconds, maybe a minute with the board. We'd just put our hands on the planchette in the middle. Gabe looked scared, so I made a joke. Something stupid about how these things never work and they're just for fun. How I was with him, and nothing would happen."

My heart clenched for a moment. It was such a big sister thing to say. He'd do anything for her, I realized. Why hadn't she come home more often?

"The words were just out of my mouth when the planchette started zooming across the board, going from letter to letter, too fast to read them," Polly continued. "I've done Ouija boards with my roommates all the time. Usually, the planchette doesn't move unless we push it. We drink a lot of cheap wine and make stupid jokes."

Alice nodded. "That's generally what happens with Ouija boards. Nothing, except for some collective suggestions. And if something sneaks through, it's not stupid enough to talk to you first, unless it's trying to learn about you."

Oak nodded. "We should check out the Ouija board tonight."

"Well, I cracked the planchette," I said. "When I stepped on it."

"That's interesting," Alice said. "I've never heard of anyone breaking the planchette. I'll have to do some research. Maybe we have a Ouija board expert at the college."

We moved into the family room, Oak and Alice taking lots of pictures, inspecting the furniture and the pictures on the walls, zooming in on various areas.

"Okay, so tell me about the different kinds of ghosts," I said.

"There's three types of ghosts, generally," Oak said. "Shadow, repetitive, and sentient. Of course, there are exceptions, and some are a little of all three, and there are people who disagree with there being three, but in my opinion, it's threeish. And I think you have a sentient one, even though she's manifesting as a shadow. Especially as you've had few problems before this. The behavior you've experienced lately seems deliberate, whereas shadow ghosts don't seem necessary deliberate. Of course, it could be the Ouija board stirred things up..." She trailed off. "I don't know. Guess you could have either one."

"I've seen lots of stuff about demons online," Polly said. "Are they a different type of ghost?"

"They're not technically ghosts, but a lot of their behavior is looped in with shadows. Ben's an expert on demons," Alice said. "You should ask him. Shadow ghosts are either ghosts that have gone into lower plains and come back with additional knowledge and strength or strong beings that are angry, jealous, or want revenge. Anything causing trouble or drama is a shadow.

Poltergeists are included here, though there is debate poltergeists are just energy, not something sentient. I could go on and on, but in general, shadows are the ones hurting people. So, the contractor getting hurt is a likely clue you have a shadow ghost. However, a sentient ghost might have wanted you to find the room and was fine with hurting someone. I don't know."

"So, you're saying ghosts are like humans. Hard to fit into boxes," Polly said.

"Exactly," Oak said with a wink.

"So why might this thing not be a shadow?" I asked. "It looked like a shadow and hurt someone."

Alice shrugged. "Yeah, but I'm not sure its intentionally trying to scare you. I think it wants something and used the contractor to get you to find the hidden nursery. And it probably caused the leak too, so you'd have to rip down walls. I'll bet you'll find the leak is centered somewhere in the old nursery."

"Then why did the plumber say it was in the master bath?"

"Maybe there's no pipes running into the nursery? We'll have to look."

Alice and Oak took some more pictures of my family room, noting the framed photos I had of my family, the small knickknacks, and a framed canvas of a landscape.

"So what's a repetitive ghost?" Polly asked.

"That's when at the same time every day, you hear footsteps or see a ghost walking through doorways," Alice said. "Sometimes you'll see the ghost brushing their hair or having an argument with someone. They're not aware of you, generally. Sometimes repetitive ghosts are also sentient, but not always." Alice folded the blanket Gabe, Polly, and I had been sitting under when we bolted. She handed it to me, and I tucked it back into the linen cupboard.

"And most of this is a theory," Oak said. "We can't question ghosts. Heck, most can't even manifest. Also, they only care about themselves, either causing problems for the living or wanting to solve a problem left over from their death. They're very narcissistic."

"So what does the type of ghost have to do with anything?" Polly asked.

"It helps us decide how to get rid of it," Alice said. "Repetitive ghosts you have to live with. They're frightening, but harmless. Sentient ghosts usually want something, and if you give it to them, they often go away."

"Into the light?" Polly asked.

"There are some reports of solving a problem the ghost had, then seeing a burst of light before the ghost disappears entirely," Alice said. "But we truly have no idea."

I showed them my office.

"This is so cool," Oak said, looking at the post-it notes stuck to any surface except the project board I'd left them on.

"Take lots of pictures," Alice instructed Oak. "We'll have to analyze them. Figure out if there's a pattern."

"Do you have photos of how it looked before?" Oak asked, zooming in to get every angle.

"No pictures, but normally, I put my post-it notes here, in the lanes designated to them." I showed them my dry erase board, with its carefully boxed-in areas for each project. "Then, when I've finished them, I put them here." I pointed to the corner on my desk where the old post-it notes would go until I threw them out, feeling accomplished for everything I'd gotten done. "It... she mixed my done post-it notes with the incomplete ones." I stuffed my hands in my pocket. I was never going to get them back into any semblance of order again. It would be impossible to remember what each note meant now that they were out of their respective areas.

"These mostly look like to-do things," Alice said, inspecting a note.

I nodded. "I'd take the notes for my post-it notes from my to-do notebook. It sounds crazy, but it keeps me organized." Pulling out the tiny notebook I kept in my pocket, I stopped, looking down at it. The pages were utterly, totally full. Circles, underlines, and Xs crisscrossed it. I'd written some of the notes on top of others. Reminders about buying milk, calling the doctor, calling my therapist, calling a furnace repair person repeated over and over. I realized I hadn't moved anything from the notebook to a post-it note since Sunday.

Since that voice had started whispering in my head that I could wait for later for everything.

Since the Ouija board.

"What's wrong?" Polly asked.

"Nothing." I stuffed the to-do notebook back in my pocket and touched the golden necklace. I'd never be able to pay Alice back.

Once the ghost hunters finished taking their pictures, I led them out of the room. I showed them the downstairs bathroom we'd locked the chest in.

"This is so pretty," Oak said, running her hands over the carvings. She tried to tug open the lid, but like before, it refused to budge.

Alice touched it, her eyes closed, and wrenched her hand away like she had this morning.

The hair stood up on the back of my neck, and I had to fight a shiver.

"I think there's..." She shook her hand like it had picked up something damp and slimy, and she was shaking it off. "I noticed it earlier today. The chest... I don't know... there's definitely some energy around it, but I can't define it."

"Are you psychic?" Polly asked.

Alice shrugged. "Something. I can absolutely feel the energy from past people in objects."

"It's pretty cool," Oak said. "We've tested her on random historical artifacts, and sometimes she just knows things. Jewelry, weapons, that type of thing. She knew stuff about the object's history, about history in general she wouldn't have known if she hadn't studied it."

"Which, of course, leads to the question—" I started.

"I'm not a history expert," Alice interrupted. "But there's no way to prove that without taking my word for it. And that's what makes parapsychology such a soft science. It's not like you can see it under a microscope."

"Yet," Oak said, taking lots of pictures of the chest.

"I want to come back to this," Alice said. "Once we're all set up, let's see if we can get it open. Might stir up some ghostly stuff."

"Agreed." Ben's voice coming through the walkie-talkie startled me. I'd forgotten about him.

The last room downstairs was the room I slept in. I winced as I showed the ghost hunters inside, the sheet and blankets still spread across the floor. "Sorry for the mess," I muttered. I didn't care about Polly and Oak, but I didn't want Alice telling the other moms my house was a disaster.

But again, the thought felt weak and faded.

And I wasn't being fair. Alice had dropped everything to help me, giving me a necklace off her body. She'd apologized for the confusion about Gabe's father and was giving up her time to help. Maybe I'd misjudged her.

"You like things in their places, don't you?" Oak said. "Your house is immaculate and organized. The ghost ripped the sheets off, right?"

I nodded and started remaking the bed. "It helps when everything is organized. It's less stressful."

"Is this need to have everything organized a new thing?" Oak asked.

"She's always been... structured," Polly said. "But when dad died—"

"Yes," I said, not liking they were talking about me like I wasn't there. "My therapist is fine with my level of organization. It helps me to control the things I can."

"Has anything happened in here?" Oak asked, her camera clicking.

"Nothing."

"Dreams? Uncomfortable feelings?" Alice pushed.

"Nope. Wait," I said. "I think I had some sleep paralysis the other night. It felt like something was holding me down. Do you think it could be related?"

Oak pushed up her glasses. "Could be, though sleep paralysis is also a legitimate medical issue too. Ever had it before?"

"Not that I can recall."

"Usually, you recall it," Alice said. "It's supposed to be terrifying."

"It was," I said, fighting back a shiver.

"Then it might be related," Alice continued. "Many people have thought sleep paralysis has an otherworldly feel to it. Just because there's a medical explanation doesn't mean a ghost didn't cause it, in this instance. Anything else?"

I showed them my to-do notebook and how I hadn't transferred anything over since Sunday.

"Oh, interesting," Oak said. "I'm betting this is a very active haunting.

Fingers crossed we get some good footage."

Polly and I went back out into the family room while Oak, Alice, and Ben from the walkie-talkie coordinated the best places for the camera set up.

The house felt different tonight. Quiet and welcoming, like it usually felt.

"Let's check out the upstairs," Alice said after a discussion with Ben on electromagnetic fields I didn't understand. "I want to see the nursery you found."

"Do it last," Ben squawked through the walkie-talkie. "Because it's going to distract you the most."

Alice rolled her eyes and mouthed, "I hate that man," to Polly and me.

I didn't know him, so I shrugged.

We went up the stairs, and I explained all the sounds of footsteps going up and down and how the squeaky step would sound at random times. I stepped on the tread and showed how it would make its sound with the slightest pressure.

Oak examined it while Alice pressed on the wood with her hand and her foot, trying to figure out the unique sounds it made.

"Okay," Polly asked. "Why does the sound the step makes matter?"

"Because," Oak said. "When I barely step on it, it makes this sound." She demonstrated, and it let out a little puff of air, a squeak like the tiniest of mice. "But when I step on it like this," she pressed harder, her foot more toward the center. "It does this." And the step wailed, the sound Gabe so enjoyed creating.

"Knowing what it takes for the different sounds helps us figure out what might make the sound," Alice said. "We can eliminate certain things when we're watching and listening to the recordings."

"Fascinating," Polly said. "Can I watch the recordings later?"

"Sure," Oak said. "We can have a viewing party. It's pretty boring though, I have to tell you, after about the first hour."

Once we got upstairs, Alice immediately went to the closed master bedroom door. She jiggled the handle.

"Isn't this the master?" she asked.

"Yeah, but I don't use it," I said.

"Why not?" Oak asked.

I shrugged. I didn't want to tell these strangers I couldn't use the room Miguel and I had slept in. The room we'd talked about our future in. The room we'd made love and tried to create another baby in.

"There's nothing in there," I said.

Alice and Oak looked at each other, and Oak stepped away to study the prints I'd hung in the hallway. "We probably need to set up a camera in there," Alice said. "Is that okay with you? Especially if the leak originated in the master bathroom. There might be a lot of activity we don't know about since it's been closed off. But only if it's okay with you."

She understood more than I gave her credit for.

I let out a deep breath and unlocked the door. Between the contractor and plumber going in and out, it didn't have the same unused feeling it once did. I pushed my hands into my pocket, ashamed I'd never cleared away Miguel's things.

Once this was all over, I'd empty this room. Get rid of his stuff. Even our furniture. This was ridiculous. I had to live my life.

After checking out Gabe's and Polly's room, we went into the tiny loft where the nursery was. I could've sworn a cool breeze blew out of the hole. Even with all the lights in the loft on, the gap was thick with shadows.

Everyone paused, and it felt like the house took a deep breath.

Alice and Oak moved closer, aiming their GoPro cameras at the opening and asking if Ben was getting the footage.

Alice stepped through the remaining drywall into the room, and we followed.

"This is wild," she said. "Someone either had a baby or wanted a baby and then closed off the room. So where'd you find the chest?"

I pointed out the dust-free patch in the middle of the floor. "We took a picture before disturbing it." I showed it to Alice and Oak. "There were flowers or leaves or something on it, but they turned to dust when I touched them."

Alice nodded. "Let's try some EVPs."

"Is anyone here?" She waited, and I craned my ears.

Nothing. No whispers, no words. I realized how quiet the house was, like how classrooms get during exams.

Oak gave Alice an enthused thumbs up. "Feeling something," she mouthed to us.

"If you're here, what's your name?" Alice boomed, making Polly and I jump.

Nothing. Nothing we could hear, at least. The air felt thick and heavy. I found I was taking short breaths.

"If you're here, can you make a noise?" Oak asked.

A slight click from downstairs made me jump. Polly yelped.

"It was the fridge," we both said. I patted my chest, feeling like my heart was going to explode.

Oak snickered. "That's the type of thing that gets all the ghost show people all twisted around. We should always look for a normal explanation."

Her words tried to cut through the tension, but if anything, the feeling of heaviness—of wrongness increased.

"Is your name Ruth?" Alice tried. This time there was a thump, like it had come from within the walls itself. We spun in circles, trying to identify it. Was it the ghost? Or just the sounds of an old house?

"Ruth?" Alice tried. "Can you do that again?" The energy was so heavy, I felt like I could hold it in my cupped hands, able to see and grasp it. I shook my head, trying to clear away fogginess.

Another thump. Whispers surrounded us. We froze, and after a few seconds, they faded away.

"Do you hear that?" Polly asked.

Oak and Alice nodded. "Ben, are you getting this?" Alice asked.

"I think there was something, but we'll have to review the footage later."

Oak and Alice asked a few more questions, but the whispers didn't come back. Within a few minutes, the house felt lighter, like after a thunderstorm had passed.

"Let's get the cameras set up on the second floor." Ben's voice boomed out of the walkie-talkie.

"I bet we got something," Alice said. "Did you feel how heavy the energy got?"

"It'll be cool to review it," Oak said. "Let's finish setting up the equipment. We may get some more stuff on camera once the ghost gets used to us."

# Chapter 25

It took an hour for Alice and Oak to set up the cameras with instructions from Ben through the walk-talkie. I stayed with Polly while she repacked her suitcases, and then Polly stayed with me while I packed a bag for Gabe and myself. I also had a list of his toys to include and ended up giving his room a good cleaning.

Now, she and I waited for Oak and Alice, sitting on the family room couch. Polly played on her phone while I fought my eyes not to close. I couldn't remember ever being so tired.

"Okay, I think we're almost done setting up the equipment," Oak said. I jolted upright.

"Drool," Polly mouthed to me, pointing at my mouth. I wiped the moisture away.

"We want to check out the chest," Oak continued. "But first we'll start with the Ouija board with the broken planchette."

Polly brought the pieces downstairs, and Alice recorded while Polly explained what happened. They tried some EVPs, but nothing happened. The house stayed quiet, the atmosphere light.

"Do you think we should burn the board?" Polly asked.

Oak rolled her eyes. "That's never been proven to do anything. I go back and forth about how dangerous Ouija boards are."

"I think there's plenty of documented cases of things getting worse in houses after someone uses a Ouija board," Alice said.

Oak shrugged. "Never know. Or it could be Polly coming home too. Maybe the ghost is feeling jealous she doesn't have Tasia and Gabe to herself."

I raised an eyebrow.

"I'm serious," Oak said. "Sentient ghosts get lonely too. This ghost has had you and Gabe to herself for a while. She's been manipulating your emotions. Maybe she doesn't want to share. Some ghosts still have all the normal human shitty behaviors."

Alice inspected the pieces of planchette, holding it up to her eyes, and then placing it onto her palm to stare at it.

"I think something paranormal touched this," Alice said. "But it might not be related to what's happening. A lot of Ouija boards are touched by the supernatural."

A chill went up my spine. Was the house suddenly getting cold, or was it my imagination? Goosebumps popped up on my skin.

I looked toward the staircase, and Oak noticed.

"Oh yeah," Oak said. "I can feel that. Something is shifting. Ben?"

"I'm not seeing anything." His voice rumbled out from the walkie-talkie, and I jumped.

"I feel it too," Polly said, hunching her shoulders.

A soft sound at the top of the stairs made Alice spin around. She and Oak adjusted their GoPros and held out their digital cameras, clicking like mad.

"I'm on you guys," Ben's voice came over the walkie-talkie. "I think the microphones picked up on whatever that was, but I'm not seeing anything."

I realized what Ben was doing. He was giving us an out, an anchor in the real world, just in case.

Oak wiped her hands on her pants and went back to taking pictures. "I thought you liked this stuff?" I whispered.

She smiled a little. "I do. But it still freaks me out. Isn't that interesting? I wrote a paper on how odd sounds or seeing shadows in the corners of our eyes scares us more instinctually than seeing the whole monster or ghost."

Another thump sounded over our heads.

"I think that's coming from the nursery," Alice said.

"I'm looking," Ben said. "Nothing's coming up on the thermal camera. Maybe it's the rocking chair, rocking."

"On it," Alice said. She went running up the stairs like she was eight, and there were Christmas presents up there.

"Can I look too?" Oak said to Polly and me. Polly had crept closer to me, her shoulder brushing mine.

"I guess," I said.

"I'll keep an eye on them," Ben said through the phone. "They'll be fine."

Polly clutched at my arm, and we held onto each other. The other two women moved around upstairs, trying to collect EVPs, asking the ghost to speak to them. I watched the stairs. If the shadow thing started walking down it, I wanted to tell Oak and Alice, tell them it had separated us. Make sure Polly got out the back door. My ears strained for anything; thumps, or any sounds outside of the ones the women upstairs were making.

"You guys okay?" Ben's voice came over the walkie-talkie, and I let out a scream. "Sorry," he said. "It's probably time to take a break."

"Yeah, I'm not seeing any movement up here," Alice said as she and Oak came downstairs. "And I think the energy is shifting again." She wrapped the Ouija board in one dish towel, the planchette in another. "We'll see if that does anything."

"You subscribe to that theory?" Ben asked, his voice full of static. "Keeping the two separate?"

"I think something came through this," Alice said. "Figure it can't hurt."

"I think it's just bits of plastic," Oak said.

Ben's voice rumbled through the walkie-talkie. "I agree with Oak, however, if Alice says she picks something up from the board and planchette, I believe her."

Alice widened her eyes in mock shock. "I can see you," Ben said.

Alice smiled, a quick uptick of her lips. She and Ben had a weird relationship.

The house felt quiet again, and I went to take our bags to our SUV. The ghost hunters had to be nearly done. Exhaustion made my limbs heavy and my head a little woozy.

Derek must have seen me leave because he met me in the driveway.

"I couldn't sit in the van," he said. "It was too hot in there. I went back to my place. Did you guys see anything?"

"Not really. They got all excited about some thumps and stuff. They'll—"

Now it was my turn to use finger quotes, "Review the footage and get back to me."

We stared at the shadows of the three people moving through my house. I thought I saw a flicker of light coming from the window in the master bedroom, but it might have just been my imagination.

He shrugged. "I'm still not sure it's a ghost. Gas leak or even collective hallucination seems more likely."

I touched the necklace. I was feeling more and more like myself. The me before Miguel died who had friends, got pedicures, and had big plans. I'd wanted to write a book on East Sacramento's history, had notes somewhere for a cozy mystery with a spunky heroine, her best friend hairdresser, and crazy aunt. What had happened to me? It had to be more than just Miguel's death.

"You okay?" he asked.

"I don't even know," I murmured, searching the upstairs windows to see if there might be another flicker. "I think that ghost's been changing me." That didn't feel right. "No, more like bringing out a bad side of me. I believe in ghosts now," I said in a whisper.

Derek stared at my house. "I don't. Ghosts don't exist. They can't. I don't know if I can do this."

Tears pricked my eyes. If he had to leave, go to a hotel, stay with a friend, I understood. He was my tenant, and we'd descended on his house in the middle of the night and literally kicked him out of his bed. Fluffy's litter box was in his tiny bathroom, and the kitten had clawed at his couch. I'd used him even before yesterday as a babysitter and my go-to whenever I needed anything. He'd filled in the male hole in my life with none of the benefits, and I'd barely even realized I'd done it to him. Why on earth was he sticking around?

"I'm sorry," he said. "I don't know what to do." He ran his fingers across his bald head.

"I'm never, ever going to be able to thank you," I whispered. My skin tingled when I touched his arm. I hadn't felt anything like that in a long time.

"Hiding in my house is not very helpful," he said.

"You stayed with the contractor and came over when I needed you to watch Gabe. When we ran last night, we went to your place. I don't know where we'd be without you. Regardless of whether you believe in ghosts."

"Well, I do have some ideas on how you can thank me." He waggled his eyebrows and winked. I forced a laugh and turned back to my house.

"When you're ready," he said, his voice a whisper on the wind.

"What if I'm not ever?" I asked just as soft.

"Then I'm happy being your friend."

"Hey guys," Polly called, sticking her head out the back door. "We're going to try to get the chest open."

"Then we'll call it for the night," Oak said, sticking her head below Polly's. "Sound good?"

"Sure," I said. It wasn't like I had much of a choice.

Derek went back to his house, and Polly, Alice, Oak, and I crowded into the tiny bathroom in mine, the chest in the middle of us. Oak knelt next to the box, running her hands over the carvings. "I've never seen anything like this. So intricate and complex."

"Alice," Ben said through the walkie-talkie. "What's your take on it?"

"I don't like the chest," she said, hunching her shoulders. "And I don't want to touch it again."

"For the cameras," Ben said. "Can you describe what it felt like?"

Alice licked her lips. "I really hate it when you make me do this."

"I know."

"It feels... wrong. There's a tingling field around it of wrongness. It feels old and knowledgeable." She paced away into the hallway. "I'm not putting it into good words."

"It just seems lovely to me," Oak said, running her fingers over the carvings again. "Maybe you're picking up on something about the chest itself, unrelated to this, or about a person who owned it before. Or even the person who made it."

"Anything's possible," Alice said. But she moved further away until she was just peeking into the bathroom.

Oak continued to run her fingers over the box, trying to find where the lid

143

connected. She shone a flashlight into the top, looking for the crack that would indicate the opening. "I can't even find where it would open." She pressed on a few of the leaves, hoping to find a hidden catch, but none of them moved or released the lid or a drawer.

Oak leaned back on her heels. "I'll do some research. Maybe it's like a puzzle chest. Like you have to press things in a certain order to get it open."

"Should we break it?" Ben asked.

"It's so pretty," Oak, Polly, and I crooned.

"Oh, that was interesting," Oak said. "Ben, do you mind tagging this time so we can look over the footage closer?"

"Already there. Alice, do you think we should break it?"

"Absolutely not," she said. "I'm not even sure we should open it."

The chest wobbled.

Oak held up her hands. "I wasn't even touching it." It wobbled again. "Ben?"

"I'm recording."

The chest lurched, and goosebumps broke out on my arms.

"Temperature's dropping," Alice said.

"If you're here, can you make a sound?" Oak called. "Ruth? Is this you?"

A clump sounded on the stairs, the squeaky step wailing. Alice moved, and I could just see her, pointing her GoPro at the stairs. "Ben?"

"I'm not seeing anything on the cameras," he said. "But I bet if we slow it down, we'll catch something."

"Agreed," Alice said. "And it's definitely getting colder. Something is trying to pull the energy from the house."

A puff of air felt against my neck, and I spun around, banging my knee painfully on the chest. It felt like something had tried to touch me.

An echo of sound, almost a laugh. "Holy shit," Oak whispered. "This is the most intense thing I've ever experienced."

"This is nothing like last night," Polly said, wringing her shaking hands. "Last night was so much worse."

We froze, and I strained for any sound, any movement around us.

The chest moved again, half a foot in one direction.

We bolted out of the bathroom and stood in the doorway, staring at the chest. My back felt exposed, and I glanced over my shoulder. Nothing there.

The lights flickered, almost going out.

The chest moved again, and whispers filled the air. I couldn't make out what they were saying, which somehow was worse. I breathed out and saw my breath puff, just a touch.

"Who are you?" Oak asked, her voice shaking a bit.

"What do you want?" Alice added. "Ruth, what can we help you with?"

Everything stopped, and silence reigned. I grabbed onto Polly's hands, her sweaty grip painful on my fingers.

What else could this ghost do?

But the temperature warmed, the clicking of the clock on the mantel sounding loud.

"Show's over," Alice said after a few minutes. "You can feel it."

And I did. It was almost like how the lights gradually came up in some theaters. It felt like the home I lived in with Gabe, not like the freak show it had become.

"The entity had to dig deep to get the energy to move the chest," Oak said. "We dropped like thirty degrees. I bet it was on empty after last night."

"Why does it get cold?" I asked, rubbing away the goosebumps.

"There's a lot of theories," Alice said. She leaned on a wall and let out a shaky breath. "But parapsychologists believe it's because the ghost is taking the energy out of the air to manifest. That's why electrical stuff behaves oddly too. Some ghosts take the energy out of those."

"Crazy," Polly said. "Can they take energy out of animals and people?"

Oak shrugged. "Maybe. Some people report being really tired after ghost hunts or experiences with the supernatural. But that could be adrenaline too."

"I think it's time to call it," Alice said. "It's nearly midnight. We're all tired. Let's have the equipment record all night. We'll see if anything gets captured, review the data, see if it lines up with the research you've done."

"We'll push on this and get you something by tomorrow night," Ben said through the walkie-talkie.

# Chapter 26

Oak, Alice, and Ben left, hopping into their cars and the van parked on the street. It looked like I'd hosted a party instead of a ghost hunt. The last time I had cars parked in front of my house was after Miguel's death, when people had stopped by to help. They'd tried to organize all the frozen casseroles, give my house a good cleaning, and watch Gabe so I could rest. I'd made it two days with their "help" and then ordered them out. Looking back, I realized I wasn't the nicest about it.

Had Ruth been manipulating me all this time? Had I lost all my friends, my support, my connections because of her? Not because of the depression and stress of suddenly becoming a single mom?

Gabe's birthday party was supposed to change it. I was going to host a fun party, invite the neighbors and other moms I'd only waved at. Now, this ghost threatened my plan, my hope for a different future. A different me.

I wasn't going to let her do that. I was going to get her out of my house.

Derek came out of the granny unit as Polly and I went out to my SUV.

"You can stay at my place another night," Derek said. "It'll be easier with Gabe spending the night at Alice's. Save you a hundred bucks on the hotel room."

Polly hopped into the passenger seat, her phone lighting her face. I sensed her watching us, pretending not to pay attention.

"You have one bedroom in a two-room house," I told him. "Three of us slept in your bed last night while you curled up on the couch too small for you."

"It wasn—"

"Yes, it was," she said. "I saw you when I got up. You were all curled up."
He'd looked... cute. And I wasn't sure what I thought about that. "You've
done so much. Taking over your house is just one thing too many. We're
going to a hotel."

"When will you be back?"

"I'll pick up Gabe from Alice's around eight, and the three of us will go out
to breakfast. Do you want to come? As the first payback for all your help?"

"I would, but I have to go to work for at least a few hours. I told my boss I
was dealing with some personal stuff, and they seemed okay with it. But it
won't last forever. I've got a billion emails waiting."

"Long as it's not a quadrillion, you'll be fine. It only takes a couple of hours
to clear a billion emails."

He smiled at my cheesy joke.

"Alice, Oak, and Ben said they'd probably have some data by tomorrow
evening. I don't know when those guys sleep," I said, looking down the street
toward Alice's wealthy neighborhood. "I owe them too. They're putting a
rush on this, pushing their other work aside. I'm sure they have other ghostly
stuff they need to do."

"What are you doing with Gabe tomorrow night when you meet with
them?"

"Polly will stay with him at the hotel," I said, mentally crossing my fingers.
I hadn't asked her, but I hoped she'd be willing to. And there was the
conversation she and I had to have about her flunking out of school. "Do you
want..." I paused, unsure of what I was genuinely asking. "Do you want to
join me at the university? Might be kind of spooky if they saw anything. But
maybe you'll be a rational voice too. You can question everything they come
up with."

I was still looking down the street when I asked, but when he paused, I
glanced over at him. He had this goofy grin on his face, like I'd just given
him the best present ever. He toned it down and stuffed his hands into his
pockets.

"I can probably do that," he said. "Dinner before?"

He was asking for more than a quick meal. More than a payback for everything he was doing. I ran my thumb over the inside of my wedding ring, so Derek wouldn't see. Derek was asking me out on a date. And while it felt like cheating, Miguel was gone. And he wasn't coming back. It wasn't his ghost haunting our house—I'd know if it was. He wouldn't scare us. He'd help us.

"Sounds good," I said, trying to sound casual, like I wasn't taking a step off a cliff and hoping the universe would catch me. "I'll find a place close to the university and text you. Five-thirty?"

"Perfect. I'll meet you there from work."

"Are you good with Fluffy spending the night?"

"She's a good kitten," Derek said with a smile. "I'll share my bed with her anytime. And I don't share my bed with just anyone."

There was a subtext there I didn't want to deal with, so I climbed into the car. "And Tasia," Derek said before I could close the door. "Let me pick the restaurant for dinner."

I licked my lips. "Okay," I said, hoping he'd pick a place I'd like and wasn't too fancy. I hadn't packed any nice clothes in my overnight bag, just jeans and t-shirts.

Derek laughed. "I promise, it'll be a jeans and t-shirt kind of place," he said.

I raised my eyebrow.

"Sometimes, it's easy to read your mind."

Yet another thing I didn't know how to deal with, so I waved, closed the door, and pulled away.

"Things are progressing nicely there," Polly said.

"Shut up," I murmured, driving the five miles to the hotel off of Howe Ave I'd found. But there wasn't any red haze or any malice in my words. Just two women joking about dating.

"Do you like him?" Polly asked. "In the bowchickawowow way?"

I chuckled and tried to be honest. "It's hard to know. He's been my friend since the beginning. I feel like my emotions have been totally out of whack since your dad died. And the ghost has been... contributing to them. I don't know if I can trust anything."

"But do you like him?"

"Maybe." I pulled into the hotel parking lot. "At least there's some potential there." We got out, and I grabbed the bags. "But I have to be careful. Gabe adores him. What if it doesn't work out?"

"You end up alone once Gabe moves out? Like Ruth? Is that better?"

I thought about her words as we checked in, went up the elevator, and walked down the hallway to the room. I unlocked the door, tossing my bag next to one of the beds. Polly heaved her suitcase directly onto the bed. The voice wanting me to lecture her about germs on her suitcase, now transferred to her bed, was easy to ignore without the red haze. I touched my necklace.

"Would you be okay if I started dating?" I asked.

She closed her eyes. "In theory, yes," she said. "It's been three years, and you should be dating. You're young and pretty, with a good career." She unzipped her bag and pulled out her toiletries. "But to be honest, in reality, I think I'd struggle. But that doesn't mean you shouldn't." She sat down on the bed, looking young and tired. "Can't put dad on a pedestal. He's dead."

I knew what she was saying. My therapist had gotten me to say similar things out loud.

"Dinner's not a lifelong commitment," I said. "Hell, I don't even know if it's really a date. And if it is, it's just dinner."

Polly smiled, though there were tears in her eyes. "I think that's a good idea. I think dad would've wanted you to enjoy life."

# Chapter 27

**Thursday**

The next morning, after tossing and turning in the crappy hotel bed, I knocked on Alice's mahogany door with its stained-glass window. You couldn't beat houses in the Fab Forties. Built between the 1930s and 1950s, they retained their historical charm, but all looked like they were out of a movie or Instagram ad, unlike my neighborhood. Elegant and perfectly trimmed maples and elms flanked Teslas, BMWs, and Mercedes parked in driveways. Large yards, Tudor and brick exteriors and expansive gardens full of blooming roses and bright crepe myrtles completed the image. Of course, the homes' insides were all recently remodeled with hardwood floors, quartz countertops, and the most expensive and exclusive gadgets. There were whole Facebook and Instagram feeds devoted to the houses in the Fab Forties.

A yawning Alice, dressed in yoga pants and a t-shirt with a coffee stain down the front, opened up the door. She'd twisted her copper hair into an octopus knot with tendrils running down her back. She looked nothing like the perfectly coiffed woman at PTA meetings and school drop off.

"Can't believe you made it at eight."

I shrugged. I was seldom late for anything.

"There's coffee," she said. "I'm sure you got less sleep than I did."

I accepted a cup, wondering how long I had to chit-chat before I could get Gabe and head to breakfast. "I'm not a fan of hotels," I said. "Always feel like it takes me a night or two for my mind to get used to the new place, so I'm not waking up at every noise."

"Me too," Alice said. "I never understood why people want to go rest at a hotel. A hotel is where you go when you have to travel. I hate sleeping at hotels, no matter how five-star they are."

I took a sip of the coffee. This was so much better than the Keurig coffee I usually drank. It was probably fresh ground, French-pressed and put through a multi-thousand-dollar espresso machine, then poured into a cup by an angel while she sang a prayer over it.

I blinked and pushed my blonde bangs out of my eyes. God, I was tired. "Thank you for letting Gabe spend the night."

She waved it off. "No problem. My nanny was happy for the overtime." Alice must have gotten a handsome settlement from her rich husband if she didn't need to work and could afford a nanny, in addition to her multi-million-dollar home. "Oak was so revved up, I bet she slept at Sac State. And Ben and I will be hitting the tech room at ten. Hopefully, we'll find you something. But I'm thinking all this activity is just Ruth. I wish we could find out why the chest is so important. Might be baby stuff in there or more journals." She shivered slightly. "I just know we can't break it open. Bad juju."

"Juju?"

"Just slang for a strong feeling."

We both took a sip of our coffee, and I looked around her kitchen. Someone, probably an interior designer, had updated it from the original design with a multi-color backsplash in subway tiles, light gray concrete countertops, dark gray cabinets, and shiny chrome appliances. Batches of herbs hung from the ceiling on a pan rack, and fresh ones filled the windowsills. It wasn't super fashionable with the white cabinets and quartz countertops everyone demanded, but it fit the Alice I was getting to know.

"How do you get a master's in parapsychology?"

"A lot of schools offer it, believe it or not. It's a fringe of psychology. And I'm actually half-way to my doctorate." She took a sip of coffee. "I mean, I was half-way before I got married. I try to keep up with things, take an occasional class, but it's hard. I keep wanting to go back full time, just get it done, but..."

"What's stopping you?" I asked, exhaustion reducing my social filter.

She rubbed her forehead and looked around at her chrome appliances, the hardwood floors, and comfortable but expensive furniture. "That's a good question. I've faced ghosts and probably some demons without a moment's thought. I've never lost sleep, scared they would come for me. Though my house is warded." She pointed at the herbs. "But going back to school, sitting down with a counselor, and putting a plan in place gives me insomnia for days." She tossed her leftover coffee into the sink and rinsed out her mug.

"Okay," she said. "Enough sharing. What are you going to do about the party on Saturday?"

"Hopefully, the ghost will be gone?"

Alice shook her head. "Hope is not a plan. Today's Thursday. And while there was a lot of activity last night, I'm not sure we're going to know enough to get rid of Ruth by Saturday. You need a back-up plan."

"I guess I could do the party at McKinley Park. It's just, I didn't reserve an area, and you know how people get."

Alice snickered. "If you don't reserve a spot, especially on a Saturday, then it's a cat-fight. And people get really mean. Maybe there's another park. I'll ask on my Facebook mommy group."

"You've done enough," I said in protest as Alice grabbed her phone and started tapping out a few words.

"Already done. And I tagged you on Facebook."

"Oh God, I never check my personal Facebook." I had a professional one for my business, but I seldom used that one either.

"You should. There's a lot of good info about the school on there."

I heard the boys' movements echoing upstairs, laughter, and a long farting sound followed by more laughter.

Boys.

Alice's eyes rolled up in her head. "Have you started reading the journals yet?"

"Only flipped through them to see if anything stood out. The writing was too hard to skim through. So my plan today is to get Gabe, get breakfast, put him in the hotel room with cartoons, and then start reading. Then Fairytale

Town and the zoo for this afternoon." I ticked off each on my fingers.

The thumping from the kids upstairs made my heart race a bit, reminding me of the thumps from my house. Was I ever going to hear that sound again without panicking?

"I wanted to thank you," Alice said.

"For what?"

"For not judging me for being psychic. I haven't told anyone else. Oak and Ben know, of course. And Gerald knew, but he... anyways, thank you."

I laughed, the sound surprising me. "I have a ghost in my house. The ghost probably made me chase away all my friends. I was horrible to Polly because of her. I almost didn't get Polly when she was drunk and needed a ride. Believe me, I'm not in a place to judge you for being a little psychic."

"Thank you," she said. "And my Spidey-sense tells me the answer to Ruth might be in those journals."

"Got it," I said. "I'll get started on them right after breakfast." Maybe I would find the answer without the ghost hunters' help.

I finished my coffee, willing the caffeine to wake up my brain.

"Time for Gabe to go," Alice yelled up the stairs, making me jump. "Let's get a move on."

The horde of boys descended in their bright pajamas, shouting and leaping around while pulling cereal and bowls out of a cupboard. Alice demanded they keep it down, and they responded with laughs and more hooting. I had the beginnings of a headache within one minute. How did polished Alice live with this much chaos?

Gabe said goodbye to his friends, and I drove to the hotel to pick up Polly. We grabbed breakfast at a convenient IHOP and then headed back to the hotel.

"Do you think Fluffy is okay?" Gabe asked for the umpteenth time.

"Yes. Derek locked her up in his bathroom so she wouldn't get hurt," I said. "I'm sure she's fine."

"Fluffy should come with us. She'd want to see the tigers at the zoo," Gabe said. "'Cuz she's like a little tiger herself. Remember how she growled at the ghost? Can we go and get her before we go? And at Fairytale Town, I can hold her when I go down the slide in the barn."

I tapped on a braided bracelet around each of Gabe's wrists. "What are these?"

"Ms. Alice gave them to me," he said. "Tyler and Nathaniel and Danny and I all got them. But I got two because it's almost my birthday."

I said a silent prayer to submit Alice for sainthood.

"So can I take Fluffy to the zoo?" Gabe asked again.

"You can't take a kitten to the zoo, silly," Polly said. "She might get eaten. And you can't leave her in the car either."

"Fluffy is fine at Derek's," I told him. "Let me get some reading done, and then we can head to Fairytale Town this afternoon."

I left him and Polly in the hotel room, Gabe watching cartoons and eating junk food while Polly took her share of the journals.

"I'm going to get coffee and read down there," I said.

"Perfect," Polly said. "I'll text if I find anything."

# Chapter 28

An hour later, Polly texted, *Anything?*

*Not really,* I responded. *She doesn't seem like a nice lady.*

*Very controlling,* Polly wrote. *Reminds me a bit of you.*

My heart dropped, and my stomach clenched. I knew I was controlling, but Ruth from the journals was genuinely terrible. She wrote about neighbors spying on her, kids riding their bikes across the lawn, and the one time she'd turned her hose on a couple of teenagers making out. I wouldn't do any of that stuff.

*I don't see it,* I responded.

*She likes things her way, the same way you do. I'm not being mean,* Polly clarified. *But you have to admit you're a bit controlling with your project boards and post-it notes.*

*It's how I stay organized. I don't forget things that way.*

*And it works, but you are controlling.*

I didn't respond but turned my phone face down on the table. It buzzed again. *You're controlling in a helpful way,* Polly texted when I looked at it. *Like in a good way. Ruth is controlling in a wrong way.*

I turned my phone face down again.

An hour later, I stood up to get another cup of coffee. My eyes were tired from trying to decipher the old writing. And my brain needed a break from the names Ruth had called her neighbors, her coworkers, the people around her. Ruth had taken the time to volunteer for committees but called everyone around her stupid and lazy. She claimed she was the only one who worked, who got things done. And the names she called the teenage girls—sluts,

155

whores, and worse.

I sat down with my coffee and fell back into Ruth's world, jumping when the chair across from me slid out. Derek sat down.

"What are you doing here?" I asked, checking the time. It was only noon. There was no way he was done with work already.

"I'm taking a long lunch," he said. "Polly said you were here, and I thought I'd come and help you read the journals."

I waved an arm at the stack of books, buzzing with caffeine after two espressos. My arm hit the journals, and they tumbled to the ground. "Damnit," I hissed, bending over to pick them up. Derek got down on his knees to help.

"Were they in any order?" he asked.

"There's post-it notes on them with the approximate years I think they're from," I said. "But I could be wrong. She didn't put years on her journal entries, just dates, sometimes. And she doesn't refer to big events often. But I'm getting the gist of who she was."

"And?"

"She was horrible. If I have the years right, she grew increasingly paranoid and vindictive the older she got. I mean, I don't think she had any friends, and there was no family. The only mentions of her husband are about how much he ruined her life, how he won't leave her alone. She thought everyone else was stupid, and she was in the right."

Derek shrugged. "It is her journals. It's not like Facebook and Instagram and how people only document the good stuff. Maybe she was venting, and it helped her be a wonderful person outside of her home?"

"I don't think so," I said. "The neighbors told Miguel Ruth was so mean the kids would dare each other to ride by her house. I mean, at one point, in her journals, she talked about putting down poisoned peanut butter for the dogs pooping on her lawn."

"Wow, that's pretty extreme. But just because she wrote it down doesn't mean she would do it. A lot of old people get like that." Derek picked up a journal and started thumbing through it. "She was married, though, right? She couldn't have been all bad."

"But women in the 1940s were supposed to get married. And she mentioned her parents were dead. So, she probably didn't have a choice financially. And she wouldn't have been able to afford the house without getting married."

"True," Derek said, picking up a different journal and flipping through it. "God, these are hard to read. Have you found anything about the baby?"

I leaned back. "I think there's references to a colicky baby. "He" won't let her sleep. But no names, no comments about being pregnant, nothing about changing diapers or midnight feedings. And that's weird, right? I don't remember seeing any pictures of a baby in the photo album either."

We both reached for it, our fingers closing on the cover. He gave mine a quick squeeze before opening it, flipping through pictures. "There's no pictures of a baby or even her pregnant."

"Did they take pictures of when they were pregnant in the forties?" I asked. "I mean, the wedding pictures look so old-fashioned. Their smiles and poses are so formal."

"But they're happy," he said, his voice soft in the noise of the coffeehouse.

I wondered what happened with his divorce. We'd never talked about it, and in all the time I'd known him, I hadn't ever seen him bring another woman home or even go out on dates. Of course, I didn't monitor his every move either, so he might have had a bunch of girlfriends. Maybe he had one now. I pushed the thought down. It didn't matter whether he did. We were only going out to dinner tonight. We hadn't said we were exclusive.

Or even dating.

"The shadow you saw was wearing a calf-length long skirt, right? Like the fifties? Or the forties. I'm terrible with fashion. Like in these pictures?" He pointed to one of Ruth posed in front of a building, the importance of the picture lost to time.

"If she lived to be nearly ninety, why would she be manifesting in a fifties style skirt?" I asked.

"Maybe she was happiest in the forties and fifties," Derek said. "In the early days of her marriage? So that's when her ghost is from?"

"It doesn't make any sense."

"None of this makes any sense," Derek said. "We're sitting in a coffeehouse in Sacramento after a couple of university students came to your house last night to perform a ghost hunt. And now we're reading journals, trying to figure out how to make your ghost go away."

I rubbed my head. "So you believe now?"

He sighed and ran his fingers across his head, then stared down at the table, not speaking.

"Derek?"

"My mother," he licked his lips. "She's dead."

"I remember when you told me," I said. "She was a widow for about twenty years after your dad had a heart attack."

He breathed out a huge breath. "A few years after Dad died, she swore she had a ghost. I didn't believe her. Thought she was just... lonely."

I touched his hand. "That may have been all it was."

"This guy," Derek said, continuing the story. "Aaron. His name was Aaron. He told my mom he could get rid of the ghost. Brought in the same stuff your ghost hunters did. Cameras, electrothermal things. Talked about orbs and electromagnetic fields. Walked around my mom's house recording the ghosts speaking, the same things they did last night."

"What did he find?"

"Pictures of shadows, voices telling her to get out." He snorted. "It was static. Trickery. Photoshop. Suggestion. He just wanted her money. It cost money, he'd tell her, to run his business. It cost money to go on ghost tours to famous locations. Cost money to run his blog."

"And she paid him?"

"Most of my dad's retirement. He bled her a little at a time. When the money was gone..." Our hands had switched places somehow, and now he was holding mine, his fingers squeezing. "I intervened when he tried to get her to take out a second mortgage."

"Oh my God."

"And then had to intervene again when he asked my mom to marry him. Had to go to Florida, had to meet them at the cruise ship terminal. It was this huge scene. But in the end, she believed me."

"Thank goodness."

"But she didn't talk to me again. The hospital called me when she died."

"You don't have to do this," I said. I pulled my hand away and folded them across the journals. "You don't have to be a part of this. I get it."

"I know you," he said like I hadn't spoken. "And I don't think you imagined anything, or Alice is trying to trick you. I still think there's a logical explanation. But I don't know what it is."

"If you eliminate all the possibilities, whatever is left, is the truth," I said, misquoting Sir Arthur Conan Doyle.

"Guess so. Maybe it is a ghost. But I'm still hoping for a normal explanation. And tonight, I'm poking holes in all of their proof."

"I'm counting on it," I said. "I'm sorry about your mom."

"It's over and done with. It's in the past and dwelling doesn't help." He looked around the coffeehouse, his eyes shadowed. "So, can I have a few of the journals? If both of us read them, it'll go faster."

I looked at my hands, closed over the top journal. I didn't want him to read them. And not only because of what he experienced with his mom.

"Polly says I'm like her," I blurted out. Ashamed, tears filled my eyes. "She said I'm controlling like Ruth was."

Derek put his hand over mine. We were doing a lot of hand holding lately. "Ruth probably used her journals to vent things she couldn't say aloud. She was a widow at a time when people looked down on women. I'm sure she wasn't a heartless bitch all the time."

"Am I a heartless bitch?"

"No."

"I was." I touched the necklace.

"That wasn't your fault. And you were never mean to Gabe or me."

I hung my head, and Derek leaned over to look into my eyes. "No," he repeated. He touched my chin, raising it, so we were looking eye to eye. "You're extraordinary and a great mother. You'll drop anything to help a client, even if you don't want to, because you understand how important their writing process is. You volunteer to help young writers learn to write. You and Ruth may have some similarities, but you're not a heartless bitch." He squeezed my hand. "I wouldn't want to hang out with a heartless bitch.

Why do you think I'm at your place all the time?"

"I have awesome coffee?" Which was a lie. All I had was the Keurig stuff. Alice had the awesome coffee.

"I love your coffee," he said with a wink. "It's better than what they sell here."

More lies.

"Buy you a cup, even if it's terrible?" I asked.

"I'll take you up on that. What journal should I start with?"

He released my hand, and an image popped into my mind; he and I holding hands, our fingers interlaced as we read the journals together. I let the image linger, but just stood up to place my order.

Balancing his coffee and my third espresso, I felt my phone buzz in my pocket. Making room for the two cups, I pushed aside some journals and pulled out my phone. "Oh!" I said. "Polly found Ruth's death certificate. She died in 2008. The house sat open for years until Miguel and I bought it and remodeled it in 2011."

My phone buzzed again. "Oh, this is interesting. She was married in 1942 to Jack Evans."

"What was going on in 1942?"

Derek and I both pulled up Google.

"It was right after Pearl Harbor, so everyone was going to Europe," Derek said. "There were shotgun marriages, quick ones where couples only had a few months together before the guy shipped out."

I looked at the wedding picture. "That explains why he's wearing a military uniform, and she's in a regular dress. It was a quick wedding. When did World War II end?"

"1945." Derek said, consulting his phone. "And everyone came home. There's that famous picture of the sailor kissing the nurse."

"A lot didn't come home," I whispered. "There were a lot of widows."

"Also, the ones coming home didn't come back well," Derek said. "Undiagnosed PTSD. I don't even know if they knew about PTSD. And there were many wives and husbands who didn't know each other well before marrying and were suddenly living together, playing house. Add in kids and family drama, and there were a lot of problems."

"How do you know all that?"

"Mad Men."

I laughed. "That makes you the expert."

"Of course."

We went back to reading, but I stopped after just a minute. "In this journal, there are occasional mentions of a "he". "He" would be unhappy with her. "He" was making noise last night. That type of thing. But there weren't many mentions, and it was from her old lady phase, I think. At first, I thought it was the baby, then I figured it was a neighbor or something."

"Do we know when Jack died?"

I texted Polly the question. "Not yet," I read off my screen. "She's still looking."

We read in silence for about an hour until Derek looked at his watch. "Nothing," he said. "She really liked the rose gardens at McKinley Park. Went on a lot of walks. But she hated the strollers."

I nodded and tapped the journal I was reading. "I think a lot of time passes in this journal. There's not many entries, and the handwriting changes. Gets shakier. But it's more of the same vitriol."

"I've also got mentions of a "he" occasionally. "He" being unhappy. "He" damaging one of her favorite dresses."

"I wonder who "he" was. I think this journal is after Jack died, so I don't think "he" was Jack."

"You'll figure it out. I gotta get back to work. If you can't find anything, let's just break open the chest tomorrow."

I sighed. "Alice says that feels wrong." And I agreed.

"If it gets this to end, might be worth it. So I'll see you later?"

"Five-thirty for dinner. Where at?" I asked.

He winked at me. "I'll tell you later. Keep you guessing. But you'll like it."

# Chapter 29

Polly and I followed Gabe beneath Humpty Dumpty's legs and into Fairytale Town. He immediately ran for the giant shoe slide depicting a nursery rhyme, and we followed, taking a seat on a convenient bench with other parents. We watched Gabe climb the ladder inside the shoe, slide down the metal ramp, then run back to the ladder.

"Does your mom know about school?" I asked Polly while we waited for Gabe to get bored and want to try another slide.

She looked up from her phone. "No." She glanced down, tapping something out with a thumb. At least she hadn't put in headphones.

"So what happened?" I finally asked. I realized I was playing with the necklace Alice had given me and said a quick prayer it would help with this conversation.

She shrugged. "Just couldn't keep up with my classes. I got put on probation last semester, and this semester hasn't been any better. Flunked a few tests. Can't make it up."

It was the middle of the year, though, around spring break. "So, did you quit, or were you expelled?"

"I was going to be expelled, so I quit," she said, staring at the metal slide coming out of the giant shoe. She smiled a little as a parent clumsily climbed off the slide behind their child. "These parents kill me, riding with their kids on the slide. Their butts don't even fit on it."

"I hated that slide when I was little," I said. "The metal edge always cut your legs a bit." When she went back to her phone, I asked, "So, what are the next steps?"

"God, I don't know," she said. She stood up and walked away.

Gabe jumped off the bottom of the slide and followed her. "Can we go to the Crooked Mile?" he asked.

She smiled. "I remember the old thing. Can't wait." Together they walked up ahead of me while Gabe told her all about the slides and buildings in Fairytale Town.

Fairytale Town was an institution for Sacramento children. A massive playground themed around nursery rhymes and fairy tales; it had opened in 1959. Multiple generations, including myself, had played on the slides and play sets. With it being across from the Sacramento Zoo, most families with small kids would hit both parks on the same day. When I'd married Miguel, Polly had been fourteen and way too old to want to go to the zoo or Fairytale Town with us. She had memories of the park with a different mother, a different family.

Gabe led Polly down the twisty concrete path, zigging between bushes while they ducked beneath trees. I heard him tell her to pretend they were in a jungle and to look for animal tracks on the concrete.

A few minutes later, Polly joined me on another bench. "He found other friends to run on the road with. He told the other kids a tiger escaped from the zoo and is hiding in the trees."

"A tiger?"

"Yeah. They're loving it. Half of them want to go after it, and the other half want to hide."

I shrugged. "Guess it's better than a ghost."

Gabe came running off the Crooked Mile path, and together we headed to the giant multi-story barn. He dragged us inside to show us the incubating chicken eggs and baby chicks. When he went to climb the ladder to yet another slide, we found another convenient bench.

"About school," I tried again. "Maybe you could try again next semester."

Polly stared at the ground in front of her feet. "I just wanted to come home," she whispered. "Just wanted... I don't know."

She sounded so sad and broken.

"I'm so sorry I was mean to you when you got here," my voice was equally soft.

"That wasn't your fault. It was the ghost."

Not entirely. She'd hurt me, disappearing after Miguel died. And then I was angry she'd reappeared and expected to move back in like the last few years hadn't happened. But the anger felt dim now. She needed me today. And if the previous few days were any evidence, I needed her.

"What's going through your head?" I asked.

She put a strand of hair in her mouth, something she hadn't done since Miguel and I were married. "Everything is harder. School. Friendships. Completing things. Dating, if the last loser was any evidence. My therapist said I was too hard on myself, but..." She shrugged and dashed a quick tear away. "I need a reset. Need to figure things out, not be stuck."

"Which is why you came back?"

"I was kind of hoping I'd be able to say goodbye to dad in your house. And then move on."

Things fell into place. "That's why you brought the Ouija board."

She ran her cheek over her shoulder, wiping away a tear. "My therapist recommended it. I was going to use it to say goodbye. Gabe saw it when I was unpacking. And I promise I didn't plan to talk to dad in front of Gabe. And I didn't honestly think a Ouija board was a real thing. Just a stupid tool to trigger some emotions and have closure. I was just going to pretend to talk to him. By myself. Just say goodbye. That's all I wanted. Just to say goodbye one more time." She was babbling, tears running down her face. She ran a fist under her running nose. "I just wanted to tell him I miss him, but I'll be okay without him. Different but okay."

"I believe you," I said, enclosing her hand in mine. "I believe you," I said again.

"I'm so sorry," she said. She was close to sobbing now. Parents were beginning to give us odd looks. "I didn't mean to wake up, Ruth. I didn't mean to cause so many problems."

"It's not your fault." I put my arm around her. She leaned into me, and I glared at anyone who dared to stare with their questioning, wondering eyes.

"Your dad would be so proud of the woman you've become."

She wept into my shoulder, unable to speak, while I held her, making shushing noises, smoothing her hair, and telling her it would be okay.

Polly had calmed down to hiccupy gasps when Gabe came running over, a big smile on his face until he saw Polly and her tears. His shoulders dropped, and Polly called him over. She went to her knees, giving him an enormous hug. He wrapped his arms around her, and tears filled my eyes. I was so glad Polly was here and so sad Miguel wasn't. But it didn't rip my heart out like it used to.

Polly whispered in Gabe's ear, and Gabe ran off toward Sherwood Forest. I stood up and offered my hand to Polly, helping her to her feet. I gave her a package of tissue.

"Of course you have a tissue," she said.

"Of course I do," I echoed. I hugged her, a long one with both our arms wrapped around each other. "You good?"

"I think I will be. You?"

"I think I will be too."

# Chapter 30

Derek awkwardly held out a chair for me at an Italian place off of Folsom Blvd. It wasn't a jeans and t-shirt kind of restaurant, but Derek had worn a t-shirt and jeans, so I guess it didn't matter. I breathed out as I took a seat, hoping he didn't see. I'd never had a meal with him without Gabe. Our meals were in my kitchen when I was paying him back for something he'd helped with—watching Gabe so I could meet a deadline or helping Gabe with his homework or dealing with the gardeners when I had to go to a work meeting. Or because he'd randomly stopped by. God, how many dinners had he had with us?

Things were changing, and it wasn't just the ghost.

"Thanks for coming with me to the university tonight," I said after our drinks were delivered. "I think Polly was a bit bummed she had to stay with Gabe, but the less he knows about the ghost stuff, the better. He's going to have nightmares for years."

"I probably will too."

"Really?"

He shrugged and took a sip of his beer. "I still don't believe in ghosts, but..." He shrugged. There were shadows under his eyes I'd never seen before. This was getting to him. It was getting to all of us.

I didn't know what to say, so I picked up the menu. We small talked about the food, debating the merits of fettuccine alfredo over chicken parmesan.

"So..." I said when we'd discussed the nuances of spaghetti sauce way too much and had nothing else to discuss. "How's Fluffy? Gabe is demanding to know," I said, pleased I'd remembered something to talk about. "I'm supposed to text him as soon as I find out the answer. He really misses her."

"That's the best kitten I've ever seen," Derek said. "Seemed totally fine, locked in the bathroom all day and didn't destroy anything. It's like she just chilled all day."

"Really? A kitten?"

"I know. It's weird. She slept with me all night, curled up on a pillow next to my head. She scratched me a few times, though."

He held out his arm and showed me a few band-aids. I winced. "I'm sorry."

"It's okay. She's just a kitten. She doesn't know better and is overall gentle."

I texted Gabe, *Fluffy is doing great but misses you a lot. She's sleeping, eating, and hanging out with Derek.*

My phone buzzed again.

*Is Derek sleeping with Fluffy? She needs someone to cuddle. But when I'm home, she should only cuddle with me.*

Not sure how to respond, I showed Derek my phone. He laughed and took my phone.

*Hey dude. It's Derek. Have your mom send my phone number to you so you can check on Fluffy. I'll send you pictures. She's doing great. Yes, she tried to sleep with me, but paced around a lot. She didn't want to cuddle with me. I could tell she misses you.*

I read the message and pressed send.

"Are you sure you want him to have your phone number? He might text you a lot."

"It's fine. I like the little dude."

Derek's phone buzzed. And Derek smiled, typing out a quick message. "He wanted to make sure Fluffy is really and truly all right."

"Maybe we can sneak her into the hotel," I said with a sigh. "I'm not sure the excitement of staying in a hotel is enough for Gabe to enjoy spending the night without her."

"Let's give it another night."

I took another sip of my wine. "Thank you again for all your help this week."

"It's no big deal. Hope the hunters find an answer, and you don't have to sell your house."

"Me too." I ran my hands through my hair. "But if we can't get Ruth to calm down, I don't want Gabe in that house. You always see it in movies with ghosts— the family moving back in again after they've defeated it. Life is good, everyone is happy."

"Until the end, when the ghost comes back and kills them all."

"So there can be a sequel."

"I think if life copied movies, we'd have heard about a lot more families eviscerated by their ghosts," I said. "I mean, from what Alice says, ghosts are pretty common."

The server came to take our order, and we each ordered the spaghetti and meatballs. Derek grinned at me.

"Guess there's no need to see whose food is better," I said. "That's always the worst when someone's food is better than yours."

"I make it a rule to always order the same thing my date does, for that reason," Derek said.

Okay, so this was a date. I took another sip of my wine. I could make that work.

Derek touched my hand. "This doesn't have to be a date," he said. "It can be a meal between two friends, too."

I ran my left thumb over the inside of my wedding ring. "It's been a tough week. But maybe this could be a date. If you wanted."

A server delivered our salads, and I flipped my napkin onto my lap.

Derek said, "There's no rush. Take your time. I enjoy spending time with you and Gabe."

"Then we'll see where this goes." He smiled at me his eyes glowing. I smiled back until things got a bit awkward and broke the tension by forking up a bite of salad while Derek launched into small talk from his day, a story about why one of his staff had been late.

"The funny thing was," Derek said, wrapping up the story. "She was telling the truth. She did have a mama possum and her babies under her car. And the mamma kept hissing at her when she got close to the car. She texted me the pictures."

He passed me his phone with pictures of red-eyed things staring at the photographer from under a car.

I laughed and passed it back. "I've heard their hiss is terrifying, even though possums are harmless."

"But that's why she was four hours late for work. I made her use her PTO—she was pissed because she was saving it for a vacation."

When the bill came, Derek and I both reached for it. "I got it," I said.

"Let me. I'm sure none of this is cheap."

I shrugged. "Insurance will help with the leak, and the ghost investigators are free. I'm assuming the ghost is making my house cold, so I don't need a new furnace. I got it."

"Let me," he said again. "It's important to me."

I let him.

# Chapter 31

It was dark by the time we made it onto the Sac State campus. Oak met us outside because, as she told us, it was "hard to find the parapsychology department."

"I'm so excited you're here." Oak walked fast, and I had to trot to keep up with her. "We got some awesome footage last night," she continued. "I'm already starting on the research paper for it. And I've written the rough draft for my blog. I'll be able to get a bunch of blog posts out of this." She paused. "If that's okay with you."

There were parapsychology journals? And blogs? What was there to blog about?

"I guess it's fine. Long as you don't identify it's my house," I said. "Or put in my address. I don't want other ghost hunters to stop by. But otherwise, it's fine."

"Awesomeness." She actually jigged a little dance, and I realized she was high on caffeine.

Had she slept last night?

"And I totally get it," Oak continued. "I won't use any identifying features. And professional ghost hunters wouldn't stop by unannounced. It's the amateurs that watch all the shows you gotta worry about."

We followed her into one of the buildings, going down hallways and through doorways to a conference room. I'd expected there to be screens everywhere, wires, and recording equipment with headphones. Like on the TV shows. But instead, it was a basic conference room with a table and chairs where Alice, Ben, an iPad, and a laptop sat.

I greeted Ben and Alice. "Oak mentioned you guys found something," I said as Derek and I took our seats.

"It's fascinating," Ben said. "I haven't analyzed everything, but I wanted you to listen to some EVPs we got along with some footage from when the chest moved. We also recorded some stuff after we left." He picked up the iPad, tapped the screen, and the giant TV mounted on the wall flicked to life.

"Here are the pictures of the post-it notes arranged all over your office," Ben said. He used the iPad to swipe through various pictures and then the same ones, only with different color circles, squares, and arrows drawn over the top of the photos. "We tried to find a pattern but couldn't. If your ghost is telling us something, we're not getting it. So we moved on to something a little clearer." An image showed up on the screen, my stairs.

"So," Ben said. "This is when the temperature started to drop when you all were inspecting the chest." He pressed play, and we watched the screen for about a minute.

"Did you see that?" he asked, pausing the footage.

I shook my head. "Derek?"

"Maybe a bit. Something seemed like it moved, but..." He swallowed and looked down.

"It's hard to see unless you're used to looking at these. I'll slow it down," Oak said, taking control of the iPad. The video crept forward, showing something dark moving down the stairs, one step at a time, like people do when they're trying to be sneaky. I swallowed, and Derek took my hand in his. His was warm and comforting, if sweaty.

"There's definitely something there," Alice said. "You can see it if you know where to look."

Oak replayed the recording. "And I agree with what you've said. It looks like a woman wearing a full calf-length skirt. Probably from the late forties, early fifties." She paused it. "You can see like this hint of curls on the top of her head. Those rolled curls they used to do? Know-what-I-mean?"

"The bouffant," I murmured.

"And here's when the chest moved," Ben said, pressing another button and the angle on the screen changing. We watched the three of us jump away from the chest as it lurched.

"Wait," I said, leaning forward. "There's something behind me." I thought about the air current I'd felt right at that moment.

Oak, Alice, and Ben descended on the iPad, blowing up the section behind me and playing the video back and forth at various speeds. They switched back and forth between the laptop and tablet.

"Agreed," Alice said. "You can just see it for a quick second. Did you feel anything?"

I nodded. "Like someone was touching me."

"I'd say something did," Oak said, her eyes glowing. "Wonderful find. Your house is so cool. And there's even more footage of the chest moving. It twitched all night."

Derek gulped and stood up. "I'm sorry," he said. "I need…" He went out into the hallway.

Alice followed.

"Deep breaths," I heard her say. "It's okay. This is a lot to take in."

My heart dropped. He believed I had a ghost. So much for the logical person poking holes in all the data.

I didn't know if I should go to him or leave him alone. Would he be embarrassed if I did, or did he need me to help? God, I hated this stuff.

Luckily, Alice came back in before I needed to decide. "He's okay," she said. "Just needed a moment. I pointed him toward a vending machine for some water. Sometimes we forget this stuff is really scary if you're not used to it. We get excited and don't remember it's not normal for you."

"Let's finish up," I said. Maybe we could be done before Derek came in. Hopefully, they'd have some answers about how to get rid of Ruth before she drove us all mad.

"So back to the chest," Ben said, his soft Texas twang soothing to my ears. Alice rolled her eyes. I wondered why she didn't like him. He seemed gentle and sweet to me.

We watched the video of the chest moving. It thumped and moved throughout the night all over the bathroom floor. "Your ghost absolutely wants it open," Ben said.

"Then Ruth should've left instructions about unlocking it," I muttered.

Again, the ghost hunters slowed down the footage to show a particularly large twitch, and I thought I saw the odd shadow in the skirt, standing over the chest, for an instant.

"Did you see that?" I asked.

"Yeah," Oak said. She paused the footage, and I saw the human-like shape wearing the poufy skirt with the curly hair again.

"I've never seen such a clear image," Ben said. "Not as a shadow. Not even in the journals or on the parapsychology websites. We might have gotten something unique here."

"I did some research on the chest," Alice said. "Just a quick internet search. I think it's from India. I believe it's a puzzle chest. You see simple versions at street fairs now, but I've never seen one so large and intricate. You have to press or pull the carvings in a certain order, and the parts of the chest will release. Then you pull out those pieces and insert them into other places. They're tricky to open. You may have to break it."

I didn't want to.

Didn't want to.

Didn't want to.

The necklace around my neck grew warm, and I touched it. If Ruth wanted the chest open, why shouldn't we break it?

This ghost made no sense!

"Keep going through the journals," Alice said. "Look for references. Have you learned anything from them?"

Continuing to touch the necklace Alice had given me, I shared how I'd found Ruth to be a bitch, but thought I'd been reading the most recent journals first. "I don't think there's any from the forties or fifties," I said. "But it's so hard to tell because she didn't date her entries."

"That is hard," Oak said. "Does she talk about current events?"

I shook my head. "None I've found. She mostly just complains about how stupid everyone around her is. She was working or volunteering some of the time because she complains about her coworkers a lot."

Alice tapped her finger against the table. "During World War II, women worked outside the home until the men came back. Then the government funded propaganda about trying to get women back into the homes. Do you remember seeing the ads of the women with the apron, the heels, and the apple pie? Those are from the fifties."

"Catered to men," Oak said. "Sexy wife who, if she's not working, has the time to wear heels and bake an apple pie."

"Not saying anything," Ben said.

"Women bought into that image too," Oak said. "The apple pie woman is smiling and seems so happy."

"If only it were that easy," Alice said. "But I think Ruth would've probably had to work if she was widowed. Found anything about a baby?"

"Not a thing," I said. "Though I don't think I've read the right journals yet. And there's no pictures in the photograph album of a baby or of her pregnant."

A green-looking Derek came into the room and sat back down next to me. I put my hand on his leg.

"Maybe the EVPs will give us some clues," Oak said. "I'm still trying to get these easier to hear. But here's what I can find." She looked at Derek. "These might be intense. Some people find them worse than the videos."

He nodded, his lips firm. I enclosed his hands in mine.

She opened another program, one of those you use when you're doing sound editing that shows the sound as a series of peaks and valleys. She clicked the mouse to start the playback, and we leaned forward. Through the speakers, we heard Alice say, "Is anyone here?"

Oak turned up the volume as we leaned forward, squinting at the screen like it would help us hear better. But all I heard was static. Oak turned off the recording.

"See this little spike?" she said, pointing at the audio file on the screen. "It tells me there's something there, but it's hard to hear."

Derek shook his head. "I didn't hear anything."

"It takes time to develop your ear," Alice said. "Let's play it again."

Alice's voice filled the room again, asking if anyone was present. I watched the screen until the file hit the little spike, and I thought I heard a whisper.

"Clothes?" I asked. "That doesn't make any sense."

Alice and Oak high-fived. "That's what we heard, too."

Ben shook his head. "I heard decomposed. And another word in front, but I can't tell what it's saying."

Derek frowned. "I can't hear anything."

"Let's try again," Alice said.

We listened to the audio file three or four times. "Maybe it is decomposed," I said.

"I still think clothes. Creeper clothes?" Alice said. "I don't know. We've tried every way to isolate it, but we can't tell what it is."

I sighed. None of this was helpful. I knew I had a ghost. They just needed to tell me how we were going to get rid of her.

"Found a couple more EVPs," Oak said. "Maybe these will help."

We spent the next hour listening to various audio files from the recorded whispering sounds, trying to decipher static, trying to see if random words hid in the background noises. In the end, we understood three more things, a voice saying, "Open it" and "stuck" and someone crying.

Derek didn't leave the room, but his hand was sweaty and shaking by the time we finished. But I wouldn't have been able to complete this without him. I'd have left too. I couldn't believe this thing was in my house.

"So what's next?" I asked.

"We'll keep looking at the footage," Ben said. "But I think we've found the easy stuff. There's likely more, but we all agree Ruth is haunting your house."

"I mean, what happens with my house? We can't live in a place where the doors are slamming, and a shadow walks down the stairs."

"I don't think you have a shadow ghost," Alice said. "But I think she's sentient. And not above hurting people to get her way. Maybe talk to her. You might be able to get her to back off."

"I don't want to be around something controlling my emotions. And what about Gabe and Polly? That's irresponsible of me to allow them to live in a house with a ghost controlling us."

"I can give you more protections."

I shook my head. "We can't live there. I'll have to sell. But then that's not fair to the people buying it. We have to get rid of her."

"I think we try again to open the chest," Alice said. "It's definitely what Ruth wants. She'll probably settle down."

"Agreed," Oak said. "I mean, we're pretty sure someone on these EVPs says "open it" right? I'll come over tomorrow afternoon. We'll get it open. She'll probably disappear after that."

"I'll be there too," Ben said. "I'll help."

"I'm supposed to have a party on Saturday. It's supposed to be..." How could I explain it was supposed to be a new beginning? A new Tasia? A new way of looking at the world?

"One thing at a time," Ben said. "Let's open the chest and go from there. You haven't finished the journals. The answer may be there."

"I still think it is, too," Alice said. "Keep reading the journals. Give it until tomorrow and then decide what to do about the party."

We said our goodbyes and walked to Derek's car. "I want my house back," I complained. "And this isn't fair to Gabe. This is supposed to be his week."

"I know," he said. He stepped close and rubbed my arms. I looked up at him, and he leaned down.

I took a step back and breathed out, my breath hitching. "This is all too much," I said. And I burst into tears.

# Chapter 32

Derek drove me back to the hotel, alternating between staring straight at the road, his shoulders hunched over the steering wheel, or glancing over at me, and apologizing. I kept wiping my eyes, staring out the passenger side windows, telling him it was fine.

The house, the home Miguel and I had made together, wouldn't ever be the same. Would I be able to live there now, even if we got rid of Ruth?

Derek walked me into the lobby and to the elevator. A mirror showed my red nose and swollen eyes. I stared over his shoulder to avoid eye contact and told him to have a good night.

"Tomorrow is Friday," he said. "I have to go into work for a few hours, but I'll be there with the others to get the chest open."

"And then what? Am I supposed to live with a ghost?"

Guests in the lobby stared at us, and the desk clerk caught my eye. "Did you need assistance, ma'am?" she asked.

Swell, now they thought I was with an abusive date.

"No, thank you," I said as nicely as I could. The clerk went back to her computer, keeping an eye on us if she needed to call the cops.

I sighed.

"Let me buy you a drink," Derek asked. "Let's talk this out."

That was the last thing I wanted, though a drink sounded good. But I didn't want to be around Derek anymore. Not tonight.

"No, thank you," I said again. "I'm tired. And just need sleep and some alone time."

Which I wasn't going to get in the hotel room shared by my daughter and son. I'd shared rooms with Gabe before—he always scattered his clothes and toys everywhere and didn't put anything away. Like at home. But unlike at home, the hotel didn't have color-coordinated boxes to put his stuff into, only a chaotic suitcase.

I dug my hands into my eyes, stretched too thin to keep crying. "I'll see you tomorrow," I said.

Derek stuffed his hands into his pocket and looked out over the lobby. "I hate leaving you this upset."

It was one of the sweetest things someone had ever said to me. "I just need sleep." For a century. "Then tomorrow I'll come up with a plan for the party. I'll be okay."

"If that's what's best," he said. "I'll keep an eye on the house and will text you if anything happens."

"And don't forget about Fluffy."

"That kitten won't let me forget her."

The pause between us grew longer. It was like a game of no-you-hang-up-first. "I'll see you in the morning," he finally said. He looked like he wanted to do something, kiss my cheek or hug me, but in the end, he just walked away.

I watched him head through the hotel doors while I waited for the elevator, images and decisions running through my head. Going to the bar and getting a few drinks with Derek until we could laugh about this. Going back to the room, curling up on the bed with Gabe and sobbing until I couldn't cry anymore. Asking Derek to come with me to the front desk and getting another hotel room for him and me for a few hours.

But that wasn't fair to him.

The doors dinged open, and I climbed into the elevator, letting the doors close in front of me.

# Chapter 33

I inserted my key card into the hotel room door, my eyes down, hoping the kids wouldn't see I'd been crying. Greeting them, I scuttled into the bathroom, turning on the water and flushing my face and eyes with water. I wiped my face dry, the make-up I'd put on for my date coming off on the white towel.

God, I was pathetic.

Taking some deep breaths, I told myself not to fall apart.

When I came out to grab my toiletry bag and pajamas, Polly met my eyes. She climbed off her bed to hug me. Gabe lay curled into a ball in his and my bed, watching a show on his iPad.

"You okay?" Polly asked in a low tone.

"It's been a lot."

"He made a move, didn't he?"

I ran my fingers over my wedding ring. "A small one. And then I burst into tears. Classy." I glanced at Gabe, and we went out into the hallway.

"What are your thoughts?" Polly's phone buzzed, and she looked at it.

I shrugged. "I don't know."

Polly's phone buzzed again.

"Do you need to get that?"

She smiled. "It's Oak. She says she knows I missed the viewing and wanted to know if I could come over to the university to watch the footage."

"Did you want to go?"

"Can I?"

"Of course. It was pretty intense, though."

"I'll be fine."

"Gabe okay, tonight?"

"He's so awesome. We walked to the McDonalds across the street, then got ice cream, and looked in the windows of the used bookstore. He told me all about the train museum. I should go sometime with him. But he misses Fluffy. And the house. We gotta figure out how to get Fluffy back to him."

"I know." In a whispered conversation in case Gabe was listening, I told her a bit about what Ben, Oak, and Alice had shared. I wondered if another hotel guest could hear us. I imagined a bored salesperson listening to our conversation, leaning against their door. Bet it was better than whatever crap they were watching on TV.

"I can't wait to watch the footage," Polly said. "So they think the shadow is Ruth, and she's trying to tell us to open the chest?"

"Pretty much."

"Sounds easy, then. Let's get the chest open."

"We're going to try tomorrow afternoon. Even if we have to break it. And then it's party time."

"Hopefully."

Polly left, borrowing my SUV to head back to Sac State, and I went into the hotel room, curling up next to Gabe. He'd fallen mostly asleep, his cartoon playing whether or not he watched it. He muttered as I cuddled close to him.

"I miss Fluffy."

"Me too. We'll get this figured out," I promised.

# Chapter 34

**<u>Friday</u>**

The next morning, my phone pinged with a text message while I brushed my teeth.

*Check your email,* Alice texted.

I pulled it up and nearly dropped my phone. What had she done?

I started typing, *What the heck are yo*—Then deleted it. I tried, *That's very kind, but*— And deleted it. Then, *You can't just invite*—

I pressed the button to call Alice and made sure I'd locked the bathroom door.

"Surprise, chickadee!" she said in greeting. "I figured with everything going on, you could have Gabe's party at my house. You won't have to do anything. I'll take care of it all. That email went out to all the parents at Gabe's class, and you can forward it to anyone I might have missed. I have a bounce house, and while the pool isn't quite open, there's plenty of room for the kids to run around and do squirt gun battles. I have plenty of squirt guns, and I can run to the store to get more for you. Plates, napkins, cups, soda, I have it all already."

Like last night with Derek, I had so many emotions. Anger she'd taken over my party. Relief I didn't have to worry about it anymore. Curiosity about why she'd done what she did.

"You there?" Alice asked. I realized I'd been silent for too long.

"Alice," I said, keeping my voice low so Polly and Gabe wouldn't hear. "I don't know what to... why? Why would you do this?"

181

"Honestly?"

"Sure." I braced myself for what she'd say. She probably thought I was a horrible mom. That I couldn't handle a party, a ghost, and my son's birthday at once.

"Because no one helped me when Gerald left. My friends took his side because no one sane would kick her rich, non-abusive, non-cheating husband out of her house. Everyone talked about me behind my back. I swear, when I went to get my nails done, the store went silent. It's been terrible."

"Why did you divorce him if he was so perfect?"

"I've had a lot of therapy so that I can say, I wanted more than to be his wife. I wanted more than the perfect life with the perfect clothes and an expensive car. I wanted to be me, and he didn't understand it."

I sat against the door in the bathroom, my knees up to my chest. It had been a hell of a week. "So, why are you helping me?"

"Because, and I'm going to be blunt... other than Derek, you don't have anyone else. Everyone left you behind. Including me. And you need help. It's just a stupid party. Please let me do this."

"Alice—"

"Because you're letting me be me. And I can't be me around very many people. And being me is more than I can ever repay.

I breathed out. And let my plans for the future go. "Thank you. I could really use the help."

# Chapter 35

I showered, and Polly and I hunkered down with the journals in the coffee-house, trying to find a mention of the chest or baby, while Gabe played a video game on my phone. But there was nothing. Just the words of an angry woman who tried to control the world and was mad when she couldn't.

Finally, after Gabe wondered for the fiftieth time how Fluffy was doing and when we could go home to see him, I texted Derek. I asked if we could stop by the granny unit, even though he was at work.

*Of course,* he responded. *It's your house too.*

*I know. But I like to ask.* I read the text message and added, *Thank you. Gabe is really worried about Fluffy.*

*Totally understand.*

Should I say something about last night? I could tell he was writing something else from the three little dots on the screen and waited to see what it was.

The dots lasted a while. He was probably texting someone else.

A few minutes later, the words popped into the screen. *Are we good?*

I took a deep breath.

*Always. No matter what.*

He responded with a happy face and a wink.

*I'll see you at three,* I texted.

*Don't go into the main house without anyone. Just in case.*

*Polly is with me. But I won't. Rather wait for the ghost hunting crew.*

*Also, I may not have cleaned up before I left. So pretend you don't see the dirty dishes on the counter.*

I snickered. I didn't know why, but his confession struck me as funny. Why did he think I cared about how he lived?

*They're invisible to me,* I responded.

"Do you think Jack was abusive?" Polly asked, making me look up. "What's so funny?" she asked.

"What?"

"You're smiling like someone told a joke."

A silly grin stretched my lips. It felt odd, like I hadn't smiled like that in a while.

"Nothing."

"Were you texting Derek? I want to see."

"Oh hush," I said, tucking my phone away. "What were you saying about Jack?"

"In the journals," she said, her small smile dying. "Ruth makes all these comments about "him" and "he." Things like "he" won't like it. "He's" going to be mad. "He'll" punish her. "He'll" hurt her. "He'll" be angry. It's throughout and mixed in with the other... stuff."

"Derek and I noticed that, too. Didn't we find Jack's death certificate?"

Polly looked at her notes. "He died in 1947. But I think these journals are after that. And the "he" thing is in every journal. Maybe she had a bunch of lovers, and they were all abusive?"

I shook my head. "She complains about the mailman not saying a proper good morning to her. You'd think if she had a lover or a slew of lovers, she'd complain about them too."

"Maybe a brother? Or her father?"

"Thought her family died." I took a sip of my cold coffee and made a face. "I wonder if she went mad after Jack died. I mean, I think she had moments of lucidity, but her anger and paranoia got worse and worse. Maybe that explains the journals. She was bat-crazy and hallucinating."

"Or maybe she was seeing her husband's ghost," Polly said.

I started to say no and then stopped. "I guess it's a possibility. Are we even sure the ghost we're seeing is Ruth?" I thought about the shadow with the skirt and the curled hair and shook my head again. "It has to be a woman.

And who else could it be?"

Polly shook her head. "Maybe it's something that wants us to think it's a woman."

"But the footage from last night was a woman's shape. A thing knowing we were filming and was smart enough to change their shape? Makes no sense."

"Then who's "he"?"

# Chapter 36

A few hours later, after Polly and I were vibrating with caffeine, we checked out of the hotel, though I warned the clerk we might need to come back. They assured us there were plenty of rooms available and would try to even put us back in the same one.

We pulled into my driveway ten minutes later. I stared at the first-story windows with their closed drapes, looking for some movement, some sign something, maybe Ruth, was watching us.

Nothing.

I unlocked the door to Derek's house, expecting from his text to see clothing and dirty dishes everywhere. But while he'd left a blanket on the couch, a plate with crumbs on the coffee table, and his bed was unmade, the rest of the granny unit looked fine.

Gabe went running in to release Fluffy from the bathroom. He yelled in excitement, and the kitten echoed it with her own meow. Gabe scooped her up like a baby, cradling the kitten, and kissing her head and belly. Fluffy purred like mad, letting out these little joyful sounds. I never thought cats could show emotion, but this cat, a puff of gray fur in Gabe's hand seemed so joyful. Gabe curled up on the floor and proceeded to tell Fluffy all about the hotel, Fairytale Town, the zoo, and every tiny thing that had happened since he last saw her.

Polly and I sat down on Derek's couch; the journals stacked on the floor between us. We kept reading, hoping for some mention of the chest or baby. After a few minutes of Gabe's chatter, Polly slipped in headphones. I was getting a handle on the spidery handwriting and was becoming increasingly intrigued by Ruth.

The further back we went with the journals, the nicer the entries got. There were random comments about sunrises and sunsets, comments about going out with friends, or the occasional party. She spoke about walks through McKinley Park, and I realized with a jolt, she'd seen the park close to our house get built, witnessed the planting of the now giant elms and sycamores that watched over hundreds of picnics and parties. She'd seen neighbors—some of them the decedents of my current neighbors—come and go, get married, have children, and die. In the beginning, in the older journals, there was hope mixed in with the vitriol.

"I got it, I got it," Polly shouted. "It's at the start of this journal. And she dated it, Jan 2nd, 1948.

"I've decided that enough is enough," Polly read. "It does me no good to dwell in the past. I will only look forward. I will shut him away, so he stops bothering me. I've had Mr. Hughes from next door put up the wall, closing off a different future and locking away the past. I've put his things in the chest Jack brought me from Germany. It's in the room, and I won't think of it again. I will move forward in a new direction. He will leave me alone if I forget him. I will forget the joy and the trials. The tears and the laughter. I will exist and persevere."

I reached for the journal, and Polly handed it over. "But how do we open the chest?" I asked the journal, like I expected Ruth to step from the pages and answer. I flipped through the pages, hoping to find something underlined, something highlighted with the word chest. But of course, the writing was too faded for any words to stand out.

I flipped to the end of the journal and read, "No matter what I do, he won't stop. He won't leave me alone. I'm so tired."

"God, I can't tell if there's anything about the chest," I said. I almost flung the fragile book down. "This is the only reference to it. We're going to have to break it open." The words were hard to say and caught in my throat.

Polly took the journal away from me. "I'll keep reading," she said. "You never know."

"What if you can't open it?" Gabe said, looking up from his video game.

"We'll take the bat to it," I said. "We'll get it open."

"And then the ghost will go away?" he asked.

"We're not sure," I told him as honestly as I could. "But we think she'll stop being so active."

"What if the ghost is dad?" He looked down at Fluffy, his hands stroking her belly, making her purr.

Polly and I exchanged a look, and we climbed onto the floor next to Gabe. I put my arm around him, cuddling him to me. Polly moved his legs, so they draped over hers. Where had this girl come from, and how I had managed so long on my own without her?

Tears filled my eyes, and I took a moment to get control. It wouldn't help Gabe if I broke down now.

"Mom," Gabe whispered. "What if we open the chest and it gets rid of dad?"

I couldn't speak. It was taking everything I had to hold back a sob.

"The ghost isn't dad," Polly said. There was a hitch in her voice, but she was steadier than I was. "I'm sure," she said, stopping Gabe from saying more.

"But what—"

"It's not," Polly said. "Tasia saw a woman ghost, and the ghost hunters agreed. I saw the footage last night. It's not dad. I promise. We would know. He would send us a message, tell us he loves us. Dad would be helping us. He wouldn't be trying to get some old chest he didn't even know about open."

"Then where is he?" Gabe whispered, petting Fluffy the wrong way, accidentally spiking up her fur. Instead of hissing or scratching, Fluffy leaned forward and began to wash Gabe's hair. It couldn't have been comfortable, but Gabe giggled, just a bit.

"From what I'm reading about Ruth," I said once I could speak. "She was a miserable person when she died. Your dad..." I had to take a deep breath. "Your dad wasn't unhappy. He loved us, he loved the house, he loved his job very much. Other than missing us, which I know he does, he doesn't have a reason to come back."

Gabe buried his head into my lap, and I ran my fingers through his silky hair. "I miss him," he whispered.

"I know, baby," I whispered. "Me too."

Polly leaned against me, and I put my arm around her. "I miss him too," she said.

"I know he'd be proud of you. Both of you, especially after this week," I said, working not to let my voice shake.

"And Fluffy?"

"Yes, he'd be proud of Fluffy." I tugged Gabe away from me, and he sat up. He'd left big wet spots on my shirt, but I didn't care. "Go wash your face," I said, adjusting Fluffy, so she draped across my lap. "I'll take care of Fluffy for you."

We were silent until Gabe went into the bathroom, closing the door after him.

"You ok?" I asked Polly.

She shrugged. "Yeah. Like Ruth. It's time to let it go. Not forget. But let it go."

I went back to my journal, not even noticing when Gabe came back. I had found the first journal, the one right after Ruth got married. She wrote about slow dances in the kitchen while dinner burned, about a picnic breakfast in the backyard, the day after Jack had planted a bunch of flowers and bushes. She spoke about waking up so blissfully happy and staring down at her new husband, marveling he was now hers. There was no anger, no hatred. Just a wonderful six weeks before he shipped out.

I closed the journal and wiped my eyes.

"What did you find?" Polly asked, looking up from her journal.

"I think the first journal, right after Ruth was married. She was so happy."

"Guess she changed after Jack died."

"Guess so."

I picked up another random journal. After a few pages, I realized this one was from after Jack had gotten back from World War II.

"Somehow, I'd thought when he came home, everything would be perfect," I read out loud.

"Maybe this is the beginning of the abuse." Polly leaned forward.

I kept reading. "But it hasn't. It's like he's a different person. He goes for drives and won't tell me where he goes. He just says he's going out and then comes home smelling like gin. I've told him I don't mind going to a bar with him, maybe we could go out to dinner, but he refuses to let me. Sometimes he doesn't even tell me he's leaving. I'll be reading outside or making dinner, and I'll hear the car pulling away. Why can't we go back to how things were?"

"That's so sad," Polly said. "He probably had PTSD. Maybe that's why he abused her."

I kept reading, flipping pages. This was a very different Ruth than the one full of vitriol later in life.

"He brought me flowers; I can't believe it. I'd made what I thought was his favorite breakfast to make up for last night." I flipped the pages I'd already read, but there was no mention of what had happened the night before. Maybe they'd argued, or he'd been impotent. I kept reading the passage. "But he threw the plate into the sink and stormed out. But and this is the best news—an hour later he came back with flowers. Daisies. My favorite. I told him they're the happiest flowers. He promised he'd be better."

That poor woman.

"He said he was sorry; he knew I was only trying to be nice. He told me things were hard, he just got angry sometimes and couldn't help it. But he would try to be better," I read out loud.

Polly blew a raspberry. We both knew where this was going.

"And he kissed me like he used to. I hope, I pray the worst is behind us. I have to believe it. There's no other choice."

"Breaks my heart," Polly said. "There was no support for abused women. It was always their fault. They did something wrong, and it made the guy hit them. It wasn't his fault, ever."

"I'm not excusing the abuse," I said. "But if he had PTSD..."

"Right. He was mentally ill, and there wasn't any help for it." Polly went back to her journal. "But there's no reason to abuse anyone."

I returned to my reading. Things had seemed good between Ruth and Jack for the next few entries, or at least Ruth had talked little about Jack. She'd talked about taking walks in McKinley Rose Garden and serving on a committee for women voters. She'd been super excited about that, but I saw some of what she'd turn into in those entries.

*And for heaven's sakes, why does Mrs. Addair insist on dressing like she's twenty? The woman was wearing a light pink sundress, completely inappropriate, not only for a married woman but for a married woman of forty. And she didn't have the figure for it—you could see the lines from her girdle. And she kept getting more and more red-faced as it cut in. The woman is fat. And needs to either go on a diet or accept it. Not pretend to be younger than she is. I promise, here in writing, I will age with grace.*

I kept reading as Polly refilled my iced tea, and Gabe asked if he could play Derek's PlayStation. Polly set it up for him as I kept falling into Ruth's world.

"I got something," I said. "Today, Jack died," I read. "A nice policeman came to tell me. Jack had driven the car into a ditch and drowned there. The policeman said Jack had been drinking. I must do the following things. One. Call the funeral home. Two. Pick out a casket. Three. Pick out a gravestone. Four. Decide what to be..." I trailed off. I'd done the same thing for Miguel. But as much as I loved lists, I'd never made one like this.

"She goes on," I said after I cleared my throat. "There's thirty-two things here. Everything from deciding what to dress Jack in, to making sure all the neighbors get their dishware back."

"Guess it was her way of coping," Polly said quietly.

I remembered putting a pad of post-it notes next to the front door when neighbors brought me casseroles and making them stick their names on the bottoms of the dishes, even the plates the neighbors said they didn't want back.

I got up and went out into the garden. The garden Miguel had loved. The garden Ruth had written about when she'd commented on the spring flowers starting to come up and the pink roses budding. I breathed deep. So much happiness here and so much pain.

But I hadn't died. And I needed to stop acting like I did.

The journal I'd been reading was still in my hands, and I went to sit on the concrete patch. Next house, I'd buy some patio furniture.

A few entries later, I texted Polly. *Can you come outside? I found something and don't want Gabe to hear.*

Polly joined me to sit on the patio, her legs curled in front of her.

"She was pregnant," I said, holding the journal out to Polly. "Found out a few weeks after Jack died."

Polly's eyes widened. "It's like a Soap."

"Only if Jack's twin brother impregnated her," I said. "And Jack faked his death."

She opened the book to the page I indicated and started flipping through the book. "Blah, blah, blah, about being pregnant. Uncomfortable in the heat.... swollen feet... didn't like the doctor."

"Oh yeah, the heat in Sacramento would be terrible without air conditioning," I said. "What happened to the baby?"

"She had the baby," she said, skimming. "A little boy. She named him Shaun after Jack's father."

I stood over her shoulder, trying to read. I pointed to a passage. "One of the neighbors came and helped with him so Ruth could get sleep."

"Yep," Polly said, turning a page. "Lots of stuff about how grateful she was for the neighbor."

"Though she didn't like her cooking," I said with a snicker. "Typical Ruth."

"Oh no," Polly said, reading faster than I was. She put her hand over her mouth.

I read the passage and felt the blood drain from my face. "Oh no," I echoed. "Poor Ruth."

Polly handed me the journal and stepped away while I kept reading. "They didn't know about SIDS, did they?"

I shook my head. "I think the Back-to-Sleep thing started in the eighties. Before that, they put babies on their stomachs to sleep." I closed the book, feeling sick. "There's another list of things to do," I said. "No wonder she got all bitter and sad." I'd only lost Miguel. I don't know what I would've done if I'd lost Gabe too.

"I bet she went crazy," I said. "For years, all she had was this house."

Derek's car pulled into the driveway, and I startled. Polly let out a little yelp. These last few days had been horrible on our nerves.

We went out to his car. "What are you doing out here?" he said, rolling down the window.

I explained what we'd found out about Ruth and how we didn't want Gabe to hear. "I think maybe if we get the chest open, we tell her we know what happened, and we're sorry for her, she'll go away?"

Derek shrugged. "Sounds as good as any other idea." He reached into the backseat. "I brought cupcakes from Freeport Bakery for Gabe. And hopefully to celebrate. With luck, we can eat them in your kitchen, ghost-free."

"Fingers crossed," I said.

Alice pulled onto the street in her SUV a few minutes later, followed by Ben and Oak. Drinks were offered and refused. Ben pulled the equipment out of the van, less of it than they'd used before.

"I thought we could record opening the chest," he said. "We'll use one GoPro, our cell phones, and a recorder mostly."

"I'll stay in the granny unit with Gabe," Derek volunteered before anyone could ask.

"Sounds good," I said.

"Let's open the chest inside the house," Oak said. "You never know. Maybe Ruth will help us figure out the puzzle. Or we'll just get some good footage. Though it'd be best if we did this at night. During a thunderstorm."

"We're not waiting for a thunderstorm," I said. "I want my house back." Even if it was just to sell it.

"I know," Oak said. "I just got excited. Maybe next house we investigate, we'll do it during a big storm."

"I'd be into that," Polly said.

Oak gave her a fist bump. "Told you this stuff is addicting."

We went inside the house. Nothing had changed. The tea and paper towels were still strewn around the kitchen, the post-it notes still in an unintelligent muddle in my office. I unlocked the bathroom door I'd foolishly locked like it could keep a ghost out. The chest sat where we'd left it, though I remembered the footage of how it had shifted throughout the room during the night.

Ben walked through the downstairs, looking at the post-it notes and the mess of tea on the floor.

Alice made a slight gesture toward him, and he shook his head.

"Everything okay?" I asked.

"I hadn't seen the inside before," he said with his Texas twang. "Just seeing if I spotted anything different. Ready to get that chest open?"

"I want to try something first," I said. "I think I know why Ruth came back and what she was trying to tell me. Maybe if I tell her I understand, she'll leave us alone?"

Alice shrugged. "It's worth a try. Some hunters swear acknowledging the ghost and talking to them helps tremendously with hauntings. Can we film it?"

"Sure. But I think I want to say it to the nursery, not the chest," I said, not sure why I was thinking that.

"Trust your instincts," Oak said. "It wouldn't surprise me if you were a bit psychic. When this is done, we can run some tests, if you want."

When this was done, I didn't want to hear the word parapsychology again. We went upstairs, and I faced the nursery.

"Hello Ruth," I whispered under my breath, feeling ridiculous. I pushed away the thought of Oak and Alice recording me. "I understand now what you were trying to say. My life won't end just because Miguel died. I'll move forward, I promise. You shut yourself away for longer than you were married. Longer than you were a mom. You didn't dream, didn't hope, and didn't plan. You just existed, miserably."

I realized the emotions I'd been feeling, all the anger that wasn't mine, was her way of trying to help. Trying to make sure I wasn't taken advantage of, as she'd been.

"I won't shut myself away. I won't make that mistake. You don't have to protect me."

Holding my breath, I waited to see if the house would respond, but there was nothing, no thumps, no sounds of footsteps. A tear slipped down my cheek. "I need to say goodbye to the future I'd planned, but I also need to keep living, right? Create a new plan for a different future. Not better or worse. Just different."

Nothing. No movement, no steps, no cold, no brushes of air across my neck.

"Did you see anything?" I asked the other women.

Oak shook her head. "Nothing. We'll check the cameras later, but the house doesn't feel different or anything. It was worth a try, though. You never know. Maybe this is over."

"How would I know?"

Alice shrugged. "It's not like there's a puff of smoke. Some people can feel when the ghost moves on; sometimes there's a flash of light, but most people simply don't see them again."

I pushed my bangs out of my eyes. "Let's get the chest open. Maybe it's what Ruth wanted."

"It's hard for ghosts to communicate, and often the message gets screwed up," Oak said as we went down the steps, our feet loud on the squeaky step. "There's some amazing articles about it. I'll send you some."

"I'll take them," Polly said. "This is so interesting."

The others had pulled the chest out of the bathroom, placing it on the blue throw rug in the middle of the family room.

"Okay," Polly dropped to her knees next to the box and ran her fingers over the carved decorations. "I did some research on India puzzle chests. I think there's buttons we need to press." Her fingers hit something, and there was a faint click. I tried the lid. "Nope," I said.

Polly pulled the leaf she'd pressed entirely out. It was shaped like a large dowel. "It must go halfway into the trunk," Oak said, leaning forward. "Clever design. You'll need to pull parts out for the lid to release."

I tried the lid again. "Nope."

"Wait, I think I felt something wiggle." Polly ran her fingers over what I thought was a vine but was actually a snake. She pulled it out. It too, was a long dowel.

"I'm getting this," Oak said when Polly couldn't find anything else that wiggled. "Let me try."

Oak pressed on a few other carvings and pulled out two more dowels. But the box didn't open.

"Come on, Ruth," I shouted to the house. "Help us out here."

The snake dowel slid across the floor next to one of the holes left by the leaf dowel. The four of us scuttled backward while Ben made a small sound. He was so quiet; I'd forgotten he was there.

When nothing else happened, Oak let out a little laugh. "Well, that got me." She picked up the snake dowel with shaking hands. "I guess I'll try it," Oak said, starting to insert the dowel into the hole

Suddenly the other dowels shot across the room, skittering into the kitchen.

"Whoops," Polly said, getting up and grabbing them. "I think Ruth got a little excited there."

Oak slid the snake dowel into the leaf dowel hole.

It fit, but nothing happened. We tried various combinations, but still couldn't get the chest open. I rubbed my arms, goosebumps popping out.

"Yep," Oak said, pushing her glasses up her nose. "The temperature is dropping. Ruth wants us to open this box."

Something clicked, and the lid popped open a crack.

I took a deep breath, which the house seemed to echo.

"Ruth," Polly called out. "Are you watching? We're opening the chest."

There was a thump overhead from the nursery, and something flung my hand away from the trunk lid.

"What the—"

The lid hurled itself open, and we leaped away from the box. I ran into the couch and fell across it. Oak hit the ground and let out a little yelp.

Alice and Polly had made it to the kitchen. Ben kept his camera on the chest but looked around the room, into the corners where the ceiling met the wall like he'd spotted something moving.

"Dramatic, much Ruth?" Oak asked, her teeth chattering. The temperature was dropping even more.

"Hold it," Alice said. "Something is really wrong." She'd gone pale and pulled her arms in around her body. She moved into the kitchen as far away from the chest as she could.

"I feel it too," Ben said.

We stared at the box, but nothing else happened. No whispers, no thumps, no slamming of doors, no flickering of lights, no sound of footsteps running up or down the stairs.

Just cold.

"Now what?" Polly asked. She blew on her hands and stuck them under her arms to keep them warm.

"Should we see what's in the chest?" I asked.

Ben nodded, but his body was tense, like he was expecting to be attacked.

"This is wrong," Alice echoed again.

"Do you want to wait outside?" Ben asked.

She shook her head and moved closer to the chest. Ben passed her the camera, and she aimed it. He moved away from us, where he could see the other rooms and the trunk.

"Go ahead, Tasia," he murmured. "Let's see what's inside."

I knelt next to the box and felt a stir of air across my neck, like someone had reached out, placing a hand on my shoulder.

"Baby clothes," I whispered, staring at the tiny bits of cloth. I pulled out a teddy bear and held it up to my nose. It still smelled like a baby.

"Oh, Ruth," I said, trying to keep my teeth from chattering. "I'm so sorry."

Footsteps sounded up and down the stairs, at a counterpoint to sudden thumps overhead. The doors began slamming again. Running feet upstairs echoed through the ceiling, skittering on the upstairs rugs with long, low sounds. Were those claws scraping?

"That's not a ghost." Ben's breath puffed out in a cloud. "We need to get out of here."

The claw-like sounds moved to the stairs, and I saw it. A shadow raced down the stairs, using its arms only, dragging leg-like things behind it. A tiny little thing, malformed, and not human, looking so different from Ruth's shadow. A baby's laugh surrounded us, and a rotten smell filled the house.

"We were wrong," Oak said.

"Get out, get out, get out," Alice shouted.

Polly and Oak vaulted over the couch, running to the back door.

"It won't open," one of them screamed. Polly jiggled the lock while Oak twisted and pulled on the doorknob.

"Ruth!" I screamed.

The door released, and Oak staggered backward. Polly grabbed her hand and pulled her out. Alice and I were a step behind, trying to get over the back of the couch. Ben grabbed us, and we hurtled out the back door, the shadow on our heels.

I sprinted across the lawn, following Oak and Polly as a terrible laugh echoed through the neighborhood. Oak turned and stopped, panting. Polly halted beside her, staring at the house.

Alice and Ben pulled up next to me, and I turned. The thing lay in the doorway, waving its shadowy arms at us. The darkness was shaped like a baby, the little pudgy body close to the ground, crawling on its hands and knees—a twisted, horrific parody of a baby. Like a psychopath had created what he thought a baby should look like.

Derek ran out of his house. "What happened? What's that sound?" He gasped and fell to his knees. I dropped next to him and hugged him.

Behind the baby-thing was Ruth's shadow. She hadn't wanted to tell me not to ruin my future, not to lock myself away. She'd wanted help. From that thing.

"We were so wrong," Oak breathed.

"I knew it," Alice panted.

"It tricked us," Ben said. "Even though I stayed out of the house, it knew. It knew enough to hide what it was."

The back door slammed, and we all jumped. Ruth was trapped in our house with the... monster, as she'd been for years. Now it made sense why she'd boarded up the nursery and locked away the chest. She was trying to lock away the... thing.

He.

"I need a drink," Ben breathed.

"We need a plan," I said. "I'm not leaving Ruth with that."

# Chapter 37

I drove a shaking Derek, a stoic Polly, and an overexcited Gabe to Alice's house so Gabe could have another sleepover. Then, with Ruth's journals, we met Alice, Ben, and Oak at a local chain restaurant advertising appetizers and giant margaritas.

Derek stopped on the doorstep of the restaurant.

"What's wrong?" I asked when I realized he hadn't followed us in.

He shook his head and went to sit on a bench, his head in his hands.

"I'll just go inside," Polly said. "I'll order a beer and a margarita for you guys."

"Thanks." I went to sit next to Derek. His knees jiggled, and I didn't think it was nerves.

I took his hand in mine, closing my fingers around his. He was clammy, his entire body shaking. I sat there, just being with him, not saying anything. Restaurant-goers came and went, some giving us odd looks but mostly ignoring us. I should've been freaking out, but it was like helping Derek was helping me.

"I don't think I can go in there," Derek said in a low voice. "That..."

"Monster," I said. "From here on out, we'll refer to it as Monster. Or "He" like Ruth did."

"I'm not sure I can live in my house, not so close to it."

"I'm selling the house," I said. "Even if we get rid of it."

"How? Ruth couldn't get... Monster, to leave."

"I don't know," I said. "But we have a couple of ghost experts inside. Maybe they can help."

"I just don't know," he whispered.

"Do you want to stay out here?" I asked. "Or you can go back to the hotel. Recheck us in."

"That okay? I mean, I don't want to leave you, but I don't—"

Before I could lose my nerve, I leaned in, and gave him a quick kiss on the lips, no more than a peck, and pulled back before he could respond.

"It's completely fine," I said. I fished my car keys out of my purse. "You know where the hotel is."

He snorted. "I can't believe that was last night."

"I'll text you when I'm ready to leave. You never know, I might need a designated driver."

"I may have a few drinks myself at the hotel bar."

"Then I'll take an Uber or get a ride from Alice. Take a break. God knows you've done plenty."

He stood up, curling his hands around my keys. He was still pale, but a little color had come back into his cheeks.

I hugged him, a full-body hug, and he buried his nose in my hair. We stood, wrapped in each other for a while before he stepped away.

"I'll see you later tonight," I said and went into the restaurant.

The others had commanded a large circular table and had the journals spread out.

"Where's Derek?" Polly asked.

"Taking a break," I said.

Alice nodded. "It hits some people that way. It's just too much."

I started to pull out my chair when I sensed someone behind me. Derek?

"Thought you were—"

"Changed my mind. I got this. Though I want the drink." He reached over and grabbed a beer, downing it in one gulp.

Polly applauded.

"I didn't know I could still do that," Derek said. "Guess my years of frat parties weren't wasted." His cheeks were now slightly green.

Ben finished his drink, something dark in a tumbler glass, and waved the server over again.

Alice had finished her wine, and Polly slurped up the last of her margarita.

"Full round," I told the server. "And I'll give you an extra twenty if it's ASAP." I started sucking on my straw, wishing I'd ordered something more potent.

We didn't speak until he brought us our drinks. Ben drained his in one gulp and asked for another.

Alice eyed him, frowning, but didn't say anything.

While we waited, I asked, "You guys are the experts. What was that thing? It can't have been a baby."

"It was a demon," Ben said. He folded his hands in front of him. "I suspect a demon is pretending to be Ruth's baby. That's why it took the form it did. And was doing it when Ruth was still alive."

"Ben's an expert in demons," Alice said. "I'd kind of wondered if maybe you had one when you reacted so poorly to wearing the necklace. So I asked him to check it out."

"I didn't find anything," he said. "Not a hint. No smells. No claw marks, and you guys hadn't been hurt. Other than the emotional piece, which ghosts can do, there was no evidence."

"Until we opened the chest," Polly said.

Ben nodded. "I think Ruth managed to trap it inside the chest, partially. The demon was desperate to get out; Ruth was desperate to keep it in."

"That's why we heard "closed" on the EVPs," Alice said. "Not clothes."

"It's why everything was so confusing," Polly said.

"Two entities," Oak breathed. "Each with different goals."

"Poor Ruth," I said. "She was trying so hard, and none of us were listening."

"That's why it's so hard to know what ghosts want," Oak said. "Everything gets muddy."

"So what do we do?" I asked. I finished up my margarita in a giant slurp, trying to hide the tears springing to my eyes. It had been a really long week. Derek's hand enclosed mine, and I blinked back the tears. "I can't let Gabe go back into my house, but I can't sell it knowing Monster is loose."

"Let's look at the journals," Alice said. "I want to get a timeline together of what happened when."

# Chapter 38

Three hours later, after three margaritas, I had a headache from squinting at the writing, and my stomach was upset from the greasy appetizers we'd snacked on.

And we had a rough timeline of Ruth's life.

"Okay," Oak said, looking up from the laptop she was taking notes in. "Here's what I have. Ruth was married in 1942 to Jack Evans. We've found their marriage certificate online. Thanks to Polly." She winked at my stepdaughter and continued. "Judging from the dates and the journals, it was one of those World War II weddings where they dated, got married, bought a house, spent six weeks in bed, and then he went to war. Ruth stayed in Sacramento, in their new house, managing all the finances as her and Jack's parents were dead." She looked around the table. "Agreed?"

We all nodded.

"A few months after Jack left, Ruth joined the workforce as a secretary and remained at the job until Jack returned. She was overall happy as a secretary, though she didn't like her coworkers, and spent her time with friends, reading books, and walking around McKinley Park. We all agree she spends way too much time detailing the rose bushes, right?"

We all nodded. Ruth's obsession with the roses had continued throughout all the journals we'd read. Even when at her worst, a trip to the rose bushes at McKinley Park had calmed her down, mostly. Unless a stroller got in her way, but knowing what we knew now, that kind of made sense.

I shivered. If I had lost Gabe, would I have become like her?

"And then we all agree Jack was at least verbally and emotionally abusive when he got back, right?"

"That's where I got confused with the "hes"," I said.

"Me too," Polly agreed.

"We also found a death certificate for Jack in late 1947," Oak continued. "No birth certificates for the baby, but thanks to the journal, we know she had one after Jack died. And the baby died, likely of SIDS, in 1948 after a hot summer."

I remembered the sweet scent of baby on the baby clothes and the teddy bear. "She loved that baby." I again found Derek's hand and curled my fingers around his.

"And then the reports of "he" and "him" started, but these are separate from the abuse she received from Jack," Alice said, taking up the story.

"And because we didn't know when Jack died, and the journals were all out of order, and didn't have dates, we thought she was referencing Jack. Or another man. Or..." I trailed off.

"We couldn't figure it out," Polly said. "We kept reading more, hoping we would get it."

"I think her reference to starting a new life and locking the past behind her with Mr. Hughes putting up a wall is about closing off the nursery and locking away the baby stuff," Alice said.

"And somehow, I think she managed to lock the demon away too," Oak said. "At least partially. Or something. May have been intentional or random. We won't know until we get a better idea of what's in the chest."

"But she didn't get rid of the demon completely," Polly said. "I mean, she talks for years about "him" not letting her sleep or "he'll" be angry with her. Some of them are only one line, scribbled like she was desperate."

Alice nodded. "I would've thought the references were to a colicky baby, not a demon thing."

The server delivering our dinners gave Alice a startled look and accidentally dropped Alice's salad plate onto the table.

"We're writing a screenplay," Polly said, trying to cover. I didn't know if the server believed us because another server brought the rest of our food out.

"The worst part in the journals," Oak said. "Were the references about being held down. How he'd stolen the breath from her. And the laugh."

"The laugh was terrifying," I murmured and finished the last dregs of my margarita.

I tightened my grip on Derek's hand, finding strength in it—no matter how scared he was, it was better than being alone.

"She'd lived with the thing for years," Polly said. "No wonder she was so paranoid and bitter when she died."

"I think she was partially crazy. Mad as a hatter," I slurred a bit.

"And now she's trapped with it," Alice said.

"We have to help her," I said. Mother to mother, widow to widow, I would help her. "So how do we get Monster out of my house?"

Oak, Alice, and Ben looked at each other.

"We can see if a priest wants to do an exorcism," Alice said.

Ben shook his head. "Those things don't work."

"We could tell it to go away," Oak said. "Sometimes that works."

Ben shook his head again. "Only with a weak shadow ghost. Not with demons. If it disappears, it'll come back. We have to kill it or send it back."

"Okay, so how?" I asked.

"No one really knows," Ben said. He picked at his chicken dish. He'd swallowed four drinks but didn't seem buzzed like the rest of us.

"Whatever we do has to be permanent," I said. "I'm not living in the house again, but I'm not selling it with a demon inside."

"You can always burn the house down," Ben said. "Most people agree fire gets rid of demons, or it'll get rid of the portal it came through."

"Let's hope it doesn't come to that," Alice said.

They lapsed into silence.

"So, what's the plan?" I asked.

"We need to do some research," Oak said. "I have some people in Scotland I can call. Let's meet back, maybe tomorrow at ten?"

"No," Alice said. "That's too early. We won't have done any research. How about three? After the party."

"No party," I said. "We're canceling it."

"There's no need," Alice said. "I won't be able to attend, but between you, Derek, my nanny, and Polly, it'll be fine."

"But—"

"Please don't argue. The party will happen."

I had the most amazing friends.

A few minutes later, we left the restaurant and went out to our cars, Alice taking Ben's keys away.

"I'll drive," Derek said. Having had three margaritas, I dug through my purse for my keys, forgetting he already had them.

"I guess it's back to the hotel for Polly and me," I said, drunkenly punching Derek's arm. He grinned and danced away from me. "Thank God for Alice letting Gabe spend the night again," I said. "He's terrible to share a hotel room with."

Polly looked up from her phone. "I'm going to go hang out with Oak. She has some cool ghost footage she wanted to show me."

"You can watch ghost footage? After what we saw?"

Polly shrugged as Oak walked over. "It actually helps desensitize you," Oak said, overhearing my comment. "And I have whiskey."

"My favorite," Polly said. She leaned forward to hug me. "I'll see you at the hotel later."

They pulled away, and Derek and I stood outside the car. I wondered why Derek wasn't getting in.

"I'm not sure I can go back to my house," Derek said, his hands stuffed in his pocket. "Not sure I can sleep tonight."

I raised an eyebrow. "Are you asking me to invite you to the hotel for coffee?"

"Kind-of."

"And by coffee, you mean..."

He shook his head and ran his fingers across his bald head, looking confused and... cute. Sweet. This was Derek. He'd been my friend for a while and was helping me through a terrible situation he wanted to run from. And he was still here. I stood on tiptoes and leaned in. He met me halfway, the kiss gentle and sweet. At first. I shivered as nerves I thought were gone sprung to life.

I'd never kissed a man with a beard before, and his whiskers brushed my cheeks, awakening tiny shivers of pleasure. He wrapped his arms around me, deepening the kiss. When we separated, I had to take a deep breath, my knees shaky, but in the right way, not in the I'd-seen-a-ghost way.

"Wow," Derek said. "I should've kissed you months ago."

I stepped away. Desire pooled deep in my stomach from one kiss. My reaction scared me; I hadn't felt anything like that since Miguel and I started dating. Well, it had been a while.

"So sleeping arrangements tonight," I started to say.

My phone buzzed, and I pulled it out. It was Polly. *I'm going to spend the night at Oak's. She said her roommate is out, and I can crash on the couch. We'll have a girl's slumber party. Want to join?*

The last thing I wanted was to talk more about ghosts.

*I'm good. But thanks.*

"Everything okay?" Derek asked.

"It was Polly. She's going to spend the night at Oak's. I think they're going to do some more drinking."

"I get it," Derek said.

"Me too," I said. I didn't want to spend the night alone. I knew Monster couldn't come out of my house, but the idea it even existed terrified me.

"Fine," I said. "You can share my hotel room," I said. "But strictly platonic. Two separate beds and everything."

"Can't," Derek said. "What about Fluffy?"

"Dang it," I said. "Sneak her in?"

"How about we go to my place? I'll sleep on the couch, and you can have the bed. We can keep an eye on the house together. And Fluffy."

I couldn't stop the shiver shooting through me. "I don't want to be close to Monster."

"Me neither."

"It hasn't come over. And I think it would've if it could."

"I think it's something to do with Fluffy," Derek said. "Right before you all went running out, Fluffy bolted under the bed. Gabe went after her and was lying on his stomach under the bed when that thing... Monster stood in the doorway, waving." Derek shuddered. "Gabe didn't see anything because of Fluffy. The kitten is somehow helping us. Helping Gabe."

"We should ask the ghost hunters," I said. I took a deep breath. "Okay," I said. "Your place. But you get the bed, and I'll sleep on the couch. That's the only way I'll do it."

"Deal."

# Chapter 39

**Saturday**

The next morning, I stood outside Derek's home on the gravel path, staring at my house, Ruth's photograph album in my arms. Nothing stirred at the windows, and I wondered if Monster watched me.

Or maybe Ruth did, with desperation.

I'd gone through the album again; there weren't any pictures of Ruth pregnant or with the baby, but there were empty patches too, places where it looked like she'd removed the pictures. She'd probably destroyed the photos or put them in the chest, trying to stop Monster from tormenting her.

She'd tried so hard to tell us. And we didn't listen.

Derek joined me outside and passed me a coffee cup, taking the heavy photograph album from me.

"How much sleep did you get?" he asked.

"Few hours." His couch had been horribly uncomfortable. And even though I didn't think Monster could come for me, I couldn't close my eyes without seeing it looming over me, with its terrible arms outstretched.

So I'd spent the night reading what we'd identified as the last journal.

"I think Ruth may have committed suicide to get away from Monster," I told Derek.

"But it didn't work," Derek said. "She got trapped." He touched my back, rubbing a little circle between my shoulder blades.

I turned to face him. "So you believe now?"

209

He nodded. "I still think my mom... I don't know. Maybe there was something. But Aaron took advantage. I know the things he claimed as proof were fake. I found some of it online. Pictures from other ghost hunts that he used Photoshop to combine into pictures from my mom's house."

"I feel so terrible for you and your mom."

"Over and done with," Derek said. "Focus on the now. We're going to help Ruth get away from Monster."

"Thank you for understanding how important that is," I whispered. Derek ran his hands up and down my arms and leaned down to give me a quick kiss. It deepened quickly, and I nipped on his bottom lip. His hands moved to my back, slipping up under my shirt to touch bare skin.

I pulled away with a gasp and said, "I'll have to sell the house, and my new one may not have a granny unit."

"I think I'll be seeing you either way." He kissed me again. What would the neighbors think? But I didn't care as his tongue slid into my mouth. Good God, he was an expert kisser.

My phone buzzed, again and again, and we pulled apart. My hands shook slightly as I pulled my phone out of my pocket.

*Where are you?* Polly asked.

*At Derek's.*

There was a long pause, but lots of dots before, *Wow, go Tasia.*

*Not like that,* I texted back. *I slept on the couch. You coming over?*

*Yep. We'll bring donuts. Me and Oak.*

Derek and I went back into his house. Fluffy had slept with me, curled next to my stomach. It was the only way I'd gotten any sleep at all. I felt spread thin, my body humming with caffeine and lack of sleep. I drained my mug. It was seven a.m., and I had four hours before Gabe's party.

"What can I do for the party?" Derek asked.

"Let's plan once Polly gets here. We're going to need a cake, favors, a game..."

"Sure you don't want to cancel? Raging Waters just opened. We can take him there and have a redo for the party."

"No. If we can make it happen, we should do it." Tears filled my eyes, though. Derek handed me a tissue and put his arm around me. I'd missed physical contact so much since Miguel had died, and it was nice to have someone to cuddle into. "This week was terrible. And it was supposed to be so special. It was supposed to be.... I was trying again. The week was going to be perfect for him."

Derek kissed me gently and then on the tears on my cheeks. "You are perfect. Have been perfect. And besides, this week was pretty awesome for him."

"How?"

"His half-sister, who he adores visited, as a surprise—" He put up a hand as I tried to explain. "I know Polly didn't come back for him. She needed to retreat, but he told me all about how Polly came back to surprise him. Then he got a kitten, pizza multiple nights in a row, went to Fairytale Town and the zoo, went to the train museum, spent the night in a hotel—he told me he jumped on the bed, by the way—and got to spend the night with his friends two times this week. He's fine."

"Well, when you put it like that."

He kissed me again. "I can't get used to kissing you," he said, pressing his forehead against mine. "Can't believe you're kissing me back. I've been wanting this for so long."

Polly and Oak knocked on the door before I could say anything.

They came in carrying coffees and donuts. "You okay?" Polly mouthed to me.

I nodded. "Just feeling overwhelmed. But we have so much to do for the party. I can make a list, and we can divide and conquer."

My phone buzzed. *I think I found a solution,* Alice texted.

*We're at Derek's. Come on over,* I responded.

*I don't want that thing to hear us. Come over here. Please.*

# Chapter 40

Ten minutes later, we sat around Alice's colossal kitchen island, munching on Polly and Oak's donuts.

Alice picked up her notebook. "So I was up all night researching shadow beings and demons. There's a lot of debate on how to get rid of them, but most people agree an exorcist might not work. We can try finding the portal and closing it using a prayer and Reiki, but Ben doesn't think that'll work on a demon. But we all agree it got out when we opened the chest, which may mean something in the chest brought it out, or its portal is in the chest. Also, it seems to be limited to the house unless it's just messing with us."

"I think if it could've come after us at Derek's, it would've," I said.

"Agreed. This thing's been locked away and unable to torment anyone for a while. It's due," Oak said.

"Back to my idea to get this handled," Alice said. "It got worse when we opened the chest. So I say we burn it. If its portal is the chest or inside the chest, it'll get rid of it."

"That easy?" I said. "Then why are there so many reports of ghosts people can't get rid of?"

"Have you ever tried to burn a huge object?" Oak said. "It's not going to burn easily, and Monster, cool name, by the way, will fight us the whole time. It may not even let us take the chest out of the house. We may have to burn it within the house."

"So it'll take all of us?" Polly said.

"And it's going to try to hurt us," Oak said.

"And if burning the chest doesn't work?" Derek asked.

Alice shook her head. "I don't know. There are professionals we can bring in to trap Monster in the chest, but those things take time."

"Got it," I said. "Get rid of the demon, free Ruth, and sell the house." The thought made me sad, but not as sad as I thought it would've. There was more than just Ruth and Monster in the house. There was the memory of Miguel, too. But it was time to move on. Keep the memories, but not the house.

A sleepy Gabe came padding down the stairs, wearing the same clothes he'd been wearing for two days. I'd packed a bag for him and me, but it was in my car, and I'd dropped him off yesterday without it. Also, we were almost out of clean clothes, let alone clothes for a party.

I picked him up and put him on my lap, knowing those days were ending soon. "Did you have fun?" I asked, as I gave him a donut.

"Yep. We played Minecraft until two a.m."

"Two a.m.?" I said in mock shock.

"Yep. How's Fluffy?"

"She's good," Derek said. "Did you see the pictures I texted you? She's behaving herself. But she misses you."

"Can I see her?"

"Soon," I said. "After the party. She's at Derek's."

"When can we go home?" Gabe asked.

"Soon, hopefully," I said. "Let's get the party done." I handed out lists. "These are the things we need to buy by eleven. It's nine now. We have to be back by ten-thirty for set up. I don't have any cash but will reimburse any money you spend. I have going to a bank on my list."

\* \* \*

The party went off the way all parties for thirty-seven eight-year-olds go. Noisy, with spillage of soda and candy, laughter, and the occasional tears. Usually, I would've run around, refilling the candy jars, mediating battle cries of "that's-not-fair," refolding napkins, refilling soda cups, and then passed out carefully measured pieces of cake with the coordinated fork to match.

But this time, I sat back and chatted with the other parents, letting Polly run around with the kids.

I'd always made fun of these school moms, and yes, some of them were judgmental and gossipy. They invited me to way too many multi-level marketing parties for lipstick, essential oils, and body wraps, but overall, it was an excellent way to spend the afternoon. A nice distraction from what was coming next.

# Chapter 41

At two, Alice appeared and shuffled all the kids and their parents out of the house. I set Gabe's presents aside, but the majority of gifts were gift cards or outright cash. I mentally shrugged; guess it was easier than trying to find the perfect present at the toy store.

A few minutes after the last child left, Oak arrived, her face long. We offered leftover pizza and cake while Alice's maid cleaned up the mess. Alice ordered the kids upstairs, and they went running, arguing about what they'd play on Xbox.

"So, we won't have Ben," Oak said once the kids were upstairs. "He got hurt."

"Oh my God," Alice said. She pulled out her phone. "I missed all these text messages. What happened?"

"He tripped and broke his wrist," Oak said. "Bad. He needs surgery to get it set."

"I should go over there," Alice stared at her phone before typing out a message.

"His daughter is with him," Oak said.

"They're talking again?"

Oak shrugged. "I don't know much about his family, but I guess so?"

Alice's phone pinged. She read the message with a grimace. He must be pretty loopy. Or typing with one hand. But I think he's saying the best course of action is to burn the chest."

"Agreed," Oak said.

My phone buzzed, and Polly kicked at my ankle. When I looked at her, she nodded at my phone.

I pulled it into my lap and glanced at the message Polly had somehow typed out.

*Ben lost his other daughter to a demon attack. He hates demons and fighting them is really hard on him. But he doesn't want anyone else to lose their family.*

I typed out, *Why do he and Alice fight so much?*

*Some sort of history. Oak says they're old friends, but they fight a lot. It's weird.*

"So burning the chest, it is," I said. "How do we do it?"

"How are we going to get the chest out of the house?" Oak asked.

"Carry it out? We got it out before," I said.

"But that was before we opened it," Oak said. "I'm not sure Monster is going to let us. Also, if we think it's tied to the chest, then it'll follow us wherever we take it."

"Are there things we can do to make it less strong?" I asked. "Crucifixes, salt, garlic, silver?"

"You're getting your fiction confused," Alice said. "Garlic is for vampires, and silver is for werewolves."

"Do vampires exist?" Polly asked.

"I doubt it," Oak said. "But you never know. Did you guys think ghosts existed before this week?"

Derek shook his head. "No way."

"Okay," Alice said, clapping her hands. "Focus. Let's make a list of everything we need and get this done before the sun goes down."

# Chapter 42

As we made our lists and Oak and Alice raided their personal stores of random objects that may or may not prevent a demon from attacking us, Derek pulled me into a hallway at Alice's house.

He kissed me until I was dizzy.

"Wait, stop," I said, laughing. "Jeez, I feel like someone who's hiding from their father," I whispered.

"Why stop?" he asked, running his hands up and down my bare arms.

"Gabe," I said.

"You don't think Gabe will be happy with us?"

I shook my head. "I think he'll be fine with it. He likes you. Just want to tell him before he sees us kissing. I'll tell him tonight, regardless of what happens with the chest."

"I have a favor to ask," he said.

"You want to stay here?" I said.

He nodded. "Do you mind? The idea of... I don't think I can. I worry I'd freeze, and... I don't think..."

I stopped him with a quick kiss to the lips, gentle and sweet. "Someone has to stay with the kids. And what if one of us gets hurt? I think you're the best person to stay behind."

He kissed my hand. "Wish you could stay with me. Stay with me," he whispered. "Let the ghost hunters handle it."

"It's my house," I said. "And Ruth needs my help."

* * *

It was nearly five when we were ready. We all wore crucifixes dangling from our belts and an entire collection of necklaces, bracelets, and rings Oak and Alice said would protect us. We'd spritzed ourselves in holy water Oak had talked a Catholic priest into giving us and had crosses drawn on our foreheads. Alice had poured the remainder of the holy water into one of Alice's super soakers after she received a text from Ben. We weren't sure how we'd use it but figured it couldn't do any harm.

Oak prepared a protection circle using chalk on the patio concrete area she'd learned from her friend in Scotland. It was full of intricate shapes, circles, triangles, and rectangles, often with little swiggles incorporated. To me, it looked like nonsense, but Alice had stepped in the middle and smiled, giving Oak kudos as Oak set rabbit's feet and burning bundles of sage at various points of the circle.

"Ben lent us the rabbit's feet," Alice said. "He swears by them."

"Are we supposed to mix all these religious symbols together?" I asked, looking at the paraphernalia.

"I'd rather risk pissing off a random deity than deal with Monster," Oak said. "And I think the deity would forgive us. Most of these symbols are Christian in origin and they like getting rid of demons."

Polly had turned on the hose and prepared buckets of water, just in case. We even had fire extinguishers in Alice's car. We all carried baseball bats, and I gripped Derek's bat, my hands sweaty, as we approached the back door. I jiggled the doorknob and pushed the door open, stepping back.

Nothing. No smell of rotting meat. No puffs of air. No thumps.

Oak stepped in.

"Come on in," she said. "But it's been busy."

I peeked my head inside and let out a gasp. Monster had opened all the kitchen cabinets and dumped everything across the counters and onto the floor. It had punched holes in cans of soup and corn and smashed bottles of soy sauce and barbeque sauce, smearing the mess all over the kitchen.

"Oh no," I said, dropping to my knees, regardless of the gooey mess. I picked the framed note Miguel had left for us. The glass was smashed, tears rent the paper, and soy sauce, ketchup, and refried beans smeared the words. I used my shirt, trying to blot what was still wet off the paper.

A gurgling baby laugh echoed through the house. "I'm not letting you do this," I screamed, my voice echoing through the house. "Get out." I sunk all my anger, all my pain, into those two words. "Get out of my house!" I screamed again. "It's mine. Not yours, and you won't chase us away."

There was no response. No thumps, no coldness, no baby's giggle.

But the house felt lighter.

"Interesting," Oak said after a minute. "Maybe it is possible to order it out."

Polly took the paper from my hands. "I'll put it in the car," she whispered.

"Try that again," Alice told me. "Tell it to get out."

"Why?"

"There's some evidence saying the owner of the house can order entities out of it, if strong enough. And you seemed really strong there."

"Get out of my house," I tried again, though it lacked the energy from the gut emotion I'd had a few seconds ago. I felt drained.

"I still think we should..." Alice trailed off, indicating the chest with a chin jerk.

"Agreed," Oak said.

We went into the family room where we'd left the chest. There was destruction here, too. Claw marks ripped the couch cushions and the picture of a landscape I'd bought from a local artist. Framed photos of Gabe were smashed, the photos torn. I hoped I still had the digital copies. The chest looked the same, though—the baby clothes and teddy bear scattered on the floor where I'd left them.

A thump sounded upstairs.

"Guess Tasia's rant wasn't enough," Oak said.

"Or maybe it's Ruth," I said.

We stared at the mess, not moving, until Alice stepped toward it and stuffed the baby clothes and teddy bear into the chest. She slammed the lid down, and it immediately sprung open, the laugh sounding again.

Oak grabbed the chest while Polly, Alice, Oak, and I circled her.

Thumps sounded on the stairs. Running feet.

Oak threw the chest over the couch and vaulted over it. I didn't want to look at the stairs, but out of the corner of my eye, I saw the thing, his body and face shifting like out of a sci-fi movie. Adult, baby, child—a multitude of faces stared out at us.

It ran at us, cackling, crying, and giggling, moving so much faster than before.

I wrenched the back door open, and Oak ran out with the chest. Alice screamed—three claw marks traced down her arm and onto her hand, dripping blood.

Oak turned back.

"Go," Alice screamed. "Get the chest into the circle."

Oak turned and bolted for the patio.

Polly shrieked. "Something's got me!"

I turned around. She seemed frozen in place, unable to take a step. "I can't move," she gasped. Her lips closed, and her nostrils flared. She let out a choky sound.

"Breathe," I ordered.

Polly's eyes met mine, huge and filling with tears. It was holding her lips shut, closing her nose so she couldn't breathe.

"Let her go," I screamed.

"Oak," Alice howled. "Light it!"

Alice yanked on Polly's arms but couldn't get her to move.

"It's not letting me get into the circle," Oak yelled.

I tried to pick Polly up, but it was like her feet were stuck in cement. Her lips were darkening from lack of oxygen. Sweat broke out on her temples. A tear slipped down her cheek.

"Let her go," I screamed. "I order you to let her go! This is my house. Let her go."

A dark shadow walked down the stairs, her skirt swaying on her hips and her hair perfectly curled around her face. I could almost hear the sensible heels clicking. She stood behind Polly. "Help me, Ruth," I whispered. "She's mine too."

Polly gasped in air and let out a choky sob. Claw marks formed down her arms, one across a cheek.

She dropped to her knees. Together, Alice and I tugged her out of the house, where she collapsed on the lawn, panting.

"Could use some help," Oak shouted.

She'd gotten the chest into the chalk circle but couldn't get to the lighter fluid. The can kept jumping around the yard. Oak's hands and arms bled from dozens of cuts.

Somehow, I got to the lighter fluid and threw it to Oak. It shouldn't have worked, but she managed to catch it. I thanked Ruth again, sure she was helping where she could.

Oak popped the top of lighter fluid and doused the chest.

Alice lit the chest. Flames licked the wood, but Oak was right; this thing wasn't going to go up in a burst of fire. Not without a lot more lighter fluid.

The demon cackled, and Oak hit the ground, yelling and trying to fight something off. A pulse of water shot by us, and the baby thing screamed. Polly was on her feet, pumping the super soaker full of holy water at Oak.

The flames went out on the chest, and Alice roared in anger. She poured additional lighter fluid on the chest, lighting the stream of liquid, and dropping the canister onto the trunk.

It exploded, and the chest caught.

We crawled away, the heat singeing our skin. I beat out a flame in Alice's hair.

The flames reached toward the sky, blue and purple mixing with the orange as the things in the chest caught fire. Something popped, and Polly shrieked again as the rest of us hid our faces.

I wondered how we were going to put it out. After a few minutes, Oak ran for the cars with the fire extinguishers.

"Not yet," Alice said, her voice creaking. "We want it to be as high as possible."

We watched the flames until the fire truck showed up and put it out.

# Epilogue

Two months later, I padded downstairs on my bare feet. The kitchen light was on, and I greeted Polly who sat at the kitchen table, doubling as my office space.

"The milk is still heating," she said, nodding at the pot on the stove.

I grunted and got a mug, the cocoa, and the cinnamon.

Polly looked up from her phone. The claw marks on her cheeks were healing, but it was going slow. Normally she hid them under heavy make-up, but tonight they looked red and raw.

"I heard Derek screaming," she said.

"Yeah," I said, rubbing my hands across my face. "He can't seem to get past the nightmares."

I looked around my new kitchen. I'd bought this house because it'd been available, affordable, and was in East Sac, but my other place was superior.

Within a week of putting my house on the market, I'd sold it and hired movers to move us out. Polly and I had tried to spend as little time as possible in the old house. We just couldn't get Monster out of our heads, though we were all pretty sure the fire had gotten rid of it. Ben, Oak, and Alice had analyzed hours and hours of data and then said they hadn't seen anything. No shadows, no EVPs. They'd even reported the house seemed warm and friendly. And the buyers thought so too, thanking me for taking such good care of the property.

But setting foot in the house made my blood run cold and my heart pound. I had to start taking anti-anxiety meds.

I hoped the fire had not only killed the demon but also released Ruth. But without seeing her, Alice, Oak, and Ben couldn't tell me for sure. On one of the few occasions when I'd gone into the house, I'd tried to reach out to her, tried to talk to her, but there was nothing. No thumps, no sounds on the stairs, and no brush of air against my cheek. She'd saved our lives, I was sure of that, and I hoped she was wherever the dead were supposed to go, and it wasn't horrible.

I pulled out a chair at the kitchen table, wincing when it caught on the threadbare and stained carpet. Who put carpet in a kitchen? I'd tried having it cleaned, but it needed to get replaced. Actually, the entire house needed work. And it was only a three-bedroom and two-bath, which meant until Polly could find a job and a place to live, I had to work on the kitchen table. And the windows leaked, which would cost a fortune to fix.

It also didn't have a granny unit. So Derek had moved in.

It was too soon, much too soon, as we were discovering, but he'd found he couldn't sleep alone. He woke from nightmares frequently, sweating and shaking. Sometimes he'd yell out or fight me as I tried to calm him down.

But it wasn't all bad either. Derek was a good cook, and although he left dirty socks scattered all over the house, he was still Derek. He would do anything for Gabe and me, whether it was the laundry or go out for a carton of eggs we needed for breakfast. And he was a good lover. I'd missed that.

"Oh, I have news," Polly said. "I'm going to go back to school in the fall. I got into Sac State on a provisional acceptance."

"How'd you manage that?" I asked.

"Oak helped. She—I don't know—worked some magic. I'm going to major in parapsychology."

"Oh," I said. "That's cool?"

"Yeah. I've been spending a lot of time with Oak, going over the data from the ghost hunts she's done. It's really awesome. We're doing a hunt later tonight. She says the more you go on, the less scary they are. Besides, most aren't like our house."

Fluffy jumped up on the table, and I curled her into me before dropping her onto the floor. "Cats don't go onto the table," I scolded. "And you're supposed to be with Gabe."

Fluffy didn't answer but started washing her face. The kitten was putting on weight and losing the cute kitten look she'd had when she'd joined our family. But she was still Gabe's shadow, following him around the house, purring and meowing to make him happy.

"And I have more news," Polly said. "Oak and I are going to start a podcast, talking about real ghost stories."

"Can you make money doing that?"

"A little. But she plans to write a book about all the ghost hunts she's gone on, so the podcast would help with promotion. And now that I have a plan, I'm going to start looking for a job. I think server at a restaurant. There's plenty of jobs, and the money is good." She reached over and touched my hand. "And I won't have to live here anymore."

I smiled at her as I placed two mugs of hot chocolate on the table. "I'm glad you have a plan," I said. "But you're welcome however long you want."

"To new paths and new journeys," Polly said.

"Not what I planned." I toasted her with my mug, my daughter in everything except blood. "But that's okay too."

# Author's Note

Another book done. When I finished Warehouse Dreams, the pandemic of 2020 was just beginning, and I was "enjoying the free time to focus on my writing". But here we are. It's still a pandemic. Millions have died. And we're pining our hopes for a future on a vaccine.

But there's good too. I finished River City Widows, and I have the beautiful, strong, and amazing Stephanie yet again to thank for this one. I was visiting Stephanie in East Sacramento and over the most amazing fried chicken, she told me about her neighbors. And one of those neighbors was a single mom with a male tenant living in the granny unit. I told her it sounded like a romance novel. She told me to write it. And I said I would have to add ghosts to it.

River City Widows is more than just a romance novel set in East Sacramento, with ghosts. It's my memories. I grew up in Sacramento and as a child, went to the California Train Museum, Fairytale Town, Sacramento Zoo and Folsom Lake. So, I spent many summer weekends in Sacramento's Old Town with my parents and brothers, visiting the tourist stores and museums along the river. When my sons were born, I took them to the same places, seeing those locations through the combination of adult and child eyes. The boys loved the zoo, circling through the reptile house, watching the lemurs and the green bird that shouted "hello!"

As a St. Francis girl, I spent much of my high school years in Downtown and East Sacramento, hanging out with Stephanie, among others. We walked through McKinley Park, paced among the rose bushes, played tag in the park (we weren't the most refined high schoolers) and after prom, went to the Lyons in East Sac (again—not the cool kids).

So, consider this story a love letter to my parents, my brothers, my kids, my most precious friends from Sacramento, and finally my husband. I would not be able to write about romance and love if he didn't love me the way he does. There are Easter Eggs throughout this book that my family and friends may recognize. Think of them as me offering you all a hug and a thank you for your love and friendship over the years.

As always, I have to thank my team for their help. Tasia was much less likeable, and it took Molly, Angie, and Sarah, my fellow Semi-Sages, to help tame her. We're on such an adventure, the four of us, and I can't wait to see where we end up. I also have an additional thank you to Sarah for a wonderful idea for Tasia that helped not only make her more likeable but added a fun twist to Tasia's internal life. I also want to thank Valerie and Steph for their help with River City Widows as well.

And a final shout out to my husband and boys for their support and love. Thank you for giving up so much so I can focus on this chapter of my life.

Here's hoping when you read this, the world is a little bit less insane. Giving everyone a COVID hug, because we all need them right now. Wear your masks, get vaccinated, and take care of each other.